BLACK MARKET NEWS

A novel by

Roman S. Koenig

Sue,
Enjoy the book!
Looking forward
to more films
in the future!
Roman

MERCURY
CURRENT

Mercury Current, LLC

This book is a work of fiction. Names, characters, businesses, places, events, and incidents are the product of the author's imagination or are used fictitiously. Any resemblance to actual events, locales, or persons, living or dead, is coincidental.

Black Market News
Copyright © 2020 by Roman S. Koenig
All rights reserved.

Mercury Current, LLC
P.O. Box 231849
Encinitas, CA 92023

No part of this book may be used, reproduced, stored in a retrieval system, or transmitted in any form, or by any means, electronic, mechanical, photocopying, recording or otherwise, without prior permission of the author.

ISBN 978-1-7342655-0-7 (paperback)
ISBN 978-1-7342655-1-4 (hardcover)
ISBN 978-1-7342655-2-1 (ebook)
Library of Congress Control Number: 2020900392

First paperback and hardcover editions: January 2020

To my family, the bedrock of every dream I have followed.

To my friends, colleagues, and mentors, whose support and feedback helped make this book possible.

To the Fourth Estate.

01: TURNABOUT

The pub's televisions were all devoted to the arrival. A full wall, a smaller TV here and there. Given the attention patrons were paying to the broadcast, one would think it was a championship game, a celebrated match, or even the latest *Star Moves* dance finale. Every personal device, from paper-thin phones to larger tablets, ran the same thing, creating a dizzying effect about the place. Shots jumped and flowed in unison tracking a polished silver jet piercing cotton-like clouds along with aerials of the downtown San Diego skyline.

None of that mattered to Quinn. He had more important things to occupy his time than watch some overblown CEO tout his latest successes as the emerging leader of California. Quinn squinted as he sifted through a mix of handwritten notes and printed pages (he was an outlier; in this age, hardly anyone wrote anything). It was Monday—President's Day—and he had a story due for the college's student news site in a few hours, and he had a major exam Wednesday. A ring of water underneath a semi-flat, half-consumed pint slowly crept toward his tablet as the spectacle of the arrival played out. He took a sip of the beer, shuddered slightly and shook his head at its bitter, stale taste, and swept the ring away before setting the glass down on the worn wooden table.

Substitute cheap alcohol for coffee and you got Coyote & Owl, the pub of choice for Quinn and his best friend, Jasper. It was the kind of place you went out of sorrow, celebration, or boredom. It was friendly and comfy enough, though. More importantly, it was the kind of place where you were left alone, which made it perfect for getting work done if coffee wasn't your elixir.

Quinn wasn't the only one ignoring the spectacle, although he was singular in his preoccupation with more serious matters. The others were a mix of the lost, lonely, or troubled. A forlorn man of about eighty, with hair Einstein would envy, sat in a booth staring ahead into who-knows-where. Nearby, a woman of about the same age, salt-and-pepper perm with a blast of fluffy hot-pink feathers, enjoyed fried zucchini and scotch, neat, occasionally glancing at the man, seemingly interested in him. At a table for two, a college-aged couple leaned into each other, arguing in hushed voices between bites of salad and fries.

"Quinn, you watching?!" Jasper yelled from the bar. Quinn gazed at the notes strewn across the corner table where he sat.

"Yeah, I'm watching," Quinn said with disinterest as he brushed away a few locks of dark brown hair from his olive-hued forehead and adjusted the squarish black-rimmed glasses over his deep brown eyes. He glanced at the coverage now and then as he continued to work.

Jasper turned to see if Quinn was actually paying attention to him. Nope. Jasper twitched his freckled nose in disapproval. He shook his head, his blond buzz cut shimmering in the light.

The excitement about the broadcast underscored its ostentation. It was a spectacle fit for a pop icon, if any such megastar could afford it.

The weather was divine, or so the slick images on screen would have you believe. It was as if God—the great CEO of all creation—was in direct contact with Bruce Haskell's entourage to angle the sunlight just right through the whitest, fluffiest clouds imaginable so his jet would cut through the sky with a shocking sparkle of perfection as it approached San Diego. It also helped that the three planes shadowing the delta-winged craft had camera crews aboard using filters to encourage the sky to look that way.

Appearance was everything to Haskell. The citizen stockholders watching his flight live across the state needed to know that his universal talents were next to virtual Godliness. Appearance was also everything to the man Haskell was coming to meet, the last man standing in California who could derail a grand experiment to outsource every aspect of life, from the election of city councils and the management of sewage systems to the ownership of schools, grocery stores, car batteries, and healthcare circuits. Haskell was set to meet the last power broker clogging his path to full eState control of California, the owner of the very funnel he had to rely on to get his gospel of corporate governance to the people—Walter Eddington.

The coverage continued with frenetic, manic abandon. Majestic jet in the clouds, its shadow gracing the skyline as it approached the airport. The landing and Haskell's stately exit from the plane. Cheering crowds waving small American flags with the California state symbol, the grizzly bear, in place of the stars. An open motorcade with Haskell donning a dark blue business suit and crimson tie, standing like an animated statue waving to the onlookers, his gelled shoe-polish black hair locked in style despite the breeze, sunlight bouncing off his chalky white skin.

The images were disturbingly familiar to Quinn. He thought about the similarities to century-old film footage he saw in a world history class a few semesters ago. Who the footage was about, he couldn't really remember at the moment. Some European dictator from one of the early world wars. Maybe something to look up again later.

As Quinn continued to work from the sheets in front of him, a woman's voice overtook the newscast. It caught Quinn's ear, as this particular voice always did. He glanced at his tablet. It was Kay Eddington. Serious. Sharp pronunciation. Beautiful. He looked at her reporting live from the *News America* studio. Her lustrous gold updo hair, light gray eyes, and vivid red suit complemented the flashy blue and white set. He brightened a little as she talked with pundits celebrating the CEO's arrival.

Haskell's presence in San Diego was not without dissent, although the news coverage would indicate otherwise. Jasper slid into the seat across from Quinn, breaking his concentration.

"There's a protest in the works tomorrow. On campus. A big one," Jasper said under his breath. Quinn's shoulders sunk and his chin dropped. His reaction irked Jasper.

"Are you serious?" Jasper asked. "Of course we're going

to cover it. How could you miss that? We've got a group of students openly protesting Haskell in full view of everyone everywhere."

Quinn closed his eyes and nodded. "I know. We have to be there. But it's just like, one more thing on top of everything else, you know."

"Forget everything else. It's the story of the year for us," Jasper insisted.

He was right, of course. Not only would Kay Eddington's garish news studio ignore it—orders from on high—but people of all stripes would overlook it out of apathy, avoid it for fear of association, or scorn it as a feckless act by ingrates. An anti-corporate protest at a public university was radical—anathema—given eState's hefty stake in such systems. The only place one might see any mention of something like it would be in the black market press. The thing people read without ever admitting it.

As journalism master's students, Quinn and Jasper had already taken courses on the development of black market news in the United States, birthed in the fallout of an era that saw massive shifts in public behavior, trust, and perception. It was the demise of the republic as people of the United States knew it. From its ashes grew an *investor republic*, a form of government that outsourced and streamlined everything in sight. Citizens as stockholders. CEOs as presidents and governors. Boards of directors as legislators.

This was also a new age of grand deceptions. Books were cooked, and so were reputations. No one asked questions, at least overtly. It wasn't because no one cared. It's just that no one thought to care. It made the career outlooks for the likes of Quinn and Jasper that much darker. The one thing they had going for them was that they were products of their time, for they never really thought to care, either. The mainstream newsies of this era were not necessarily deep thinkers. Yet.

In this context, covering a significant protest was an amusement, a sideshow, more than anything. It was fun to watch people willingly troll public figures only to be hassled in return.

Before Quinn tackled this latest bit with his best friend, aside from the two projects already ahead of him, he had some business to tend to first.

{ }

A blue smoke-like fog cast a pall across the deserted park. Quinn wore a black hooded sweatshirt to guard against the evening chill. His black sneakers, a throwback design to perhaps the 1920s, were slippery on the moist grass. The acrid plastic-scented mist dampened his shirt and jeans as he approached the platform of a nearby commuter rail station.

Through the haze, he spotted a shadowed figure. A rail car glided away from the angular mid-century-style platform as the figure turned to face him. It was a woman in her late fifties. Short red hair. Gray raincoat.

The closer they got to each other on the platform, Quinn could make out it was Theresa Bell, his contact. They met quietly for several weeks at this spot, an out-of-the-way station on a minor route owned and operated by Haskell's eState monopoly, as labels and posters everywhere proudly displayed. eState normally had its eyes and fingers over everything, but small stations such as this were overlooked either out of miserliness or negligence.

Theresa appeared weary. There was nothing remarkable about her generally. In fact, were it not for the dim, icy lights of the station itself, she would disappear into the gray landscape in a mere blink. But there was something about this woman. Something about her lack of remarkable character that suggested this was not her natural condition, but one that was thrust on her. Her eyes showed it. A certain sadness. A longing for answers. More importantly, a longing to be heard.

Theresa took a deep breath. A puff of mist wafted from her lips. She worked up a sorrowful smile as she and Quinn met face to face. Quinn shivered, glanced about the place.

"Cold night," he said.

Theresa pulled her right hand from her coat pocket and shoved a wafer-thin memory card toward him. It was barely visible in the dark aside from two tiny golden components that glistened in what hazy light there was.

"This can't be ignored anymore," Theresa said.

Quinn took out a small tablet from his sweatshirt pocket and connected the card. The tablet's screen cast a harsh glow from below his face. He scrolled through a series of files. There were terms that raised immediate red flags.

... *transfer funds* ...

... *schedule payments* ...

... *no trace to eState activity* ...

... *divert attention* ...

... *execute Operation Stakeholder* ...

... *terminate hazards* ...

Quinn was skeptical. "What university would order a hit on a student?" he asked her.

"eState, an eState university. My daughter!" she said with a break in her voice.

"What would that serve them?" Quinn pressed.

"Those are Pamela's files. Her contacts in eState got her those," Theresa explained, increasingly emphatic. "The chain is there! The proof!"

Quinn paused to consider it. He nodded.

"I can give you two thousand," he said.

Theresa curled her lip in relief and gratitude. "I can afford a memorial with that."

Quinn grabbed a wad of old, tattered cash from under his sweatshirt and handed it to her.

From behind Theresa, out of her view, two figures quietly emerged from the fog. A trace of guilt moved through Quinn. Theresa must have caught it because the look on her face dropped immediately. She glanced behind her, then turned back to Quinn.

"No," she said softly, almost in disbelief. Then the reality settled in. "No!"

The two figures were now clear in the rail station's overhead lights—officers, men in black overcoats with small unlit digital badges and eState Safe Harbor patches at their right shoulders. They were surprisingly calm, compassionate in their demeanor. One looked to be in his forties. His crew-cut brown hair glistened with highlights of silver. The other couldn't have been older than Quinn, who was twenty-six. The guy was tall and lanky with a swish of black hair covering his forehead. The older one gently grabbed Theresa by the arm.

"Ma'am, please," he said in a low voice, sounding almost like a counselor.

Theresa looked back toward Quinn.

"My daughter will not die in vain!" she said indignantly. "She will not die in vain!"

The older officer led Theresa away into the darkness. The younger officer held out his hand. Quinn gave him the card.

"Great work on this one," the guy said. He looked in the direction of his colleague, who was now out of sight. He shook his head. "Conspiracy theories."

{ }

Quinn and Jasper were back at Coyote & Owl. It was late, and there was nothing else better to do. They each downed a shot of richly colored whiskey, slamming the glasses down next to several more waiting to be consumed.

"What did you make?" Jasper asked.

"Ten-K," Quinn said.

Jasper raised his eyebrows, impressed. "Damn. Calls for another one." He shoved the next shot over to his comrade.

They raised their glasses again. Jasper let out a satisfied sigh after drinking his.

Quinn's second shot didn't agree with him as much. He winced and looked at the glass with suspicion. "What did you get us?"

"Can't remember," Jasper said.

Quinn played with the glass, tapping it, attempting to spin it on the table. In the pause between them, he gazed into the glass, noticing the small bubbles and imperfections.

Jasper was concerned. "You're not having second thoughts are you? That was a big hit."

Quinn shook his head. He said nothing more.

{ }

The newsroom of Pacific State University's student newspaper was not the sharpest facility on the campus. It was tucked away in a corner of the vast property in an outmoded administration building dating back to the 1950s or early 1960s. The architecture was classic industrial of the time. Boxy, utilitarian, with windows only across the tops of the walls where they met the roof. The beige paint was peeling in places, making the turquoise doors stand out all the more despite their own worn-out state. Immaculate landscaping gave the impression that gardening crews made every attempt to avoid even touching the sidewalks up to the grass and shrubs.

The one thing going for the building—which also housed other somewhat forgotten disciplines of the arts and humanities—was the trees, many of which appeared to be as old as the structure itself. A wisp of wind through the population of pines and sycamores had a calming effect. From the inside, the view of the treetops from the high windows was equally soothing.

Quinn stared at those treetops in the brief trance of a hangover from the previous night's overconsumption of shots. It was often what followed his work with eState agents—a journalist posing as a journalist to stop whistleblowers from outing the truth of the giant corporation and its rotten underside. He thought about Theresa. Just how true were her claims and those files on the card? He generally doubted them, although he knew there had to be some truth in what she offered. He wondered where she was, what the agents really did with people like her.

What he knew for certain was that he had enough money to get by this month. It was late February, the height of the semester when assignments—and bills—were coming due. He had to get work done. He had to eat. And he had to sleep. This all ran through his mind as he watched the trees sway through those ancient windows.

Quinn snapped out of it. He looked around the room. A small group of his colleagues worked at a collection of secondhand tables, which were as old and run-down as the building. On the north wall of the rectangular space, a two-hundred-centimeter screen displayed the live site of *The Pacific State Sun*. Quinn and his colleagues worked on tablets, a bit smaller than letter-size paper and practically just as thin as a sheet. Small black boxes, wireless hubs, were at every other table. The tech seemed out of place in such an outdated environment.

Most importantly, though, there was coffee. Lots of it. The rich, homey scent competed with the smell of stale ceiling tiles, carpet, and furniture. The coffee won out. Quinn took a sip and smiled with relief. He tapped a couple of commands to connect his tablet to a hub. A soft chime followed. A home screen appeared with a blank page and cursor waiting for direction.

"Upload all," Quinn said.

A flood of his notes, photos, and video immediately populated the file.

"Ready," a kind feminine voice replied.

"New story," Quinn continued.

A new blank page appeared.

"Story open," the voice replied.

"Compose draft one," Quinn ordered.

A news story began to craft itself on the screen, line after line of instant text. Occasionally, there would be a pause where a word or partial sentence would appear, replaced by two or three versions until the software determined it was the right construction.

Quinn looked at the faculty adviser's open office door. He got up and headed there. Quinn entered, closing the door behind him.

Behind the worn oak adviser's desk sat Noel Appleby, seventy-five, a man who looked as dated as the fixtures and building around him—frazzled white hair, eyes of gray with a toss of sawdust, light blue button-down shirt open at the neck, taupe trousers, and well-worn brown leather shoes. Noel stared, chin to chest, all-knowingly at his student. He motioned for Quinn to sit.

"What are you going to do with the ten thousand?" Noel asked as Quinn took a seat.

"Buy some food, pay for my classes, rent," Quinn replied.

Noel didn't move a centimeter.

"Doubts?" Noel followed.

Quinn shook his head.

Noel leaned forward, cupping his hands in the shape of a triangle, elbows on the table.

"You wouldn't be in here if you didn't have them," Noel said. "What about the woman's story? You saw her evidence before you handed it over. Was it legitimate?"

Quinn blew off the question. "eState conspiracy theories are like pennies. They're not worth anything."

"It was worth something to her," Noel noted with a disapproving look.

"Why would a corporate steward like them kill their own customers?" Quinn asked, shrugging at the absurdity.

Quinn's attitude flabbergasted Noel. Then the implication behind Quinn's question sank in, to the point Noel appeared to stop breathing for a moment.

"That's a sorry justification for what you did last night, especially when I know you better ... I thought," Noel replied. "Why are you here? What are you about?"

"I'm about making a living with the talents I have," Quinn said. "I'm good with words, I'm good with questions ..."

"Not the right ones," Noel interrupted. "Writing, okay, fine. But you ask questions that are convenient, not significant. And the problem is, even you're not sure about your own outlook. You fight against your own independent streak. I can see it on your face. Every time we have this conversation. And it's getting old, frankly."

Frustration built inside Quinn. He wanted approval for what he did the night before, yet he asked his mentor knowing full well he wasn't going to get it.

"*What I did was right.* That's what I want to hear from you," Quinn demanded.

"You're not going to. Ever." Noel leaned in further, placing his hands flat on the desk. "Your other teachers will throw that nonsense around, but not me. I took my first reporting job when this industry still meant something. I'm a relic trying to save souls like yours."

Quinn had no easy counterpunch to being called a lost soul. He barely opened his mouth to respond before Noel stopped him, only this time with more fervor.

"Your job is not to tow the line of authority or some pop culture candy, it's to help people like that woman you sent to jail last night! Tell *her* story!"

Quinn wrestled with the idea that Noel was right. He grew up in a vastly different culture than his mentor. He was the child of an educational system that taught to test, not to think. Yet Quinn was a thinker. He always had been. It was as if he was trying to force himself to be otherwise.

Quinn stood, gave Noel a terse "thanks," and headed out.

"Quinn," Noel said in a soft plea. Quinn looked back. "That woman's story might never see the light of day now. Put yourself in her place. It could be your story that's never told."

As Quinn returned to the newsroom, he thought more about the events of the past day. The arrival. His method of earning money at the expense of his sources. He found that he just didn't seem to care. Then there was the protest happening in a few hours, the one he and Jasper were covering. Did he really care about that?

{ }

It was Tuesday, after President's Day. Time: 2 p.m. High clouds partly obscured the sun. The quad was silent except for the sound of the California eState flag snapping in the wind. Such banners were fabricated of some synthetic material to be heard as much as seen. With every puff of a breeze, the flag flew or came to rest with a distinct *whap*.

Forty-nine Pacific State University students stood in a row. Several eState-contract police officers took positions nearby, holding sets of white plastic cuffs, ready for the right time to haul the protesters away.

The forty-nine had their mouths covered with straps of duct tape, each with a message written across. Among them:

Free Speech
No Corporate State
E-State Kills
Transactional Death
President's Day, Not CEO's Day

Their arms were linked. They stood tall, looking forward, their eyes wide with commitment. Occasionally, a few of them would break their concentration with a glance as the officers moved around them. Other than the protesters, officers, and Quinn and Jasper there on assignment, few students or faculty were in sight. Some who walked by lowered their heads and quickened their steps as they passed. The vast majority had no reaction at all, as if they were walking by some commissioned art that had been there for decades, part of the grounds.

Quinn and Jasper stood a few paces apart, press credentials hanging from lanyards around their necks. Jasper held up a tablet, capturing video. Quinn took notes using a stylus on his. He observed every sound—or lack thereof—and sight around him. The constant *whap* of the flag cut through the tension, almost to the point of distraction. Quinn practically flinched each time the flag hit.

A distant high-pitched *whir* grew louder as Quinn continued to write. He stopped and looked skyward. Four small drones approached, camouflaged by their sky-blue color, uniform from the bodies to the propellers. They were designed not to be seen unless they were nearly on top of you.

Jasper noticed them, too.

"What do you make of them?" Quinn asked as Jasper walked over to him.

"Aerial shots? Law enforcement?" Jasper replied.

Quinn pondered the possibilities.

"Get some footage, I'll find out," Quinn said.

He left Jasper and headed to one of the officers, who was standing alone observing the drones.

"You know what these are?" Quinn asked on approach. Before Quinn could come any closer, the officer put his hand up and waved Quinn off, shaking his head "no."

The drones were oddly attractive in their sleek design and mysterious purpose. Quinn smiled curiously as they came closer, floating just above the event. Then the machines continued their descent.

Quinn started back toward Jasper, but one of the drones blocked his path. It appeared to observe him as it hovered. Then it slowly spun, scanning the scene. Quinn looked at Jasper, who was still a short distance away, and pointed with amusement at the machine.

The drone backed away, landing in unison with the other three drones, strategically placed around the protesters and everyone else.

In less than half an instant—the sharp *crack* of a whip—Quinn felt the sensation of flying through the air, slamming back into the concrete with such force that he lost all sense of feeling and place. He had been thrown into a food processor, with his remains melting into the floor. That's what he felt.

Was he in a nightmare of some kind, lucid in the midst of the experience? Was he alive? Such disembodied thoughts ripped through his mind as he struggled to focus on the torn fragments of the flag attached to the pole above him, through the smoke and smell of burnt fabric and flesh. His face turned ashen as his blood drained. He heard nothing, until the muffled sound of a woman's scream. Then the screams of more people. Cries for help. Police calling in assistance. He didn't dare move. He wasn't even sure he could.

Jasper cowered under a nearby bench. Aside from a few slices from darting debris, he appeared unscathed. Yet he remained frozen in place, his blue eyes anchored to the gruesome scene of his friend and everyone else before him.

A tear rolled down Quinn's face as he tried to turn his head in Jasper's direction. Quinn opened his mouth, fought to speak. Nothing came out. Jasper slowly crawled out from under the bench. He struggled to stand, his legs rubbery from the explosion and the horror of Quinn's injuries. He glanced about the scene in suspended terror.

Quinn's head began to clear. He saw his buddy standing nearby. He felt better knowing Jasper was there with him, that he was alive. Quinn was aware that he had no sense of time, so despite the seeming eon it took to witness Jasper's dazed state, he knew it was likely just a few seconds. Perfectly understandable. But Quinn also knew there was something terribly wrong. Whether it was with him or Jasper, he couldn't figure, but his own sense of survival told him not to move.

Stay put. Jasper's here. He'll help, or he'll find it.

Quinn was right. There was something wrong—with Jasper.

In reality, Jasper's lack of action wasn't just a few seconds. It literally was a sort of eternity, like his internal wiring got fused in the burst. Quinn's relief molded to confusion as he observed Jasper's behavior. Jasper looked back at him, increasingly terrified. Then, Jasper made a move—backward. He turned away from Quinn with a look someone might give when they discover they've been betrayed. Sudden death or injury, or simply a shocking event, can feel that way.

Jasper backed away slowly, lightly bumping into the bench he hid under. He slid sideways to the right, brushing shrubbery along the way. There was no doubt. Jasper was not staying.

Quinn was alone.

02: NEAR-DEATH REMEMBRANCE

Quinn struggled to keep his face above water. The current pushed hard against him from behind, and as he fought to catch any breath to survive, he was certain his life was about to end. His left foot got caught between two rocks, wedged in such a way that he couldn't pull free. Without the ability to break away and at least try to swim, he was done for.

"Grab my hand!" Jasper yelled above the rush of the flood.

Quinn couldn't see him even though he was within arm's reach at the shore. Jasper reached out, precarious on the sandy bank, perched on a boulder just centimeters from falling in himself as the flash flood ate away more of the soil. If Jasper wasn't careful, the boulder would give way and wipe both of them out.

"On your left! Follow my voice!" Jasper shouted. "Here!"

Quinn pushed with his arms in Jasper's direction. His ankle was twisting, but he didn't care at this point. His left hand was barely above the water. Jasper grabbed it solidly just as a branch swept by, scraping Quinn across the right cheek.

Grip established, Jasper worked to pull Quinn closer. He grabbed Quinn's arm with both hands. Quinn got a clear look at the shore. He furiously yanked on his foot as Jasper pulled.

Finally, Quinn's shoe slipped loose of the rocks just enough for Quinn to free himself. Jasper held firm as Quinn breached the inundation that would take him downstream. He climbed up the bank, chunks of sand giving way underneath him and falling into the surge of muddy water.

Jasper helped Quinn up the rest of the way. He was safe. But Jasper lost his footing and fell into the wash, hitting his head on the boulder as he went.

"Jasper!" Quinn yelled, running to keep pace with him in the deluge. "No, no, no, no. No!"

Jasper wasn't unconscious, but a small cloud of blood surfaced as the water carried him away. There was no way Quinn could keep up in the sand, which was the consistency of wet cement. He plodded clumsily, the best he could do.

{ }

Quinn walked—devastated—down the trail beside the torrent along stands of silver cholla cactus, creosote bushes, cheesebush, and palo verde in the eState-branded Kofa National Wildlife Refuge. He had no idea whether Jasper made it out anywhere along the arroyo, which had been nothing more than a dry wash a few minutes before the flood. The sky was cloudy. The temperature had cooled slightly as the Arizona summer monsoon gave birth to thunderstorms around them during their hike.

The two friends were nature enthusiasts, athletic in general. The hike was an easy one—or should have been. They actually knew better than to trek along dry washes during monsoon season, but they couldn't resist. Now, Quinn's heart raced. He wondered where his buddy was. He would've made an emergency call, but his phone, an instrument less than half a centimeter thick, was lost in his fight for life.

The arroyo's flow lightened as Quinn continued his hike back toward the trailhead. The sound of the water would've been a pleasant companion were it not for the battle that transpired several minutes before. Then Quinn spotted someone up ahead—a man sitting on the ground under a palo verde, arms around his knees, head lowered, blood trailing down the side of his head, drying in small dams through his buzzed hair. Quinn approached him. There was no doubt who it was.

Jasper looked up and stood as Quinn trotted to him. They heartily embraced, patting each other on the back with relief.

"Sorry I couldn't return the favor," Quinn said.

Jasper chuckled, shook his head. "That was too close, man. For both of us."

They walked past a modest wooden trail marker with a camera unit the size of a tarantula and an ominous posting from eState: *Watch your place in our beautiful refuge. Park safety is your responsibility.*

The breeze picked up. Quinn heard a soft, steady, repetitive chime in the distance. It wasn't a wind chime. The sound was mechanical, almost like a computer. No, a medical device of some kind.

For a moment, Quinn felt out of place. Like he really wasn't where he thought he was. It was as if he was tangibly reliving a memory.

{ }

With a slice on the cheek and a gash to the head, Quinn and Jasper weren't the most presentable figures for the job they were in Arizona for. They were Pacific State University freshmen on their mandatory Summer of Service before entering their sophomore year, a requirement of enrollment. Given that eState was a sponsoring donor of the institution, it was a default for students to do service with a company-related cause.

Quinn still couldn't shake the feeling that he was living in a memory, a waking dream. The chime he heard earlier had faded, but he couldn't recall how he got to where he was now—a large conference hall in Yuma. He and Jasper wore white business shirts, thin black ties, black slacks and shoes, and name tags designating them Observers. Quinn seemed to be preprogrammed when it came to his thoughts and actions. He knew something didn't feel right, yet he was unable to divert from the script he was playing out.

It was Election Day, and Quinn and Jasper were participating in one of eState's major experiments in shareholder democracy. They walked around the hall, holding tablets with rolls of voter data and real-time updates of residents signing in and preparing to vote on site.

Neighborhood polling places had been eliminated. Instead, large groups of people were called in like jurors for duty to register their votes at regional hubs on a secure system of portable screens, reused for every session throughout the day. Crowd after crowd arrived at central locations across the state in one-hour intervals until 7 p.m.

Quinn and Jasper, as observers under a federal watchdog program, were among a posse of about a hundred to watch the election process in the city of Yuma and nearby communities. The observers were expected to look professional and keep silent as they witnessed the proceedings—tough to pull off when you practically had the marks of a brawl on your face.

"What the hell happened to you?" a disapproving female voice grumbled from behind Quinn.

He turned around to see a short woman, bowl-cut brown hair and cat's eye-shaped glasses, navy blue dress with white polka dots, giving him a judgmental once-over. It was his supervisor, Mrs. Jansing.

"What's wrong with your face?" she asked. "You and your friend."

"We got hurt on a hike yesterday," Quinn replied.

Mrs. Jansing raised her eyebrows.

"Ah. Well, I'm glad you're okay but you look like you were in a bar fight," she said. "eState doesn't mess around with image. We all need to look the part."

Mrs. Jansing walked ahead, keeping her eye on the other observers. Jasper caught some of the interaction. He shrugged, opened his hands, and mouthed, "What was that about?"

Quinn shook his head.

eState doesn't mess around with image. Mrs. Jansing's remark stuck with Quinn. eState's entourage was diverse in ethnicity and gender, yet the corporate managers running the show were uniquely powdery in their appearance no matter their skin shade, all matching the look of their guru, Bruce Haskell, whose portrait served as master over the hall from the massive projection screen up front. Haskell's subordinates looked like androids, with monocles over their left eyes, the glass faintly glowing yellow.

Trumpets sounded from speakers in the ceiling. The screen turned white, showing a simple *eState* logo with a red "e" and blue "State." The first group of voters in attendance, numbering about two thousand, took their seats in rows of perfectly aligned chairs.

Once the call of the trumpets was complete, the screen transitioned to a full shot of the American flag, a single large star in place of the former fifty. A vapid rendition of the National Anthem began to play. The shot pulled away slowly.

"I pledge allegiance, to the flag, of the United States of America," Haskell recited over the music.

The longer the shot pulled out, the more it revealed Haskell—his back toward the camera, right hand over his heart—staring nobly at the revised Old Glory.

"And to the republic, for which it stands, one nation, under God, indivisible, with liberty and justice for all."

Haskell turned to the camera, his face occupying the screen with the flag behind him. All of the eState overseers on hand stood at attention as he smiled. The emotion was artificial. The message was canned, used for every session. Quinn had heard the oration several times already.

"The sacred right of voting in these United States is unique among nations, singular in human history," Haskell said, the anthem continuing under his address. "As citizen shareholders in your local communities and in the greater American family, your vote matters now more than ever."

Arizona was an early adopter of eState governance.

In addition to its national portfolio, the company had full local and statewide control locked in a seventy-five-year contract. To remind citizens of that achievement, as Haskell spoke, images of the state's natural resources and key legislative victories rolled across the screen. Parks with eState-branded signage. A cheering delegation in the U.S. House of Representatives. Headlines proclaiming the elimination of the Interior Department and numerous federal and state agencies deemed archaic, inefficient, or redundant. The President signing legislation to such effect, proudly showing his big, bold signature to dignitaries and reporters in the Oval Office.

It was emblematic of an embedded suspicion of all things *government*. The new buzz phrase—*private stewardship*.

"Today, you elect local boards of directors, CEOs, presidents, vice presidents, even your congressional representatives," Haskell continued. "As citizen shareholders, you hold more power over government than anyone in American history, with eState as your partner along the way. Your tax dollars are the stock upon which modern America is being built. State by state, politicians are making the right choice to truly heed your voices by contracting with us to run the most important aspects of your lives."

Haskell's confidence and penetrating emerald eyes energized few members of the crowd. In fact, aside from those who were mandated to listen because it was their job, no one else particularly cared about the speech. Most of the attendees fidgeted, talked with each other, played games on their personal phones, or checked their private text messages.

Quinn watched and listened, but he was also indifferent.

Growing up in a cosmos of technology and masterful mass marketing, such an overt system of subtle authoritarian means was a no-brainer. By the time Quinn started college, eState was ubiquitous. If it wasn't the practical owner of government, it was the mother conduit of digital commerce, all forms of media, the means of production from steel to soybeans, medicine to military.

"eState's ability to govern begins with you," Haskell said. "Your vote counts. And with eState's safe, stable, secure system of elections, your vote is more powerful than ever. You stand united with us. And we stand united with you. In these grand United States of America. The greatest nation on Earth."

The National Anthem's conclusion swelled with Haskell's stilted smile. The video faded. Voting was set to begin. But there was a glitch.

Quinn noticed two eState officials quietly, hurriedly approaching a member of the voting audience—a bald, mustached man in his sixties who was leafing through an old-style print newspaper. Something called *Phoenix Phake News*, a tongue-in-cheek play on the "fake news" trope. From what Quinn could see, the paper's lead headline referred to "candidates for sale."

One of the officials, a young woman with poofy red hair, wrested the paper from the man, who yanked it back. Quinn tried to make out the hushed argument that ensued, but chatter from the crowd masked anything specific.

The man turned red-faced, refusing to do whatever it was the officials asked of him. Two burly, armed Yuma County law enforcement officers, wearing official silver emblems and eState Safe Harbor patches, walked up to the man. More words were exchanged. Then the officers grabbed him by the arms, forced him to stand, and escorted him to the rear doors.

The crowd went silent as the argument became a spectacle.

"What about my vote?!" the man yelled, echoing from the back of the hall. "I'm a registered voter! Do I still get my vote?!"

The officers shoved the man out and exited with him, slamming the doors behind them. The attendees returned to their business.

The incident may have been somewhat shocking, but Quinn, Jasper, and the other election observers marked nothing on their tablets. The man's rights had not been violated. There was no irregularity. He surrendered his privilege to vote because of the black market newspaper he carelessly read in public, and on eState turf.

"The Constitution doesn't apply," Quinn overheard Mrs. Jansing whisper to an observer, who looked like a young-adult duplicate of her supervisor. "It's a private enterprise."

The big screen lit up again, this time with a list of elections. First on the docket was the Yuma County Board of Directors, followed by the naming of its Chief Executive. Light discussion spread through the crowd as the screen listed the nine candidates.

"Welcome," a pleasant female voice announced over the speakers. "Please review candidates for Board of Directors, Yuma County. Vote when ready."

The list of candidates appeared on voters' tablets. Participants started tapping *X* next to their choices.

For Quinn, there was a persistent two-dimensional quality to the experience, like he was a witness to the events in front of him from some bodiless state. It was a similar sensation to what he felt the day before when he and Jasper almost didn't make it out of the flash flood.

Was that yesterday? Wasn't it earlier today? Quinn asked himself. He couldn't tell anymore.

The sound of that distant, repetitive chime returned. Quinn listened to it carefully. The more he paid attention, the more the chime matched the rhythm of his pulse.

{ }

"How boring was that?" Jasper said after finishing a pint, setting the glass down with a thud on the table. "At least they let us drink."

Arizona was a choice destination for college students on their Summer of Service. It had become known as an "eighteen state"—drinking was legal at the official age of adulthood.

Quinn and Jasper sat at a table outside a Yuma pub. The humidity clung to skin like a magnet. It had to have been about thirty degrees Celsius. And it was close to 10 p.m. Thunder rumbled around them. Lightning flashed close by.

Again, Quinn sensed a time gap. He tried to figure out how he jumped from trail to convention center, then to the pub. He experienced everything as it happened, followed his memory just as the actual events unfolded. But something was different here. Quinn was breaking free of his bardo.

Light rain began to fall. It was the kind of weather Quinn loved. He closed his eyes for a moment as mist from the rain, smelling sweet in the desert air, brushed across his face.

Increasingly lucid in the reverie, Quinn grew angry. He

couldn't grasp why at first, but the reason slowly formed as he looked at Jasper sitting across from him. Jasper seemed foreign, a specter of someone he thought he knew.

"Why did you walk away?" Quinn asked.

Jasper crimped his brow, caught off guard in the middle of a second beer.

"Walk away from what?" he replied, the rim of the glass near his lips.

"Why did you leave me?" Quinn said.

The shower turned to a downpour. The lightning was brighter, virtually overhead. The thunder was sharp, deafening, and immediate. The quiet, rhythmic chime returned to Quinn's ears.

The downpour seemed to morph into the sound of rushing water. Suddenly, Quinn found himself standing on the trail along the wash where he nearly drowned. Jasper walked ahead of him. The chime droned on.

Past and present merged. Quinn remembered. He couldn't reconcile the friend who saved his life that summer after their freshman year with the one who left him at the scene of the bombing now.

"You can't leave me here!" Quinn yelled.

Jasper appeared to ignore him.

"Don't walk away from me!" Quinn shouted, desperate, hurt.

Crash. A burst of thunder. Quinn was knocked off his feet. Instead of hitting the trail, his back slammed into the concrete of the Pacific State University Quad. He was bloodied, mangled, in a kind of pain so deep it didn't feel like pain at all. Worse than pain.

The sun above turned into the hovering white lights of a surgery table. A caretaker machine looked after Quinn's vitals. Its chime was sedate, a gentle messenger reminding him that he was alive.

03: THE COST

Quinn counted time in the friendly beats of a heart monitor. His vision was turbid at best during the few occasions he assumed he was awake. Mostly, he dwelled in a shapeless, viewless, colorless vacuum. He didn't know exactly how many days had passed since the bombing. It must have been close to a week, he figured, but that was a loose estimate based on half-understood conversations of doctors, nurses, and therapists, muffled in a cloud of blinding lights from a ceiling above, sensations of being put to sleep, awoken, cut into, and reassembled.

At this particular moment, Quinn heard Kay Eddington echoing from the hospital room television, the professional voice of certainty that calmed him just as much as the pings of the monitor tracking his vitals. It was the first time he heard Kay's reporting. Quinn was finally waking up, lucid enough to take stock of his surroundings.

Saturday, he thought to himself. *She said it's Saturday.* It had been four days. That was the first solid fact he could count on.

There was one other thing that occurred to him. *I haven't seen them*, he realized.

To his recollection, as best he could tell, there had been no visits or inquiries from his father (with whom he was estranged) or his best friend. He was left to navigate eState's medical system half-consciously with no help. Who knows what decisions were being made on his behalf.

He latched onto a snippet Kay reported, something about eState streamlining and fully covering victims' medical expenses. That should have been good news, but Quinn was too much of a mess to know either way. One of Quinn's doctors, an exceptionally tall woman in her fifties, graying light brown hair tied back, walked in as the news broke. She confirmed the information with a nod and an encouraging smile. She leaned—towered—over Quinn.

"You're getting the best," she said.

{ }

Kay looked out of place in her tailored powder-blue business suit and dark brown overcoat, an A-list presence among a short line of average-looking people standing at the door of a run-down industrial building in some who-knows-where corner of San Diego. She didn't feel uncomfortable, though. Kay was there for a specific purpose, and she actually found the people fascinating. In the cloistered circles of the upper class, she often didn't have the chance to interact with common people—those who watched and listened to her on a daily basis. As fascinated as she was by them, Kay also found it refreshing that they didn't seem to either care or know who she was. These people—a mix of the curious, conspiracy theorists, and black market journalists—were there for the same purpose she was. Information.

At the front of the line, a short, well-built guy in his early thirties served as the event's bouncer, scanning every entrant across the face with a small device that emitted a cobalt-blue light. Kay noticed her competition ahead in the queue. It was Olivia Boyce, forty-three, shaved black hair, umber eyes, skin the color of deep myrrh. Were it not for Olivia's serious, almost official manner, she would blend perfectly with this crowd in her jeans, amber mock turtleneck and black coat. Olivia's eyes darted corner to corner, tracking the people around her. She turned to the left, blowing an icy cloud of air through her lips, and spotted Kay. They exchanged a quick nod.

The bouncer scanned Olivia, followed by a few more people. Then it was Kay's turn. Such procedures were common at these events, methods for the organizers to know whether the people attending were who they said they were. Kay was widely known, so her appearance anywhere was immediately noticed even if people pretended they didn't know. Still, no chances. Kay stood expressionless as the deep blue light of the scan moved across her face, forehead to chin. The bouncer checked the screen. He waved her through.

The building's interior was a cavernous yet inviting space. The floor was empty except for eight rows of well-worn, formerly white metal-frame folding chairs, eight chairs to a row. The state of the vaulted ceiling's wood and corrugated metal suggested perhaps a century in age. It was a pleasant rustic interior, partly thanks to the warm glow of the clear incandescent light bulbs hanging from the ceiling.

Kay reviewed the premises like an agent stalking a tatty property to gentrify. *Perfect for a restaurant,* she thought, smiling to herself as people gathered and talked in small groups before taking their seats. *The area could use some redevelopment.*

She took a seat as close to the middle of the rows and chairs as possible. As others found their seats—about two-thirds of the chairs were ultimately taken—a frosty-haired man in his mid-fifties wearing a rumpled gray suit entered from behind a shoji at the front of the room. Whether his hair was messy because it was styled that way was tough to tell, but his demeanor indicated he was the ringleader for tonight, the auctioneer selling a single prized item.

A rectangular table draped in black cloth had been placed ahead of the first row. A wooden gavel rested on a circular green weight.

The auctioneer carried a small, locked wooden box under his arm. He walked to the table and surveyed the assembly. It was 7 p.m., time for the evening's business to get underway. He placed the box on the table, slammed the gavel against the weight, and the remaining strays took their seats.

A lanky, shabby giant of a man sat in front of Kay. She leaned left and right, struggling to catch a full view of the auctioneer.

"Remember this is a cash-only transaction. Cash only!" the auctioneer said sternly. He unlocked and opened the box. It contained a memory card—the one Quinn scored from his source just a week before. The auctioneer held it up for the audience.

"There's one item tonight. This drive," the auctioneer continued. "It contains interior eState documents directly linking it to last week's bombing at Pacific State University."

If true, this was a stunning find to score on the black

market. Murmurs spread through the crowd. Kay could not leave this auction without that card. The more she heard was supposedly contained on it, the faster her heart raced.

"Purchase records of materials, internal emails and phone conversations, and more," the auctioneer described. "The record is incomplete, however. This information is a starting point. The seller is anonymous. Bidding starts at three thousand dollars."

Kay stood and launched her hand into the air. The auctioneer nodded.

"Three thousand," he acknowledged. "Do I have three-thousand-one-hundred? Three-K-one?"

"Three-K-five," a woman's voice countered. Kay turned in the voice's direction. It was Olivia, who was seated, relaxed, her hand up barely past her head.

"Four thousand," Kay replied.

Most of the other participants shook their heads in resignation, some continuing to whisper. No one else was going to touch this auction.

"Four-K-five," Olivia said, still calm if not somewhat put out—but not surprised—that there was a battle.

"Four thousand, five hundred," the auctioneer confirmed. "Do I have four-K-six?"

In a fit of bratty impatience, Kay waved her hand again: "Fifteen thousand!"

{ }

Walter Eddington's Citizen Group was a massive monolith of a media company, and he made sure San Diego knew his national reach by building a gargantuan, angular concrete complex of two to six stories, situated at the center of fifty acres of neatly trimmed grass. Without another structure in proximity (he bought properties around it just to tear the buildings down), Ground Zero of his business empire looked like the center of the universe, a complex of giant gray tablets perfectly placed by God's hand. The eyes and ears of God's locale? Beautifully designed transmission towers, dishes, and solar panels peppered around the parklike setting—part sculpture garden, part planetary base.

It was Monday morning, and Kay rolled up to the main building's entry in a silver electric sports car. She was the passenger; there was no driver. She stepped out in a charcoal business suit and pillbox hat to match, carrying a thin, gray metal briefcase. The car closed its door and silently departed as she headed to the atrium-style entrance with a slight smirk.

Eddington's office on the top floor of the tallest tower was his sanctum. He had other offices and buildings around the nation, entire skyscrapers including three in downtown San Diego alone, each with a top-floor office reserved just for him. But even if such an office sat on the top floor, none compared to the throwback comfort of the dark walnut-paneled lair of his main media complex. Even at just six floors up, a wall of windows looked southwest down upon the rest of his campus in such a way that it could be more than a hundred stories above. The view was not for the acrophobic.

Eddington sat at his desk, the steam of fresh coffee rising from a branded *News America* mug in lively red, white, and blue. The light of a digital tablet cast a sinister glow on his face as he studied the morning's latest headlines, stock market notes, and political updates. Three large flat-panel monitors played news broadcasts from his various holdings. eState CEO Bruce Haskell's face was plastered across all of them as he gave a speech showing some approximation of sadness and compassion concerning the terrorist bombing the week before. Eddington glanced at the show with mild annoyance, sipping his coffee in between furrowed eyebrows, mild frowns, and scoffs.

Haskell's words weren't all that important to Eddington. Although they were both masters of business, they were polar opposites in almost every other way. Eddington's tall stature, wavy silver hair, frost-blue eyes, and chiseled features gave him an instant, intimidating yet affable air of authority that Haskell had to artificially force upon an audience. Where Eddington was sharp, Haskell was slick. Where Eddington held to a moral and ethical code, Haskell held fast to the idea that he himself *was* the ethical and moral code. Eddington was the dinosaur. Haskell was the next generation rising fast. Sandwiched between these power positions were people like Kay, Quinn, and Jasper, the third generation trying to navigate around, and make sense of, such doyens.

Kay burst through the double doors of her father's office. Eddington was unfazed, his eyes fixed on the tablet.

"There's a receptionist out there," he said flatly.

Kay walked up to her father's desk and placed the briefcase in front of him. She opened it and took out the memory card from the weekend's auction. She held it up and smiled.

"I got something on the black market last night."

That got is attention. He looked at her, waiting for the pitch.

"This drive has material directly linking eState to the bombing," she quickly announced, barely able to contain her excitement. "I opened it when I got home and you won't believe what's on here. Meeting notes, emails, receipts ..."

"Let's discuss *on the black market*," Eddington interrupted impatiently.

"Dad, I have to go there because our reporters are too shallow to sniff out the facts for themselves," she said.

"Which is very convenient for me," Eddington mentioned.

Kay's pride shifted to puzzlement. "This was murder, and it's news."

"Not now!" Eddington said sharply.

"Something called Operation Stakeholder?" Kay added.

Eddington's eyes flared. Then he paused and took a breath.

"There isn't an outlet that'll run it," he told her. "Just about all the majors are owned by eState except for my holdings. Why do you think Haskell paid me a visit? If they win a hostile takeover, you are out of a job and I'm out of ... everything. It's not running."

There was no point in Kay arguing. Her father's decisions were edicts, and whether the situation was professional or personal, there was usually no swaying him. She had her ways, but she could tell this wasn't one of those days. She placed the card on his desk, masking any reaction of defeat.

"Well, I bought it for you anyway," she said. "If you won't run it, not even the black market will now."

"Assuming it's the only drive," he noted.

Kay always had a Plan B when it came to spinning discussions with her father—make it sound like a win-win.

And in this case, it really was. With their ownership of the information, eState's dark secret of its involvement in the bombing was quashed. For now. Eddington had a habit of acquiring such information for future weaponizing.

There were other things to worry about, however. Underground trading of such information was illegal under eState's management of the justice system. No one was immune from the consequences. Eddington and his family were no exception. The information on that card, if confirmed, was still worth pursuing in due time. Eddington pondered that possibility as Kay began to leave.

"Kay," he said in a gentler, more fatherly tone. She stopped and turned around. "Don't go to those auctions. I don't need my daughter in jail for trading. It doesn't look good for either of us, especially when you're the face of the network."

Eddington gave it another thought. "See if you can find someone in the newsroom you can trust and we can quietly afford to lose." He held up the card. "How much?"

"Fifteen thousand," Kay told him.

Eddington huffed in exasperation. "I'll reimburse your account," he said.

Kay smiled, quite satisfied. "Thanks, Dad."

{ }

There's always that certain pit, so deep that you can't see to the top, so black that you can't see the walls for the rungs you could grasp to climb out. Quinn was there. He spent days trying to locate those rungs using nothing more than a match for light. For every one he grasped, medication and surgery wrested his hands away, sending him falling back to the bottom. All he knew was that he had to keep clawing his way upward until he could at least spot a beacon at the top.

What saved Quinn in this space was the knowledge that the rungs were there. If he could find them, work at grabbing them often enough despite the forces restraining him, he could fight his way out. But as he approached that beacon, all he saw were mirages of the people who should have been there for him—his mother, his father, and his best friend. Their combined absence should have left a void, but that was caused by only one of them. Jasper.

Monday marked six days since the bombing. Quinn was now fully awake, finally able to assess the consequences of the event that shattered his body, perceptions, and potentially a friendship.

Quinn's eyes wandered, unfocused, as he tried to conjure some imprint of the mother he never knew. Quinn was an only child, raised by a single father who never remarried after his mother was hit and killed by a rogue automated car when he was a toddler. He knew the story, recalled the details. He laughed slightly as he weighed which tragedy was now to be the heart of his family tale—his mother's untimely death, his own survival, or his father's lack of presence at the hospital. Quinn sometimes felt a presence that he chalked up to the spirit of his mother—an odd breeze past his ear or a fleeting scent of perfume that she wore—but he wasn't feeling it now.

Where are you? Quinn wondered.

As for Quinn's father, he was just as much a ghost to him, maybe even more so. As a son, Quinn was an academic parental curiosity. Quinn figured that if his father were present now, he would analyze how Quinn was going to forge a new life out of this devastation, a dispassionate observer standing behind the doctors. That emotional distance was so intolerable to Quinn that he left home after graduating high school and never looked back. Despite all that, in this moment, Quinn was torn. He longed for one of his father's bot-like emails spouting cliché advice about life, love, and work, or maybe a zinger like "... if you had your head on straight about a career." At the same time, as far as Quinn knew, his father had no idea his son was involved in such a catastrophic incident. And frankly, Quinn didn't want him to know.

Hell with him, Quinn dismissed.

Quinn was most saddened by his best friend's absence. Stuck in a hospital bed for a seeming eternity, Quinn had ample time to dwell on that friendship.

Jasper tended to be uninhibited, a bit of a tough guy with a great sense of humor, willing to leap on a dare. Quinn recalled one night during their freshman year as roommates when Jasper pulled him along on a drunken quest to dig up a piece of an exotic plant from a neighbor's yard simply because Jasper wanted one of his own.

"That's someone else's property, you're going to get us in trouble," Quinn scolded at the time. Jasper rebuffed him with a simper.

But that rambunctious flair was a facade. Quinn remembered holding Jasper tight as he wept when he got word that his younger sister had died, the one sibling of three whom Jasper felt closest to in an estranged family of extreme religious and conservative values.

"My God, why?" Jasper wept, Quinn recalled.

He understood Jasper's cry now more than ever.

Quinn was inquisitive, brainy, compassionate, dedicated, optimistic—traits similar to the mother he never really knew—with an athletic side that attracted him to martial arts. Jasper had similar interests, but from a completely opposite family—two devoutly religious, strict, smothering parents full of expectations, one older brother, and two younger sisters. As friends, the two built a brotherhood out of their mutual frustrations over family rage and isolation.

Jasper was often oblivious to consequences, a trait that Quinn had to keep an eye on.

Quinn's reflections shifted to one time they were sparring—kickboxing—at a dojo. Quinn held a set of pads as Jasper threw a series of combinations. Jab, cross, hook, uppercut. Jasper launched a surprise kick that was so hard it propelled the knuckles of Quinn's own hand into his nose, nearly breaking it. It was bruised for days, but Jasper's remorse over such an incident could last for months.

All of this and more played on repeat in Quinn's mind as he dwelled on the future, of how he was going to rebuild his life, rebuild a friendship he feared had been jeopardized when he saw Jasper cower that day of the bombing.

Quinn wasn't sure who would feel more guilty about the whole thing. Deep inside, he didn't honestly care that Jasper reacted the way he did. No one knows how they would react in such a violent situation. Quinn understood that. He hoped Jasper would. The only problem was that Jasper had yet to visit him in recovery. So there was Quinn, alone in the hospital, facing months if not years of healing, with the one brother he chose in his life nowhere to be found.

Aside from the sounds of various medical devices, the constant visits from ostensibly every medical professional in existence—and eState investigators asking what he witnessed—his most important companion was Kay Eddington. She didn't know him, but he felt he was getting to know her better and better, watching her newscasts daily about the status of the investigation.

Despite Quinn's smarts, however, he was part of his generation's stock, a population raised on instant media and marketing who generally lacked the ability to question anything beyond the superficial. It's not that the masses were any less bright, it's that the application of thinking and believing reflected different values, established by the Bruce Haskells and Walter Eddingtons of the world. That was all starting to change as more people began to see through that veil. It took a near-death experience for Quinn. As he saw replay upon replay of footage on the TV above his bed, he began to question.

"... And the body count only goes up from last Tuesday's terrorist bombing at a Pacific State University protest," Kay reported. "One more student and a security guard died of their injuries overnight, bringing the toll to nine with scores more injured."

Tears started to stream down Quinn's face.

"There's still no claim of responsibility for the bloodshed, although eState CEO Bruce Haskell believes the protesters themselves are to blame," Kay continued.

The video cut to press conference footage of Haskell, standing atop the steps of eState's San Diego headquarters, wearing an expensive tailored suit just as black as his hair, giving his skin a ghostly pale look. At fifty-six years old and below-average height, Haskell's posture hinted at a man who should be taller. His face was stonelike as he talked. A monocle Haskell wore over his left eye shook as he pounded fist to hand for emphasis.

"We know there's a violent faction to these protest groups that will kill their own members to stop progress," Haskell told the reporters gathered around him. "This is absolutely true, and we saw that play out on Tuesday. Don't let any so-called legal or military experts tell you otherwise."

Haskell's claim only deepened Quinn's hurt and confusion. He was there. He saw the drones land. He saw the faces of the protesters. There was no way those people would have inflicted the ensuing carnage on themselves. As one of the severely wounded witnesses, it made him even angrier that his statements were not taken seriously by eState's investigators (who also happened to be contractors representing all levels of law enforcement).

No one's asking the right questions, Quinn thought.

Jasper had been standing at the door, listening to the report. It wasn't the coverage that stalled him from making his arrival known to Quinn. It was the fear of seeing his friend for the first time since the blast. Jasper's eyes were diverted from the TV by Quinn's injuries. His heart was in his throat over them.

Quinn shifted himself in bed, wincing through the process. He instantly smiled, wiped his tears, and relaxed when he saw Jasper, who still hesitated to come in. Quinn shrugged as if to wonder what the big deal was.

"What? You're afraid of me, man? Get in here," Quinn said encouragingly.

Quinn reached his hand out to Jasper, who grasped it. The handshake became a hug. Tears returned to Quinn's eyes as Jasper tried to hold in a cry.

"What do we do, Quinn?" Jasper asked, his voice muffled as he buried his face in Quinn's shoulder.

It was a question that took on so many connotations. Quinn looked toward the ceiling. For the moment, he had no answer.

04: FOR THE RECORD

Names.

That was the thought Kay had at the end of every broadcast since the campus attack. eState Safe Harbor was forthcoming about all sorts of information, for the most part. The numbers of dead and injured. Property damage estimates. The suspected "terrorists" who seemed oddly undefined and apparently impossible to catch.

In all of the reporting done by Kay and her colleagues, the *who* of the tragedy was an elusive angle.

Names, she thought. *That's what I need to humanize this story.*

"Well, if you get them, you sure as hell aren't going to run them," her father said, sitting behind his desk, glaring at his daughter standing across from him.

"Why?" Kay asked.

Eddington cupped his hands around his face in frustration.

"eState, Kay. Remember who I'm tiptoeing around."

"That makes no sense to me," Kay said. "How would publishing victims' names cause trouble for eState?"

Eddington was exasperated by his daughter's insistence.

It pained him to ask her—"Are you really that clueless?"

Kay's face turned red as she tried to tame her fury at the insult. "Are you serious?"

Eddington appeared equally insulted that she would honestly think he meant it.

"Of course not, sweetheart, I just don't know what else to tell you."

Eddington pondered Kay's initial question. He took a deep breath.

"Names and faces are powerful things. Control them, and you control the entire story," he explained. "If I know Haskell and his apparatus—just as you do—eState has to keep the story on the attack, not the victims. That makes eState the victim."

Kay was dejected. "But their stories ..."

"They'll be told in time," Eddington interrupted. "Hopefully."

"I'm still going to get them," Kay pushed.

"Even if you do, they're not airing," Eddington restated. "You're not to hunt them down. You're not to report a single word. Our independence banks on it."

{ }

Kay squinted in the late afternoon sunshine outside the main building of her father's campus. The sun was low to the west, adding a lively glow to her goldenrod suit. She spotted her car heading up the driveway. There was a folded note wedged under the driver's side windshield wiper.

The car stopped where Kay waited. She grabbed the paper

and opened the driver's door.

"Destination," a male voice said from the dashboard control panel.

"Hold," Kay ordered. She opened the note.

Kay looked out the windows to make sure no one was near, especially her father or any of his associates. Then she began reading.

A detailed map took up most of the letter-sized sheet. It included a set of directions to an abandoned suburb—North City West—about thirty kilometers north. Below the map was a street name with a vague address.

East on Quarter Mile Drive, turn left at marker 101.

No other instructions were needed. Given the barren environment up there, Kay was likely headed for a house that would be the only one occupied for blocks around it. By evening, such a dwelling would be the sole building with any light except a stray streetlamp along the way.

Kay was loosely familiar with North City West, a formerly dense community of houses, schools, and commercial centers that fell on hard times in recent decades. Few people lived in such regions anymore. Her knowledge of the area was based more on word-of-mouth descriptions than her own excursions.

The abandoned neighborhoods weren't known for any crime or other dangers. Nonetheless, the location disquieted Kay. Cities and crowds were her preference.

No matter the auction's location, Kay wanted those names. She had taken too many steps to skip the sale now.

She withdrew cash from her company account. Her contacts with the underground—a chain of people to scatter any breadcrumbs that could link her with a direct source—surreptitiously placed the note on her car for delivery. The one thing she couldn't allow was the car to drive itself.

"Manual pilot. GPS off," Kay said.

The car adjusted its settings. Kay took the steering wheel, hit the accelerator, and peeled off like a seasoned driver.

{ }

Kay's journey north was uneventful, but she was edgy. Such a trek reminded her of the disconnect between the dense metropolitan centers she was familiar with and the nearly dead, largely unoccupied suburbs, left to time's erosion and people's short memories.

Driving on a manual setting in this realm made sense to Kay, not just as a deterrent against digital footprints that could trace her movements, but to dodge roadway obstacles along the neglected freeways and side streets void of inhabitants. Just on the freeways alone about twenty kilometers out, Kay navigated lanes closed for construction never finished and various flotsam in her path.

By the time Kay arrived at North City West, she was vacillating between depression over the state of the world outside her bubble and wonderment about those few souls who still managed to live there.

She was close to her destination now.

{ }

The neighborhood was lined with crumbling relics, homes that hadn't seen use in years. There were hints of the formerly tamed landscape, but the yards, medians, streets, and sidewalks were overrun by weeds and native vegetation.

Not far ahead, Kay noticed one house that countered everything she had seen. It appeared as pristine as an insect trapped in amber, perfectly preserved. A two-story throwback frozen in time from the year it was built, from cream-colored stucco and dark brown trim to red-tile roof. The light from the windows made it a welcoming beacon among its dusty, forgotten brethren. Her unease evaporated, replaced by curiosity.

There was a small, professionally printed sign on a wooden post jammed into the dirt of an old yard across from the house: *Park here.*

Kay counted seven cars parked along the street, mostly older models. Two newer vehicles were the same model as hers, one light aqua blue and the other black. She parked near them and walked to the residence.

Judging from the number of cars and the lack of people, Kay concluded that this auction was a smaller, more intimate affair. She heard talk and light laughter as she walked to the front door.

She knocked. Several seconds passed until she heard someone approach. Kay was surprised when the door swung open. A tall, glamorous woman of about sixty in a vibrant red pencil dress stood at the doorway like a model at a swank reveal. The outfit's long sleeves and high neckline gave the woman a noble appearance. Her silver beehive hair, slate-colored eyes, small gold earrings, bracelets, and brilliant diamond wedding ring seemed as out of place as the pristine 1980s-era house, a piece of retro perfection among a ruined landscape.

The woman recognized Kay on the spot. "No need to scan you," she said with a smile.

The familiarity was mutual. "Elki?"

The two knew each other relatively well. Elki Reyes Stone was a unique mix of technology entrepreneur and wealthy socialite. When Elki's husband, Zyler Stone, sold their social media empire, Communion, to eState without her consent two years ago—and joined the eState fold himself as an executive alongside his lover—her divorce and lawsuit for breach of contract made headlines across the country. She kept the ring and continued to wear it.

The "Stone Split," as the scandal was branded, was one of Kay's first major national stories.

Elki was also a vocal critic of eState. She was philosophically opposed to its monopoly and rich enough to express her dissent without repercussion. That put her at odds with the Eddington family on occasion. Nonetheless, she built a good relationship with Kay on a professional level. Kay was de facto ambassador of the media empire as its lead anchor, so it only made sense to foster a friendship to promote her philanthropic pursuits.

At the moment, however, Kay was trying to make sense of how Elki ended up in such a peculiar place. Elki could tell.

"Yup. My auction," Elki said as she welcomed Kay inside.

Kay stopped her in the entryway. "How did you get the list?" she discreetly asked.

Elki put her left hand at Kay's right shoulder. "You'll have to fight for this one."

Kay understood what Elki meant as soon as they entered the living room. Past several finely dressed guests, at the sliding glass doors facing west, Kay saw Olivia Boyce talking to a rumpled professor type—Noel Appleby. Between Kay's posh suit, Elki's attire, and the upper-class threads worn by the rest, Olivia and Noel appeared the sole representatives of anything close to the middle. Olivia wore midnight black head-to-toe, including a messenger bag. Noel was his usual shopworn self in an open-neck shirt, slacks, suit coat, and loafers, all various shades of tan.

Olivia spied Kay across the room and raised her wineglass, which was filled with a small amount of chardonnay. Kay's presence was disappointing, though not surprising. Noel detected Olivia's concern.

"She can't get those names. They'll go straight to daddy," Noel told her.

"I know," Olivia said.

Olivia opened the back door and stepped out with Noel. They took in the scarred landscape of melting homes and half-dead trees.

"What the hell was all this for, huh?" Noel said hopelessly, shaking his head.

Olivia looked back at the house, around the well-maintained yard of shrubs, grass, swimming pool, and outdoor furniture, everything a mid-1980s museum piece.

"What do you make of this?" she asked.

"Word is she owns it," Noel shared.

"*Stone* ?"

Noel raised his eyebrows and nodded.

They watched Kay through the glass—pouring herself some red wine, toasting, sharing a laugh with the event's enigmatic host.

"That list is your domain, Liv," he said. "She can't have it."

"She won't," Olivia assured him. "I'm still curious why it matters to you so much."

Noel avoided her observation, returning his attention to the forgotten landscape around them.

Olivia tried to lighten the mood. "Elki doesn't allow a lot of special guests to these things, so you've got to give me something."

"I have two students on that list," Noel finally volunteered. "One of them is in pretty bad shape, that's all I know. Quinn. I want you to meet him, and a friend of his."

Then he looked down in self-reproach.

"I should've visited him a long time ago," he told her. "But I gave him some advice that ended up applying to him in a way I didn't intend. I'm afraid if he saw me, I'd be nothing more than a walking 'I told you so.' "

"Oh, I doubt it," Olivia said, trying to encourage him.

"I have to make a visit before I put my career to bed," he resolved. "I want you to come with me."

He looked at her with renewed energy. And a sense of urgency. "What he's gone through, my gut tells me he's a candidate."

Olivia slid the door open. "I better catch up with Kay before this thing gets started."

Kay surreptitiously monitored Olivia's movements. Then the two met eyes across the room. Once she realized Olivia was headed in her direction, she broke the small talk with Elki and a couple of the guests to greet her halfway.

"The setup for this one is a bit odd isn't it?" Kay said.

"It is," Olivia tepidly replied.

Elki and some of the guests couldn't help but notice their interaction, flashing side glances between bits of conversation and cheese and sips of wine. Such improvised meet-ups between the two were uncommon, even in limited settings. Were it not for the nature of the information on the block this time, they still would have kept their distance. But the names of the bombing victims were the missing human element to an appalling attack. The story was incomplete without them, no matter how much time had passed.

Olivia wondered if that gap in the reporting was by design on behalf of Kay, her network, and her father. It was the reason Olivia wanted to speak with her.

"What would you do with them?" Olivia candidly asked.

"With what?" Kay answered.

"The names," Olivia said, annoyed by Kay's blatantly false ignorance. "How would you use them?"

Kay stared at her without an answer.

"You bought that drive over six months ago and you've reported nothing," Olivia pointed out. "Is that what you're doing? Buying information to sit on?"

"My dad ..."

"Yeah, your dad, I know," Olivia interjected. She looked away. "Boy, do I know."

Olivia's reaction baffled Kay. *What's that about?*

"You should give me more credit," Kay said. "I'm serious. I want to run them."

Elki stood behind a table that held a spread of hors d'oeuvres. She took an empty wineglass and tapped it several times with a small knife. Her smile was broad and kind.

"Thank you all for being here," she said cordially. "I'm so proud to run this auction because the proceeds from tonight's item will go to a cause very dear to my heart. I grew up in these neighborhoods not long before they started to die. Many of the people who remain here still live well, but it's also home to those who lack food, regular water, and other basic resources. The kinds of things no corporate overseer like eState will bother with out here. Well, I won't forget, and neither should you."

Elki held up her left hand, asking the group to wait. She stepped away, out of sight, down the hallway to her right. Light conversation ensued among the participants. She returned carrying a short stack of papers, which were bound together with a black clip. She waved the stack above her head.

"This is what you're here for," she said. "And one hundred percent of what you pay will go to the Suburban Relief Fund."

Light applause erupted from the gathering.

To this point, Elki appeared to be running the operation alone. She had the poise of an elite cocktail party host, not the gritty manager of an off-the-radar intelligence sale.

Hidden cameras, maybe? Kay speculated. *A gun under the table?*

The questions were put to rest when two men entered the room from the hallway. Their black suits clung to their muscles. Metallic webbing between the fingers of their left hands indicated they held stun weapons of some kind. Both were in their mid-thirties, one with dark bronze skin and black hair in a mohawk fade, the other freckled with his red hair pulled back and tied. They held small pads of paper and pens, one for every member of the party.

For Olivia, the gathering felt more normal with their presence. She expected such measures at these events.

Elki motioned to the men, and they distributed a pad and pen to each guest.

"Please write your name and an opening bid, fold the paper, and place it on the table in front of me," Elki instructed.

Kay was not happy with this method. She had no way to know who she was competing against.

Bidders dropped their papers on the table. Elki opened each one, maintaining an impartial look as she read them.

"I have a high bid of twenty thousand," she announced.

Kay fought to hide an arrogant smirk, satisfied that her first bid set the mark. She looked at her competitors for reactions. Many shook their heads and chatted softly with each other. Others stood alone, keeping their poker faces. Then there was Olivia, whose eyes widened slightly at the bid.

Gotcha, Kay thought.

Olivia also noticed Kay's reaction. Now she knew who she was up against.

"Another round?" Elki asked.

Only three participants dared a second bid—Kay, Olivia, and a stout elderly lady in her eighties wearing a boxy kelly green blouse and dress. She glanced at her white leatherette purse before writing another bid.

The three dropped their papers on the table. Elki looked them over.

"Next high bid is fifty thousand."

Kay clenched her jaw. Who just outbid her? She looked at Olivia. No reaction. Then the elderly lady. No reaction, either.

"Again?" Elki asked.

The elderly lady looked around the room. She appeared sullen as she declined. Olivia immediately jotted another amount. Not to be outdone, Kay did the same.

Kay and Olivia placed their papers on the table. Elki reviewed them. She paused.

"One hundred fifty thousand."

The price spurred derisive grumbles among the gathering.

"Again?" Elki repeated.

Kay was stuck. There was no way her father would allow such an expense, especially after he rebuffed her buying the information in the first place. How much would these names be worth if she couldn't do anything with them? If her father refused to pay for them, such a personal expense could set Kay back months. She was unsure how much that was worth, too.

"No?" Elki said. "Congratulations, Olivia. The sale is yours."

There was hardly a reaction from anyone, signaling the other participants' resignation. The guests said their goodbyes quickly, dropped their pads and pens at the table, and began to leave just as hurriedly. Noel looked at Olivia in disbelief. He leaned toward her.

"Impossible," he whispered. "You ... that was impossible."

"You wanted me to get the list, you're not going to complain now," Olivia said in jest.

She walked toward Elki and the prized list waiting for her.

Kay was astonished. Her black market rival just blew past her with an offer she knew was patently unaffordable. She had to talk to Olivia.

"How did you pull that off?" Kay asked, mildly impressed.

"Saving pennies," Olivia replied.

"Maybe we can work together on this," Kay offered. "Split the cost, share the reporting."

"Or you can report the scoop that my people have," Olivia proposed, knowing that Kay couldn't mention anything coming from a black market outlet on her show, let alone the network.

"You're a local sheet under some really dark shadows," Kay chided. "Those names were worth fighting for. I could've given them a national audience."

Kay smiled half-heartedly at Elki, acquiescing to Olivia's victory, then left just behind the elderly woman in green.

Olivia was pleasantly surprised by Kay's determination. There was an authentic quality to it. But her track record was dicey. Olivia couldn't forget what Kay pulled a few months ago when she snagged the drive full of information only to bury it. Kay's motives and actions were always suspicious, as far as Olivia was concerned.

Elki looked at her two henchmen. "Make sure everyone's out and lock the door," she quietly ordered.

Olivia could see that Elki was undecided about Noel's presence, even though she knew who he was and allowed him as Olivia's personal guest.

"I need him to stay," Olivia told her.

Elki nodded.

Still, something wasn't right. An undertone of regret.

That was the only way Olivia could interpret Elki's changing mien. If Elki was having second thoughts about the deal, Olivia had better seal it fast. Olivia prepared to reach for the cash she had in her messenger bag.

"I brought my half as agreed," Olivia said. "I have enough on me."

Noel looked between the women, confused.

"Your half?" he asked.

"The bid was *ours*," Olivia explained. "Whatever it took, we'd split the cost. Seventy-five thousand, it ends up. It was a gamble, but it worked."

The moment should have been triumphant, but Elki was mournful. "You don't owe me anything."

Olivia's instinct was right. "And why is that?"

"Walter Eddington gets the list tonight," Elki admitted. "There's no price you could've bid to change that."

Olivia easily could have felt double-crossed, but given the twists these auctions often took, it was an outcome not altogether unforeseen. *Part of the game*, she kept in mind.

"So no one runs it," Olivia reckoned.

"He told me you and Kay would fight for it, and we both knew either of you would win over anyone else," Elki told her. "It's better she didn't get it. It saves him from yanking it out of her hands himself."

"I don't care how it spares his conscience," Olivia argued. "I know the pitfalls of dealing with him. I want to know *your* reason."

Elki's lower lip quivered. It was a symptom of the grief she could no longer hide. "I don't want her name published."

There was no way Olivia and Noel could have known

that Elki had a loved one on the victims list, and they were touched as they learned that was the case. Whatever the reason Elki feared to keep the name private, Olivia chose not to force the point. If the list could not be hers, however, she wanted to satisfy the second part of her mission—to see the names, at Noel's urging.

"Can we have a look?" Olivia requested. "At least that."

"It's important," Noel added.

Elki silently approved, clearing the water from her eyes as she unclipped the list. Olivia and Noel joined her on the other side of the table and began combing through the names and associated photos. Smiling, innocent faces, mostly from student identification cards. Printouts of brief biographies with marks of *deceased*, *injured*, or *whole* next to the names. Olivia first had to know who Elki was referring to.

Stone, Tiffany: Deceased

"Your daughter," Olivia realized aloud. "Elki. I'm sorry."

Elki appreciated the sympathy, understanding that they, too, were searching for victims. "I hope your people are okay."

"Look under Craig and Kellerman," Noel reminded Olivia, who continued to leaf back and forth through the pages.

While Noel knew his students had been hit in the attack—and survived—he was in the dark about the extent of any injuries they suffered.

Craig, Jasper: Whole
Kellerman, Quinn: Injured

Jasper's entry indicated survival without trauma—at least physically. The description of Quinn's injuries, however, fractured even Olivia's solid composure. Her mouth fell open at the horrid description of his mangled lower body. Noel closed his eyes.

"To survive something like that," Olivia said.

"He did," Noel considered. "And now more than ever, I can't see him. I told you why. I was on the fence before. But look at this."

"No," Olivia insisted. "You absolutely have to go. And so do I. I want to know these two."

05: TRANSMUTATION

Quinn sat alone, shivering in the hot air of a humid summer afternoon.

It was early August, yet he might as well have been in a meat locker. It was a jagged, icy sensation he couldn't shake. Quinn's eyes showed the pain and wear of adjusting to a body now repaired and ready for use. His eyelids were a pinkish red. The whites around his pupils were wrapped in vines of inflamed vessels.

The hospital's rooftop garden was pleasant enough. Green bonsai. Various shrubs and flowers. A calming waterfall. The sound of the water, the sky peppered with puffy subtropical clouds, brought to Quinn's mind the summer in which he almost drowned. The friend who saved him then—Jasper, who inexplicably abandoned him in the bombing—was no hero today. While Quinn sat in a wooden chair in the garden, Jasper sobbed silently in a Reflection Room nearby.

Even though Jasper spent virtually all of his free time with Quinn in the months since, Quinn was unable to forgive him for his desertion. It was an attitude that belied a more sensitive temperament. Quinn wrestled with the possibility that Jasper's abandonment was nothing more than shock, the kind that jars one so deeply that any behavior defies explanation. That was the reasonable conclusion. Quinn, however, was not in a reasonable space. He hadn't been for some time.

Quinn felt badly for the jab he threw at Jasper a few minutes before, yet part of him believed that his lack of patience and compassion for Jasper's own pain was only fair. Jasper still came out of the bombing with the better deal.

Today's trek from the rehabilitation floor to the roof should have been cause for celebration. Quinn made the journey on his own power for the first time. But the toll it took in pain and fatigue was too much. There was a point where Quinn couldn't get his new right foot up a shallow step on the rooftop garden's deck. Quinn was using a cane, balancing himself on it with his left hand. Jasper grabbed Quinn's right arm, an offer of support. But Quinn repelled him with a rapid shove to the chest.

"Too late," Quinn chided through his clenched teeth.

Jasper's feelings were hurt. He backed away and thew his hands up, leaving an opening for Quinn to assail him further.

"I could've used your hand on President's Day."

The two stared at each other briefly. Jasper, dejected, walked away and hid in the Reflection Room while Quinn tried to take in the summer air.

Quinn knew his words stung. But his own pain outweighed that concern. He quaked in a freeze, yet his lower body felt afire deep within, a scorching sensation beyond description or comparison. Organic nerves attempted to connect with new synthetic counterparts. As he sat in the chair, he looked at legs that were his, yet not. The sense of touch was foreign. He felt nothing of the surfaces against him—sweatpants, socks, shoes. When he stood, moved, or sat, the sensation was dull and nondescript.

The new links being forged were overwhelming him. The clashing signals threw his body into chaos. The result: A warm, muggy summer day felt like winter below zero.

Quinn heard the glass doors behind him slide open. He looked over his shoulder. Noel, his university news adviser, entered the garden carrying a small, plain cardboard box under his left arm. Not counting Jasper, this was Quinn's first visitor. Quinn worked up somewhat of a smile.

Noel sat beside him, looking just as rumpled and outdated as ever in a white Bahama shirt, tan slacks, and dark brown loafers. The sunlight cast deep shadows into the lines of Noel's face. It was a mask that seemed to be of two people—kindly laugh lines around his mouth and eyes; stress-worn creases between his eyebrows and up his forehead.

"How are you?" Noel said, noticing Quinn's shiver.

"Getting there," Quinn answered. "It took you a while to find me."

Noel shook his head. "I wasn't sure you'd want to see me."

"Why wouldn't I?" Quinn asked.

"Well, like I told a friend of mine yesterday, I thought I'd be a ... how did I say it ... a big, blaring 'I Told You So.' "

"Yeah, but you were right," Quinn conceded. "So now I'm here. And no, there's nothing wrong seeing you. I'm glad you're here."

Noel handed him the box. "This is not supposed to be on the premises, but the nurses said you were a special case."

Quinn carefully opened it, revealing a bottle. He didn't take the bottle out for risk of dropping it, but the cork told him all he needed to know. An EAB logo was burned into the top. A fine bourbon.

"And not an eState brand," Noel said. "Hell no."

Quinn smiled. "Oh man, this stuff's good."

"I did have to make a deal with them. The nurses, I mean," Noel warned. "That bottle isn't to be opened until after you get out of here, so no sneaking sips in a paper cup."

Teacher and student shared a transitory laugh. Quinn sensed there was more to Noel's visit.

"Your dad? Anything from him?" Noel inquired.

Quinn shook his head. "Just a call." His eyes were damp enough from the pain to disguise any dismay. "I don't think I'll be seeing him for a long time."

"You'll be fine. No doubt about that."

Quinn could barely hold in a whimper. "I don't think so," he said as he looked at the distant hills to the east.

Noel's shoulders sunk. He realized just how profound Quinn's misery was. Noel briefly observed the rooftop garden. It occurred to him that someone was missing.

"How's Jasper? Has he been to see you?" Noel asked.

"I think I made him cry."

It took a couple of seconds for Noel to understand Quinn's answer. He knew the friendship was a volatile, conflicted, brotherly mix. He knew Jasper saved Quinn's life during that summer between their freshman and sophomore years. Jasper must have visited Quinn during the past several months.

"I don't think I'm a very likable person," Quinn said.

"*That* is absolutely not true," Noel asserted. "Look at me now."

Quinn side-glanced Noel, fighting feelings of shame for a whole host of things. Selling out a grieving mother—for his own gain—when his conscience should have prevented it. Dismissing the plights of the afflicted. Questioning little to nothing.

Noel's stare drove right through him. "Does that matter to you?"

"It depends," Quinn answered. "For the right reasons."

"There are no right reasons," Noel argued. "You're tussling with whether you like yourself. You wouldn't have come to me all those times otherwise. Your gut, that's what it's all about. You've got to follow it. You didn't before. Now you have to. You can start by doing two things."

Quinn tilted his head, waiting to hear more.

"You're going back to school, I take it," Noel said.

Quinn nodded.

"Good."

"Taking more classes from you," Quinn said.

Noel paused. "No."

The answer rattled Quinn. For a moment, he feared he was the reason for Noel's rejection. Perhaps it wasn't him specifically but what he embodied—the kind of student Noel frustratingly tried to reach but couldn't.

"I'm not going back," Noel confessed. "I took my retirement at the end of the semester. I'm yesterday, Quinn. The world has to belong to you."

Quinn was relieved. Still, he was disappointed that he wouldn't get the chance to truly absorb what Noel had to offer just as he was coming to value it.

"Keep in touch, then?" Quinn asked.

"Can't really say. My partner and I are leaving the grid as much as we can. Consider me unplugged," Noel declared with melancholic pride. "So, thing one, get back to your studies. We got that covered. Thing two. There's someone I demand that you meet. You and Jasper both."

Noel directed his eyes to the box. "Look in there again."

Quinn noticed a folded sheet of paper wedged between the bottle and one of the sides. Quinn reached for it, but Noel stopped him.

"Not now; wait."

"No, I'm going to look," Quinn lightly insisted.

Quinn fought the shiver running through his body as he worked the paper free. It vibrated in his left hand. He motioned for Noel to take the box from his lap, which Noel obliged. There was a note scribbled on the paper. The state of Noel's handwriting—barely legible—surprised Quinn. The concern on Quinn's face was evident.

"I'm having my moments lately," Noel granted. "Time to retire."

Remember Quinn,
You matter, and so does your work, now more than ever.
All my best,
Noel

Quinn rubbed his eyes, fighting the urge to cry.

"There's someone you'll want to know in the years to come, maybe even work for," Noel said. "Just meet her, talk to her."

Noel got up and headed for the doors. He walked through

as they slid open. Quinn was in too much discomfort to wonder why Noel left so abruptly.

{ }

The windows of the Reflection Room faced east to the medical center's garden. It wasn't a big space, at most the size of a large bedroom. The wooden ceiling—low and arched—looked like it had been taken from a ship's cabin. The walls were paneled in the same wood, the floor covered in thin burgundy carpet. There was nothing religious about it. Just the windows, a couch, and a few chairs facing the garden view. And silence.

In the half hour since the blow-up with Quinn, Jasper sat on the floor, leaning against the wall opposite the windows. He spent the time sobbing quietly, replaying the bombing's aftermath in his mind. Jasper could see Quinn lying in a bloody mess on the concrete, increasingly smaller in the distance as he backed away from the scene.

Jasper thought of his sister—Thea—for whom he could do nothing as she wasted away from so-called *glacier flu*, a mysterious superbug traced to a major ice melt that spread rapidly across the continents in less than a decade. Then he thought about the time he rescued Quinn from that rain-swollen wash in Arizona. He risked his own life then. He wished he could have when Thea got sick. How could he have abandoned Quinn after the drones detonated?

Pray. Find an answer.

He jettisoned that notion. Jasper split paths from his family on the power of prayer some time ago. There had to be something he could *do*.

Jasper caught a glimpse earlier of Noel talking with Quinn. He hesitated to join them. Now, he shook off the heartache as best he could. It was time to catch up with his old professor and show Quinn that, despite whatever battles they might have from here on, he was determined to stay.

I can find an answer on my own. I'll find a way to make it up to him.

{ }

About five minutes passed until Quinn heard the doors open again. Noel returned. Olivia followed a few steps behind him. Quinn struggled to stand so he could greet the unexpected guest.

Olivia was considerably shorter than Quinn. Still, she was imposing with her shaved hair, plum high-neck shirt, black sport coat, slacks, and boots. Quinn's right hand trembled as he offered it to shake.

"I'm Quinn ..."

"I know who you both are," she interrupted, nicely enough but cool and to the point. "I've seen the victims list."

Olivia gripped Quinn's hand and shook it. He had a strong grasp despite his weakened state. It impressed her.

"Olivia Boyce," she said as the three of them sat. "Where's the other one?"

"I don't think he's coming back," Quinn told her.

Olivia studied Quinn's shiver, the crimson vessels permeating the whites of his eyes. She knew enough of his backstory from the victims list to understand the source of his agony. If Quinn got this far in recovery, Olivia sensed, he would make it.

The doors to the garden opened again. Jasper stood at the entrance. He waved timidly at Noel, then looked at Quinn. No words were necessary for Quinn to say *I'm sorry*. Jasper could tell from the look on his face.

Olivia locked her eyes on Jasper as he approached them, sizing him up like a cadet. She was indifferent as they exchanged brief introductions and he sat with them.

"I hear the two of you want to be journalists," Olivia said.

"We *are* journalists," Quinn told her.

"Not yet, you're not," she contended. "First you were in college, then you got hurt."

Quinn fixated on her—a judge skeptical of a lawyer's argument. She respected that. It was ironic, too, since she was also the one judging them.

"Algorithms can write stories. But humans ask the questions," she continued. "When your family gets sick because the soil under your home cooks them with radiation, you learn to ask questions. The right ones. And you get answers."

Quinn speculated about a hint he heard in what Olivia said, the reference to being "cooked with radiation."

Parthia? he thought. *Interesting.*

The eState company town in southeast Missouri was built about twenty years ago as a testing site for alternative energy projects. The ill effects on the community's residents were mysterious and slow to develop, but they were survivable. For those untreated, however, the results were gruesome and deadly. So it was rumored. The truth about what went down in Parthia was scarce, dismissed as *fringe-fact* circulated by crackpots.

Whether Olivia experienced the town's demise herself was unclear to Quinn, but he surmised that she either had relatives working at the site or was interested enough in the case to chase it early in her career.

"That's how I got my start," she told them. "I was in school like you, getting taught to paint by numbers, worrying more about social platforms and smiling faces, plugging in the pieces for the Cloud to do the thinking and writing for me."

Olivia was particularly interested in Quinn's reaction. Noel told her about Quinn's tendency to double cross sources on the black market to make money. It was a trait she was wary of, but she hoped the bombing might have reshaped his mind-set. That's what she was there to find out.

"What's your interest in us?" Quinn asked.

"I want to know what you care about, where you want to be in a few years," Olivia told him.

Quinn shrugged.

His reaction surprised Olivia. After all he had been through, Quinn had to have some idea of where his life would be headed from here on. More to the point, he had to care about something.

Maybe it was the fact it was a bad day for him. He couldn't even enjoy the warmth of a summer afternoon. He was exhausted as his brain and nervous system adjusted to the synthetic reality of his replacement limbs. He snapped at his best friend.

Olivia's inquiry did have an answer, however. Quinn cared about one thing—the lack of serious questions about the bombing and its aftermath. He recalled the pang he felt as news reports glossed over eState's contention that the protesters would bomb themselves and cause such collateral damage. In the months that followed, eState's proof of that assertion was vague at best.

Olivia had no way to know what Quinn cared about, but she wondered if the tragedy he endured would shape him into the kind of journalist she sought.

Quinn noticed a thin, black shoulder bag that Olivia brought with her. Its shape was perfect for papers. When she saw him look at it, she took that as a cue. Olivia opened the bag and handed him what appeared to be a folded newspaper.

The Observator

Stories raking muck about eState dominated the black market paper's front page. Two headlines caught Quinn's attention.

CIA operative missing in eState espionage probe
eState execs' kids fast-tracked into top universities

"You ever read one?" Olivia asked.

Quinn sneered at the question. The paper was a trigger that ignited memories of the days when he derided such underground media.

"You know how much in here is fringe-fact?" he told her. "I turned over sources trying to push this stuff."

"Were you injured by a conspiracy theory?" Olivia argued.

Quinn resisted the urge to resent her, but the challenge

thrown at him by this stranger was beyond his tolerance.

"We're done," Quinn said.

"Quinn, think about what she's saying," Noel pleaded.

"I'm freezing here on a summer day, I'm hurting all over the place, I'm just barely learning to walk," Quinn said impatiently. "I've got enough to think about."

Then he looked at Olivia. "And I don't know you."

There was something about Quinn's eyes that told Olivia he wasn't as abrasive as he appeared. His scathing comebacks seemed to be a trait that he held underneath, a magazine discharged only when he deemed it necessary. Otherwise, his eyes conveyed a softness, a sage quality. That was in contrast to Olivia, whose abrasiveness was pure. She was affable enough, but when it came to business, she would push to the point. She had little patience for empty gab, and she made no apologies for it.

"In time, I hope you do. I certainly want to know you." Then she looked to Jasper. "Both of you."

Quinn tossed the paper on a small table next to him.

"Keep that," Olivia offered. "Just don't go parading it around the hospital. Look at what's in there. You'll find the kinds of stories you'll never see mainstream. That's the stuff that really matters. If you still want this work, it has to matter to you, too. How long have you got left in your studies?"

"At least a year when we start back," Jasper answered.

"Plenty of time to think about it," Olivia replied as she got up to leave. "Oh, one other thing. The black market's not the place where you're going to get rich. You barely make a living, but you do the work because you care."

Olivia walked toward the doors. "You'll find me if you're ready," she said without turning back. "When you're ready."

Noel watched Olivia leave the garden. Then he turned to Quinn.

"It's your story now."

06: THOUSAND DAYS POST

It was an odd little device. Made of wood and metal, it looked like an old-fashioned telegraph key designed to tap messages in Morse code. Exposed wires—red, black, green, and yellow—connected pieces of the device together, all fixed to a dark cherrywood base. A black power cord exited the back. The device could very well have been a repurposed antique. New or vintage, it was designed to send something quite different than a coded message. It was there to provide comfort, ease pain.

Measured drops of clear liquid fell from the tap onto a heated metal plate a few centimeters below on the wooden base. Each drop instantly sizzled and evaporated, leaving a brief trail of vapor and a sweet, earthy scent. A small glass vial filled with the liquid was attached to a component just behind the tap. The quiet, steady sizzle was a soothing sound. The resulting vapor combined to take Quinn's mind off whatever pain was troubling him, be it physical or emotional.

The drop maker, small as it was, had prominent space on the top of Quinn's dresser, in front of the diploma for his master's degree in news curation, the goal once sidelined but now complete. Quinn was first taken by the gadget's woodsy aroma a couple of years ago as he concluded his post-bombing rehab, what he came to call the first of his two graduations.

Quinn's eyes were bloodshot, half open, and watery from the high. He was at home, lying in bed, somewhat awake, dwelling on the event that almost killed him and challenged his perceptions of truth and purpose.

Yes, Quinn rebuilt himself in the thousand days since the bombing. But even fully healed, he still didn't feel entirely whole. As the drops evaporated, Quinn thought about Theresa Bell, the woman he sold out to eState authorities the night before the attack. She crossed his mind occasionally, and he accepted the twist of Karma that just as her story was never told, his hadn't been either.

Guilt aside, right now, he was free of the shocking, zinging, electric sensation that ran through him since the explosion that racked his body. Quinn had learned to live with it, to embrace it as a reminder that he was alive. But even in those times when the sensation wasn't there—thanks to a narcotic or the simple fact his body decided to give him a break—he was still working through the sense that physically he only half existed now, however unfair a perception that might be.

Quinn rubbed his face as he worked to clear the haze in his head. He took in one last deep breath of the ambrosial forest-scented vapor. He looked at the dimly lit digital clock on the nightstand, which cast an amber glow across the room—12:25 a.m. He had to be at the first of his two jobs in about an hour.

{ }

Pounding taps fired off in succession like automatic weapons. The sound wasn't particularly loud, but to the untrained ear of someone living in this period, it would be startling. The taps would fire off inconsistently, almost as if they were being shot at intervals by hand. Several machines going at once, at efficient factory pace.

The sharp bursts echoed around a run-down office space with an open ceiling to the rafters, part of a large converted warehouse. The room was large and poorly lit, mostly with desk lamps. Desks were scattered in loose rows. But the sound that could be fearful to the modern ear was actually quite harmless, unless you were the specific target. The machines responsible for the noise weren't guns or other such weapons. They were electric typewriters, a kind of machine not manufactured for decades, held together and maintained using ancient reused pieces, parts recreated by artisans and small entrepreneurs, or personal hacks by those who used the instruments.

The journalists sitting at these desks at 2 o'clock on a Monday morning weren't using this old analog machinery because it was quaint. They were using it to keep their work off the digital networks—the tentacles—that belonged to eState, its subsidiaries, and allies. Everything about this operation was analog, from pen and pad to printing press and finished copy.

This newsroom reflected the first of Quinn's decisions when Jasper asked him "What do we do?" that day in the hospital where he sat broken in recovery. It was an answer to the challenge posed to Quinn by his mentor, Noel, the final time he saw him. "It's your story now."

Quinn and Jasper sat across from each other at their desks, typing stories on deadline for the next edition of *The Observator*. Reading, let alone producing, such a publication was technically illegal by eState standards. Reading this sort of so-called "fake news" could result in harassment by eState's security apparatus, fines of various levels, possible jail time if the material found in the paper was considered a security threat. The rules were nebulous, barely justifiable constitutionally, and casually enforced. But when they were, the action was swift and the consequences were unpredictable.

Despite that, people produced and read this content for the very reason that it was *not* fake news. It was the counter-punch to the Eddingtons of the world who walked lightly around eState to keep themselves in business and power.

The baronial entrances of eState officials so beautifully produced, packaged, and delivered through Walter Eddington's holdings were not to be found underground. Instead of the perfect smiles, handshakes, and self-aggrandizing compliments the purest of dictators would love, black market news shared the real stories, off the grid and out of eState's reach. The payoffs to local and state officials to conveniently resign and hand off government control in the form of "contracts" that would "streamline" government services and turn voters into citizen shareholders. Dark and dirty secrets of eState managers and leaders. People missing or mysteriously dead. Soldiers and law enforcement officers killed through incompetence in training and leadership. Lackluster regulations of medicine, food, environment, everything the master company touched.

It was Quinn's answer to his own pain. The lesson learned from his near-death experience. He had become one of eState's quiet statistics, and now he was working on the black market. But that wasn't the whole story. This was only one of his jobs.

Quinn's eyes were still inflamed as he flipped through handwritten notes and typed at efficient speed.

Headline: *San Diego Council Paid Off to Quit; Votes Itself out of Office with Millions in Payoffs from eState.*

Olivia Boyce, *The Observator*'s editor, entered from a nearby hallway. She scanned the room, singling out Quinn and Jasper for casual scrutiny. Jasper looked at Quinn as he continued working, eyes fixated on his typewriter. Olivia walked to her desk and sat. She thumbed through a short stack of assignments.

Jasper leaned forward to Quinn.

"You've got to lay off the drops," he advised at a near whisper. "It's getting obvious."

"They're legal," Quinn said, keeping eyes to paper and typewriter.

Olivia was perturbed. "Quinn. Over here, please."

Jasper shook his head and got back to work. Quinn stood stiffly, took a moment to steady himself, and walked over to her.

"Yeah," he said impatiently.

"Cut the drops. You were late again tonight," Olivia told him.

Jasper shook his head again, overhearing the conversation. Quinn nodded and turned to leave.

"Hang on," she said. He turned back to her. "If you're in pain and you need a break, just tell me. I'd rather give you time off than have you come in here high. Finish up."

Quinn walked back to his desk.

{ }

Everything about the operation these journalists worked in was beyond old-school. Throughout the late night and early hours before sunrise, stories, photos, and graphic elements were all produced using equipment dating from the 1960s to maybe the early '90s. Staff members in the paste-up department processed rolls of photographic paper and laser print, slicing and waxing pieces into place on large pages, prepping them for the presses. By 3 to 4 a.m., copies zipped at blurring speed through two giant presses in a plant attached to the newsroom. It was an incredible sight that was out of place and time yet more relevant than ever given an interconnected world in which every A through Z, every face in a photo or piece of video, was traced and logged by watchful corporate eyes.

It was now about 4:30 a.m., and Quinn and Jasper were in a side room off the presses, stuffing copies of the basic black-and-white *Observator* into gray canvas bags for delivery. The duo wore black, from shoes to hoodies. Their road bikes were at the ready against a wall.

The early March sky was just starting to turn a deep blue at the horizon as Quinn rode his route, which changed week by week, sometimes day by day, to prevent easy identification. He sped by rows of newer townhomes, tossing copies of the paper as he went, always keeping the hood of his sweatshirt low and his eyes out for busybodies who might not appreciate the unsolicited free deliveries. The streets were empty, as they should be for this time of morning. Aside from autonomous cars and trucks, and commuter trains, automobiles of any kind were increasingly rare and usually not on the roads until about 9 or 10 a.m. Quinn kept to the center of the road to avoid full illumination from the few streetlights dotting the way.

Something caught his eye a few houses ahead to the left. He could barely make out the figure in the dim predawn light. He swayed farther to the other side of the street to avoid any interaction. As Quinn approached, he was able to make out a rotund woman in a white robe, hair under a flower-patterned cap, probably in her late sixties, walking a small, black poodle-like dog along the sidewalk.

Quinn eyed the woman as she observed him with what he deemed a suspicious look. That's the kind of busybody Quinn always had to be wary of. He skipped tossing papers to some of the houses near her. He passed her by.

"Excuse me. Sir?!" she said in a surprisingly friendly tone.

Should he stop?

Quinn kept going.

"Please!" the woman yelled. "You got the paper?!"

Quinn stopped. He turned around. He could tell by her voice that this was not one of those busybodies. It was against his better judgment, but he went to her.

He shrouded his face in shadow as best he could. A bit of light reflected off his glasses in the darkness. He stepped off his bike and handed a copy of *The Observator* to the woman. Her dog pretty much ignored him.

"I know you guys don't like being seen. Thank you," the woman said as she took the paper.

The woman's dog neared Quinn's right foot as it sniffed around the grass strip between the sidewalk and curb.

Suddenly, the dog snuffled, jerked back, and looked at Quinn's leg. Quinn looked down, wondering what the dog was doing. The dog slowly, cautiously approached Quinn's foot again. Something just didn't add up for the pet. Quinn moved his foot away slightly, and the dog again acted surprised.

The woman smiled as she hid the newspaper under her robe. "He knows," she said, observing the dog's behavior. "So do I. It's all right."

Quinn nodded, got back on the bike, and sped off.

{ }

It was now about 7 in the morning. Quinn closed the front door behind him. He squinted from the bright red-orange sunlight cast across the wall from the living room windows. He parked his bike next to the door, the burlap sack now empty of newspapers. He shook his right leg, wincing in a fleeting shock of pain. He took off his glasses and hoodie, revealing a tight black T-shirt underneath. Quinn tended to be reserved, intellectual in his demeanor, but his athletic build also indicated someone who cared about how he felt physically. This juxtaposition of personality and appearance often drew people to Quinn. It frustrated him because he never considered himself anything particularly special.

Quinn sighed, rubbed his forehead, and headed for the bedroom. He was still fairly groggy from the drops he inhaled before dawn, and now he was tired from the dark hours' work. A shower was in order.

Quinn's work was nowhere near done. He had another job, and he was due there by 9 a.m. It wasn't unusual for anyone to have two jobs, even three or more. What was unusual for Quinn and others in his field was the willingness to walk the line between light and shadow. The work was more exhausting mentally and emotionally than physically. Quinn had to be two people, maintaining facades for two audiences. That weighed on him sometimes, but the work was also his passion, part of his reason for being.

There was little time for sleep during weeks like this, when work was heavy at both jobs. The steady rain of the shower was a relaxing substitute, though. Quinn could spend a good ten to fifteen minutes just standing under the warm water, emptying his mind, thinking of absolutely nothing. It was the kind of escape he appreciated because it didn't require a narcotic.

{ }

Refreshed from his respite at home, Quinn was now his second self. Hair sharply styled, brown Henley, black slacks, a fresher pair of his favorite black sneakers, a case containing his work tablet by his side. He sat alone in a row of seats aboard a commuter rail car, the world sweeping by in a blur beyond the windows as the train traveled at high speed.

Aside from a stray civilian, the car was occupied by members of eState's management class—men and women in upscale, repetitively styled business suits wearing wireless earpieces and monocles glowing red or green. Some of them had empty stares. Others' eyes darted back and forth as if they were reading something. Several appeared to talk to themselves as they typed and swiped on tablets.

Quinn was disquieted yet encouraged by this set. Watching

them, he observed how mechanical they all seemed—beings who looked human but no longer were. He was relieved because their seeming lack of human presence reminded him that—synthetically enhanced as he now was—he was still fully human. Quinn struggled with his sense of humanity, what it felt to be alive, since the blast three years ago. He often worried that he was actually only half alive, living half a life. The people on this train were a message that his impressions were wrong. He was alive. Whole. They were not.

{ }

Bruce Haskell contorted his right hand into a tight ball, crunching the latest edition of *The Observator* in his fingers as he stood facing his nemesis, Walter Eddington. The front page's top headline peeked through the creases of the paper: *San Diego City Council Paid Off to Quit.*

Haskell threw the copy on Eddington's office desk. Eddington, calm and amused, leaned back in his chair, his hands cupped in a triangle below his chin.

"Did you see what's on that front page?!" Haskell barked. "I want answers from you, Eddington! No one knew about this deal!"

Eddington smirked. "Someone did."

Haskell was incapable of lightening up. One of the things he couldn't buy was a sense of humor. He took the paper and shook it at Eddington.

"It made it onto the black market!" Haskell ranted. "It's accurate!"

Eddington's smile widened a little, but his gut tightened.

Haskell just confirmed the report was true.

"So eState did buy off the council at seventy-five million a pop."

Haskell would not tolerate that interpretation.

"It was a buy-*out.* A severance package."

"Like every good politician deserves," Eddington replied. No one could win a war of words with Walter Eddington.

Three years after his last entrance from the clouds, arriving to the corporate rescue, Haskell was in a weaker position than he expected. He was in Eddington's castle trying to explain away an act of basic chicanery. *How the hell can I clear this moron off the plate?* Haskell thought as he stood across from the silver-haired irritant.

Haskell tossed the paper back on the desk. Eddington quickly grabbed it. He got up and walked over to his foe, waving the paper for emphasis.

"The only glaring omission in this piece is the PR campaign I waged for you to take over this state in the first place," Eddington said as he guided Haskell to the office exit, through to the foyer.

"Well it wasn't good enough," Haskell challenged. "*You're* are not good enough! I shouldn't have to travel incognito to make my deals. That's what your PR is getting me."

Time had not been kind to Haskell. The eState executive was the monopoly's golden boy, and he set up shop in California personally to slay the biggest bureaucratic beast in the United States and fold it into the behemoth's family. Rumors persisted, however, that eState was behind the university bombing. Haskell's efforts to quell that suspicion were only partly successful. Pockets of resistance in the big cities—Los Angeles,

San Diego, and San Francisco—were nagging, annoying pests to his success. The crisply produced media packages showing his love of the people and their adoration for him in return gave way to quiet arrivals in unmarked jets, with Haskell spirited away in smoke-mirrored vans to his destinations.

Behind closed doors, Haskell's hustle to sell eState's vision to regional power players worked, but only so far. Much of California—the inland and northern counties—were fully under eState contracts. High-tech hub San Francisco was the first major city to fall under its spell. Then arts capital Los Angeles. San Diego was the last holdout, the state's locus of biotech and advanced medicine, which Haskell thought would be an easy customer.

But Haskell met his match in Walter Eddington. It was Eddington's own leviathan that kept Haskell and eState in check, largely because Eddington held power over the message.

So how could Haskell undercut his nemesis? By doing what he did throughout the state, what was common practice throughout the eState empire—buy off civic leaders and bureaucrats under the table. The message was clear to a dwindling number of resistant politicians and institutions. If you wanted to stay in the game, either you played by the rules of new masters or you left the board.

What Haskell couldn't understand was how people could think in any other way. Basic rights, commerce, security, governance. All of those were for sale, weren't they? It infuriated him that the black market press had its eyes and ears so close to his furtive methods to gain control. He was irate that Eddington—the mainstream incarnate—didn't seem to care.

"That information came from somewhere in this

organization, I'm convinced of it!" Haskell barked again, half-circling Eddington like a small dog trying to exert dominance over a bigger one as they walked toward an elevator past the foyer. "You need to keep your people in line!"

Eddington calmly dodged Haskell's blocks, but he was growing tired of the man's tirade. He hit the down button at the elevator and whipped back to Haskell, gently pressing two fingers into Haskell's chest.

"I've backed every move eState's made over the last several years, shy of calling for the governor's assassination!" Eddington said with a tense jaw.

"Then find out who's leaking our business to the black market press!" Haskell insisted.

Haskell had a point, but Eddington didn't dare let him know it. Journalists were journalists, and it was entirely possible that information was being shared across the lines.

"I will get to the bottom of it. But on my terms," Eddington said.

The elevator bell rang and the doors opened. Eddington and Haskell walked in, the doors closed, and they headed down. Haskell flared his nostrils and briefly shook his head at the elevator's odd marijuana-like scent, something Haskell complained about in some form every time he had to visit the building. The scent was a running joke since the complex opened. It was definitely not the narcotic, as the scent also carried a petrochemical note. Whether it was the faux light-wood paneling, the metal and plastic accents, flooring, or hydraulic fluid, no one could determine the source.

With another ring of the bell, the elevator stopped at the fifth floor, Commissary. Haskell blinked impatiently. Quinn entered, his eyes widening for a nanosecond realizing the Goliaths he just joined. The elevator continued downward.

Awkward silence reigned as the two titans stood alongside Eddington's employee.

Eddington glanced at Quinn.

"Good day so far?" Eddington asked.

Quinn nodded. "Yes, sir. Yours?"

Eddington side-glanced Haskell. "Productive."

The bell rang again and the doors opened. Third floor. Quinn exited, followed by Eddington, who threw one last look at Haskell as the doors closed on him.

Quinn and Eddington headed in the same direction from the floor's entryway to the newsroom of *The Citizen*. This was Quinn's second job (unknown to Eddington and all but maybe two others on the staff).

The Citizen was San Diego's major metropolitan daily news site, housed in the same complex that held Eddington's nationwide media empire. The floor above it was the domain of *News United*, the seat of Eddington's video and audio networks anchored by his daughter and her colleagues.

The newsroom walls were plastered with large media screens running the day's productions, including the website, which blared a massive headline in bold type: *San Diego Council Hands Torch to eState*. It was a vastly different take on the story seen in print on the streets that morning.

A staff of about seventy worked at large open tables (cubicles were considered obsolete). There were spaces for five people per table where staff members had tablets docked at ports connected to larger screens running along the center of each station.

The room was streamlined and antiseptic in its beige hues, metallic gray accents, and navy blue carpet, yet there was a buzz about the place—coworkers discussing their work, sipping coffee, watching the broadcasts from upstairs. It was an engaging place to be despite the clinical ambience.

The environment in this newsroom was starkly opposite to that of *The Observator* in most respects, however. The camaraderie was similar, the energy of the work, but here the stories were shallow, mundane, and largely unimportant.

The next top headline in rotation on the site: *Pint-Sized Brainiac Wins Over 'Star Moves' Audience.*

Very little actual writing took place anymore, superseded by algorithms and artificial intelligence. Quinn and Jasper, and others like them, preferred the rough-around-the-edges feel of old-school style. But the more secure jobs, reputation, and "real world" opportunities were in Eddington's realm.

Quinn sat at his station, next to Jasper. Eddington headed to the editor's office several meters away toward the other end of the floor, closing the door behind him. Jasper observed Eddington out of the corner of his eye as he worked on a story. Quinn docked his tablet. A soft chime rang.

"Enter instruction," an automated woman's voice said.

As he did in college, Quinn spoke commands into the tablet to construct a story. The woman's voice echoed repeatedly throughout the newsroom, activated by Quinn's colleagues for every project.

"He's pissed about something," Jasper quietly noted as he covertly watched Eddington through the editor's office window, shaking the copy of *The Observator* and berating the editor, a man in his early thirties wearing a plaid shirt, high-and-tight hair.

"There's nothing to worry about is there?" Jasper whispered.

"I don't know," Quinn replied, keeping his eyes to the tablet.

Brassy, newsy music rose from the room's television screens. Vivid red, white, and blue graphics moved across: *Final Word With Kay Eddington.* A swift camera shot pushed in on Kay's face as she looked up with an air of smug confidence.

"What would you rather be? Citizen or shareholder?" Kay asked her audience. "I vote for shareholder."

Quinn and Jasper paused to watch. There was no way not to watch her, actually, since her face was practically on every wall, big screen and small.

"eState has been rolling out its corporate governance model across the country over the last few years. The final holdout? Of all places, San Diego, the business-forward biotech hub of our nation," Kay said, cool and persuasive. "Every state, and the federal government itself, signed on to put an end to corruption and big government by contracting with eState. Except California, thanks to San Diego. But my hometown finally saw the light. And today, we can be shareholders with the rest of you."

Quinn was mildly amused by her editorial. He got back to work.

{ }

Kay sat at the studio news desk, resolute, the stage lights giving her blonde hair a vivid, almost blazing appearance.

When she shared a report or opinion on her show, her confidence and charisma left no doubt that she was a well-studied authority.

Her sponsor, Chillax Cola, certainly believed so. A can of its product—black, emblazoned with caution-yellow type screaming its name—was prominently displayed at the end of her broadcasts. It was a seal of approval for millions of young watchers. Chillax was, after all, an eState brand. If Kay liked Chillax, her audience would like her even more, and collectively, somewhat subliminally, they would all love eState.

The studio was empty of human involvement except for Kay. The cameras were fist-sized and operated by program or remote, attached to bendable poles and dollies on the floor and tracks on the ceiling. Their tentacle-like behavior, snaking around the studio to capture all sorts of angles, could be a terrifying sight to an untrained observer. Tiny red lights above the lenses directed Kay where to look. Although she rarely used teleprompters, several were strategically placed throughout the space to match the camera directions.

Her director, behind a window at the back of the studio, called out instructions remotely to a miniature earpiece.

"Citizen equals taxpayer. And where do your dollars really go?" Kay asked her audience with a shrug. "When you're a shareholder, you have a personal, financial stake in what your community does on every level."

She leaned in slightly toward the cameras for emphasis.

"You live in this country, you invest in this country. Shareholders demand, and get, a return. Citizens don't. So are you a citizen or a shareholder? As of today, we're *all* shareholders." Kay punctuated the point with a supportive smile. "It's a change you're going to like. Join the conversation at News United, hashtag Chillax and Final Word."

Kay held the smile as the lights dimmed. She looked to the can of Chillax on the desk, raised it, and took a hearty drink. Viewers would never know she hated the stuff.

Theme music echoed over the studio's comm speakers. The cameras began to back away. Kay held the pose, waiting for her bombastic, deep-voiced announcer's outro.

"From America's finest city in the golden state of the world's greatest nation! News United with Kay Eddington!"

Kay was expert at masking her glance to the studio's *On Air* light, desperately waiting for the music to fade and the light to go dark so she could separate that horrid can of pop from her lips.

It was a ritual she endured for every broadcast. Show after show, she had to quaff the molasses-sweet mystery substance the color of atomic orange. It stained her tongue and teeth every time. If she didn't wear lipstick, Chillax could do the job.

The light finally shut off. She relaxed and shuddered with the last gulp.

She threw a perturbed look across the studio as she stood to leave. There were no smiles here behind the cameras. Once the production was off the air, the pretense was gone. The only behind-the-scenes smiles came when local breweries and distilleries brought in their latest concoctions—again sponsored—for the production staff to scarf down. But none were on hand today. Probably for the better, Kay figured. The Chillax aftertaste would not mix well.

Kay pushed the studio door open with a thuggish slam. She met her producer in the hallway.

"Good show, Kay," the short bespectacled man said.

"Would somebody tell my dad to get me another sponsor unless he's trying to kill me?" Kay asked, deadpan. She was absolutely sick of that soda.

Before her producer could answer, she brushed past him. "Never mind. I'll tell him myself."

{ }

There were times Quinn felt he was the punch line of some universal joke.

He grew up thinking those who questioned society's machines were conspiracy-theorist nutjobs, only to become the injured party to one of those conspiracies. He joined the resistance while working for—he thought—one of its biggest targets.

It was a conflicted existence, but Quinn had grown to embrace it. The lines of enemy and ally were more clear to him these days, even though he worked for both. He was a traitor to neither. The way he saw it, he was part of a circulatory system of checks and balances. Both pieces of that system gave him employment.

Time: about 6 p.m. Quinn had been up since not long after midnight. Fortunately, he had a few upcoming days off from *The Observator* (it didn't publish daily, and Olivia knew he also worked for Eddington). He looked forward to nights of better sleep, perhaps even free of drop-induced pain control.

First, he had a task for his underground alter ego.

Quinn's face was partly obscured by his black hoodie. He walked, hands in pockets on this clement evening, along the sidewalk of a relatively deserted portion of an urban shopping district. The massive project of apartments, shops, ice rink, luxury theater, elementary school, among other amenities, had plenty of nooks for covert meetings.

A man in his mid-thirties came upon Quinn from the opposite direction. The guy also wore a hooded sweatshirt (virtually an underground dress code), black but with white stitching. He was an informant with knowledge of eState's failures in law enforcement across the state. The guy's face was narrow, sunken, with green eyes and a bit of stubble blending into his sandy complexion. Quinn knew little about him other than a cursory Army background check and his name. Morgan. The two had been in contact for weeks thanks to a tip from one of Quinn's colleagues at *The Observator.*

They met, nodded, shook hands.

"What've you got?" Quinn inquired.

"eState's losing control in L.A.," Morgan told him. "Nine officers died in the riots last week. My buddy barely got the information out."

"L.A.," Quinn said grimly.

"These guys are walking dead. You've got bad training in urban tactics, furloughed pay, unqualified leadership. They get knocked off trying to control the streets and their families don't get told what's happened to them."

Quinn needed more. "What's the proof?"

"I got names and photos. That's all I have right now."

The guy took out a tiny drive from one of his pockets.

Quinn put up his right hand. "No downloads. They can

be traced. I need hard copies."

Morgan put the drive back in his pocket and instead took out a small red plastic case about fifteen centimeters wide and seven centimeters tall. He opened it, revealing tightly folded paper printouts and photos.

Quinn pulled out a wad of worn hundred-dollar bills from the right front pocket of his pants. "A thousand, that's the best I can do."

Morgan took the cash. But when Quinn took the case with his left hand, the guy immediately grabbed his wrist. Hard. The case and papers hit the ground. Quinn resisted, winced in pain, as the informant's grip tightened, contorting the wrist to near breakage.

"I don't want to snap it," Morgan said.

Quinn was betrayed, and he felt like an idiot for allowing it. He was better than this.

Betrayal was a risk of this line of work, as Quinn knew from being on the other side. But then a fair amount of panic began to set in. It hit him that being arrested for trading meant his activities would be revealed to his day job. How would Eddington's outfit respond to that? What would Haskell do? Quinn's name might not have been on his stories in *The Observator* (no one was stupid enough to put bylines on their work underground), but any charges of subversion against him now would have repercussions of some kind.

Quinn still managed to put the fear aside and ask: "Is it true?"

The undercover agent nodded, revealing some regret, then forced Quinn around and placed a small handcuff device across his wrists. It collapsed around them with a *zap*.

Quinn looked ahead blankly. He got his information. But no one would know.

The agent gave Quinn the boilerplate as he led him away: "You're under arrest for the trading of black market news. Statute BM795J. The eState grievance network is available should you wish to file a complaint about this action."

{ }

Quinn buried his face in his hands as he sat on the bench of a rectangular holding cell. It was a spotless room, white tile, floor to ceiling. The chamber could easily be repurposed for spa use, it was that impressive. The brushed metal bench ran the length of one wall facing another entirely of security glass. The only split in the glass was the door, which had no handle, only a small digital pad to scan cards and enter commands.

An alarm squealed from the panel. A husky, solid-faced, fuzzy-haired guard entered. An eState Safe Harbor patch sat underneath the man's badge at the top front left of his navy blue shirt.

"You're clear. Let's go," the guard said.

Clear? Quinn looked at the keeper for an explanation.

The guard was impatient. "You're being released. Come on, move."

Quinn obliged.

As he walked toward a registration window, Quinn noticed a familiar figure, the back of an ally.

A balding, round man in a nicely styled brown tweed jacket turned to face him. It was Elliott Day, the now-former mayor of San Diego.

"Mayor Day," Quinn said with relief, and some surprise.

"He's been processed, you can take him," the guard said.

A mousy woman in a canary yellow uniform returned Quinn's belongings at the window. The guard officially handed him over to the politician's custody. Day's wide, tight-lipped smile brought out a touch of rosacea in his light skin. His cheeks pushed upward into his drab eyes. Day put his hand on Quinn's shoulder as they left the building.

Quinn wasn't sure what time it was. There were no clocks anywhere. It was still night, judging from the color of the partly cloudy sky beyond the facility's doors. *That's encouraging*, Quinn thought. Had it been daylight, he knew he would have lost a night's sleep and might have been late for work at Eddington's media palace. He could rest easier now.

Outside the building, Quinn turned to Day.

"How did you pull that off?" he asked. "They got me for trading, you know what that means."

"A blown cover, for one. And out of a job," Day said. "I might not be the mayor anymore but I've still got some good friends in eState circles. As soon as I got word about you, I started making calls. Now, I've got some new info for you, but it'll have to ..."

"What is it?" Quinn pounced.

"... *wait.* It will have to wait."

Day motioned for Quinn to keep walking.

"It'll be worth it."

07: INTERVENTIONS

Quinn often frequented a lakeside trail, a largely forgotten piece of old suburbia that fell out of favor over the past couple of decades as people moved into increasingly dense civic centers. The trail circled Lake Miramar, a neglected man-made body of water of dubious quality. The overgrown reeds, sagebrush, and other native vegetation obstructed nearby hillsides of unoccupied, decaying single-family homes.

The crisp, clear start to the day was perfect for an early morning run among this unnerving mix of quiet nature and forsaken neighborhoods. Quinn enjoyed running here.

He was methodical, almost to mechanical perfection, as he darted down the roughly paved trail. In fact, he ran exceptionally fast this morning simply because he could. Despite the speed and the impressive length of his nonstop sprint, he appeared to break only the slightest of sweat, moderately winded.

Running was an interesting pursuit of choice for Quinn given that it wasn't one of his favorite things to do before the bombing. He was athletic, but running was something of a chore, a means to an end when it came to training. He still loved martial arts. But these days, he feared he could literally kill someone with a roundhouse kick. He shied away from it as a result, at least until he truly felt he could exercise a new level of self control.

It had been a few days since Quinn's close call with eState authorities. With a brief break from his duties at *The Observator*, he was able to live some semblance of a good old-fashioned, nine-to-five life. To sleep before midnight, to rise by 6 or 7 in the morning. Into work for Eddington between 9 and 11 a.m. depending on the shift.

Quinn savored these breaks. He knew they would always be short-lived. It was not something he minded.

Elliott Day stood waiting a short distance away down the trail, enjoying a leisurely walk, dressed in jeans and a tan faux-leather coat. He squinted as he watched Quinn approach fast from the east, first a tiny figure, then within virtually no time at all a human bullet barreling toward him. Quinn broke his run as he got closer.

Quinn wore a yellow hoodie (there was no need to hide from anyone here) and black full-length running pants. No glasses. He slowed to a walk the closer he got to the former mayor. Then he came to a stop, leaning forward on his knees to catch his breath. Day met him with a wave.

"You know, I thought our business was finished after I left office," Day said facetiously.

Quinn appreciated the humor. Breath in check, he stood to greet Day, who pulled an old-style cassette tape from his right coat pocket.

"This is the last information I have," Day said. He handed the tape to Quinn. "I'm out of the loop now."

Quinn was apologetic as he took it. "You've got to name a

price this time. Seriously, I can pay you something."

"Eddington barely pays you and neither does that black market rag," Day replied, dismissing the idea. "After what's been happening, this is the best public service I've offered in my career. That's good enough for me. I can retire as a mayor on seventy-five million pretty easily anyway. Save your money so you can eat."

Day patted Quinn on the shoulder and turned to leave.

Quinn studied the cassette, fascinated by the old tech. The case was off-white. Only the A-side label had something written on it in blue ballpoint pen: *Final.* The spools holding the brown tape inside rattled when Quinn turned the cassette on its sides.

"What's new on here?" Quinn asked.

Day stopped and turned back.

"That seventy-five million we all got didn't come from eState. It's all there, everything you need. With one final knockout blow."

Day departed.

"What do you mean?" Quinn asked.

Day didn't stop this time. "You'll see."

{ }

Eddington sat at his desk, leaning back in his chair with that usual triangle hands-to-the-face look when something was perplexing or worrisome. An eState security executive stood across from him with a look of concern.

"And this has been going on for how long?" Eddington asked.

"Years probably," the man said. "Dad, I'm the one who has to handle this."

eState's tentacles spread far, so much that Eddington's own son, Owen, was a top-clearance member of the company's security apparatus. Owen knew secrets about eState and its executives—notably one—that could untangle much of its dominion across the country, and certainly in California at this critical juncture.

In public, Owen Eddington looked and acted "eState"—sharp black suit tailored and pressed to perfection, the signature eState monocle over his left eye. He was thirty-two, at a height and build similar to his father, with a shock of corn-silk-colored hair shaved to the skin on the sides, pompadour on top, and eyes of a color between his sister's gray and father's blue. His entry into eState's security chain came through his service in what was left of the Navy before it was folded into the corporate machine.

In private, during time with his family and close friends, for example, Owen's monocle was "off the grid," as he would say. It was then that Owen would tell them about the company's grimy underbelly, the rotting foundation on which the empire was built.

Eddington digested Owen's most recent news, made more challenging by eState's blatant role as its own enforcer.

"Self policed," Eddington said distantly. "That's going to spell trouble in years to come."

Eddington's brow crinkled as he looked at his son. "You think it's wise to be telling me this?"

"As long as I'm offline, it's all right," Owen said. Even then, there was no mention of the crux, the focal point, of this latest intelligence.

The "this" of the conversation was so potentially explosive that neither of them would dare speak it aloud again. But Eddington knew that "this" could also solve his nagging Haskell problem. Eddington's son could undo eState's CEO from the inside.

Owen grew uneasy. He searched for his next words.

"I just ... you need to know that if there's any trouble from me trying to pursue this, you're the last line. The public has to know."

"*Will* there be trouble, Owen?" his father asked.

Kay burst through the doors in a chipper mood. Eddington pointed back with his usual perturbed reminder: "Receptionist."

Owen turned to greet her. "Happy birthday, sis."

The siblings hugged.

Eddington grabbed a small jewelry box off the desk and walked over to her. Kay opened it, revealing a simple, classy silver necklace. She was surprised and delighted.

"It's beautiful, Dad, thank you," she said, followed by a kiss to his cheek.

Owen gave her a departing nudge on the shoulder and headed for the door. "I've got some business to take care of. I'll see you at dinner." Owen stopped and looked back at his father. "Joining us?"

Eddington shook his head.

"Sorry, kids. Late night for me," Eddington replied. Then his mood darkened. "Good luck."

The exchange caught Kay's ear. *What was that about?* Owen was out the door before she could ask.

{ }

Golden late-afternoon sunlight cast a stinging glow across Owen's face as he walked briskly down a hallway in eState's San Diego hub. The walkway's ceiling was three stories above, with widows almost reaching that height, giving the space a cathedral-like aura. The abundance of sun negated artificial light during the day.

Owen's expression was impassive. It was the kind of face a cardplayer would covet, and with the business at hand, Owen needed it. As a key cog in Bruce Haskell's security network, he had to hide what he knew—what he was about to confront. He masked a deep rage, aimed at a man who for too long got away with abuses of power that walked a fine line legally but were in a sinkhole morally.

Owen was about to confront "this."

{ }

In his opulent eighty-seventh-floor office, with a commanding view of the city's skyline, Haskell sat across from San Diego County's chief medical officer, once a public employee but now part of eState's local system.

The woman appeared cautious, eyes wide with barely a blink, as Haskell leaned toward her casually, like a good friend.

"The work your division's doing with the flu outbreak has gotten a lot of attention," he told her.

Haskell had an odd charisma in these private settings. He was cool, collected, yet mannequin-like, with eyes that looked into your soul and told you he had bottomless belief in you.

If you could see through that veneer, however, life could be hell. So it was for Sandra Mott.

The stout, no-nonsense doctor with tightly curled black hair was quick with a simple "thank you," but it was evident in her look that she had something on her mind, no matter the fear she felt otherwise. Before she could add anything, Haskell had to jump in with praise of his organization.

"This is what private stewardship of public resources is all about. You're one of eState's best cases right now."

The praise seemed so earnest that it could melt the heart of the most solid bureaucrat, but Mott remained steadfast as she pursed her lips and took a breath.

"I do have an observation," Mott said.

Haskell's eyes narrowed, his lips thinned, as he nodded. "Of course," he said in his best attempt to sound open-minded.

"There's been an unusual amount of fatalities with the new vaccine," Mott said guardedly. "I'm sure you've seen the numbers."

Haskell's tight lips crimped into a distorted smile, feigning concern.

"As a physician, that must trouble you greatly. I understand," he said.

Mott shifted in her seat.

"I'm concerned Pharma's release of this new shot is premature," she told him with clinical frankness. "The county shouldn't be a testing ground for medications that aren't fully vetted."

Haskell nodded impatiently. "Testing continues," he blurted. "I'll consider your feedback."

He stared at her briefly. Then his eyes widened. He leaned into her even more, disengaging his monocle and taking it off.

"She really is beautiful," Haskell said warmly.

Mott squirmed in her seat again, almost as if she was tied to the chair and couldn't stand. She adjusted the blazer of her teal suit.

"You know how things work here," he continued. "You know what I appreciate. I have to tell you, you're not the only one who's expressed concern about the vaccine. Your voice adds to that, to the point I'm convinced. If you'd like it pulled for more testing, I must ask one thing more of you. It's for your job, and for this."

"What would that be?" Mott said in a trembling near-whisper, knowing where the conversation was headed.

"I would be honored to spend a full evening with your daughter."

There was only one answer Mott could give, so she said nothing.

"Excellent," Haskell said, lightly patting his thighs. "Anything more?"

Mott glanced back toward the closed office doors. "No, that's all I have right now."

Haskell stood. He smiled with suggestive expectation.

"Good. Good. Bring her in, then," he said buoyantly.

Mott exited Haskell's office and went to her daughter, Alexis, who sat waiting in the foyer. Alexis stood to greet her mother. A tear rolled down Mott's left cheek as she gently held her daughter around the neck.

"I'm sorry, sweetheart," Mott said gently. "You'll be okay?"

Alexis nodded, and they walked back toward the office.

Haskell was admiring the city view when he heard the doors open. He turned around. His smile widened to a grin at the sight of Alexis, who had long, wavy obsidian hair, her mother's hazel eyes, and almond skin. He approached mother and daughter, giving a favorable once-over to Alexis' white blouse, black capris and saddle shoes.

"Alexis," he said. "Beautiful. Come here. It looks like we've got a full evening together."

Haskell held his hand out to Alexis, who walked around the desk to meet him. He looked at her like a doting relative wanting to catch up after a long absence.

"I heard you had a birthday recently. Your eighteenth?" he asked.

Haskell caressed her hair. He turned, smile intact, to her mother.

"Thank you, Doctor Mott. You can leave us now."

{ }

Owen spotted Mott as he approached the foyer. He had that stare of an officer on a mission, his enemy in sight, ready to pull the trigger.

It had been nearly ten minutes since Mott left her daughter with Haskell, and she sat dejected, lost in grief, on the couch. She turned and stood immediately when she saw Owen, just a few steps away.

"Are they in there?" Owen said urgently as he walked up to her.

Mott nodded. Tears returned to her eyes.

"Stay here. I'll send her out," he said.

Owen stormed through the doors. Haskell and Alexis were in a suggestive embrace. They appeared to break a kiss as they turned to face him. Haskell looked at Owen like a predator interrupted mid-feeding—calm, unsure of the threat, assessing the intruder.

"I'm busy," Haskell said with flat arrogance. "Whatever it is has to wait."

"*It can't*," Owen pressed.

He looked at Alexis, who stared at him in desperate silence, her eyes pleading for release.

"Your mother's waiting for you," Owen told her.

Alexis rushed out of the room. The two men studied each other in a standoff.

{ }

Kay was often out of the loop when it came to her brother's work with eState. It was a necessity she never questioned. Even so, she was annoyed by her unintended intrusions on the occasional closed conversation with their father. She sometimes wondered if it was part of the reason their mother maintained a distance from their father in recent years—roundabout exclusion from confabs only the men of the family were allowed to share.

The siblings were close nonetheless.

Owen kept his promise of a birthday dinner with Kay despite the corporate intrigue. They sat at a small table for two in a bistro populated by their rich counterparts—well-behaved men and women in varying degrees of dress-casual to semiformal clothing, faultless faces and hair, forced light laughter, reasonably behaved children.

There was no need for a lot of conversation or shallow small talk for Kay and Owen, though. They were simply happy in each other's company, away from the heavy weight of their jobs and lives.

Owen watched his sister with reserved joy as she closed her eyes, her face illuminated by the light of a single candle atop the creamy icing on a fluffy piece of coconut cake. She smiled, blew out the flame, then immediately dug into the cake with a silver fork and savored the first bite. He was often cheered by his sister, especially at times when her professional facade gave way to the occasional terse and bratty annoyance with things around her, or the warmth and childlike excitement he watched in this moment.

Something didn't seem quite right to Kay, however. Owen noticed her occasional glances beyond his shoulder to something behind him during the entire dinner—five people seated at two back-to-back tables with the siblings in their sights, three men at one table, what appeared to be a couple at the other.

Owen knew the people were there. What he didn't realize was that Kay recognized at least two of them, Owen's colleagues in eState security. Unless they were there for a surprise birthday visit, Kay's common sense told her their presence could not be a coincidence. Their dimly lit green monocles were also a partial giveaway. Company executives frequented this spot. Upper-crust monocles glowed red. Other divisions such as law enforcement glowed green.

Finally, Kay had to ask him.

"Do you have a detail with you tonight?"

Owen's eyes shifted a bit. "No."

"I recognize some of them," Kay replied, looking at the group again.

Owen nodded and tossed his napkin on the table.

"You know what?" he said. Then he paused. "Excuse me."

Owen left his sister and walked over to the covey's lone woman, whose bun-tied brown hair, black slacks, sport coat, and white blouse almost gave her the look of a warden. Muted conversation ensued.

Kay observed the scene like a well-practiced agent in her own right. She looked down toward the cake and cupped her hand behind her ear as if to massage it, just enough to enhance her hearing to catch at least a few words or phrases.

"Maybe it's better if we leave now," Kay heard Owen's colleague say. "I can read your rights outside."

"My rights?!" Owen snapped.

While Kay couldn't parse the context of what she heard, the implication stirred panic in her.

"The order's from above any of us. Way above you," his colleague disclosed. Kay noted some compunction in the woman's voice.

There were a few more words Kay couldn't catch. Owen returned to the table, somber. He didn't sit. He only placed his hands on the back of the chair, ready to break some news.

"I have to go," he said.

Kay was heartbroken. Her instincts told her this was not a normal call. There was a palpable undercurrent of anger in Owen.

"What do they want you for?" Kay demanded. He didn't answer. "Owen?"

He leaned toward her. His colleagues stood, waiting for him to depart.

"There's trouble, Kay. Pursue it."

{ }

Kay sat alone in the car as it drove her home. She couldn't banish the questions that vexed her. *What just happened? What kind of trouble?*

When Kay was frustrated, agitated—when she couldn't come up with easy, instant answers—she took control of the wheel. She would literally drive the bogeys out.

That was the thing about cars that irked her. What was the point of a steering wheel if you weren't going to be a driver?

"Pull over; stop," Kay ordered to the car's control panel.

It stopped along a busy street in downtown San Diego, mostly occupied by basic driverless cars with no options for human operation beyond emergency breaks.

"Manual pilot," she said.

The car changed its configuration to allow her to drive. Sports cars of this price range allowed for such a luxury. She waited for a clearing in the traffic, then sped into an open lane.

Kay darted between the common vehicles at daring speed, well above the mandatory twenty-five kilometers per hour.

An annoying bell-like *beep* blared from the car's console. It was her phone, which was routed through the car's control panel. She glanced at the number—blocked. This raised her curiosity. *Owen?*

"Kay Eddington," she answered.

"You won't be seeing him for a while," a distorted female voice told her.

Kay's eyes froze, staring at the console. "Who is this?"

"I'm in a position to know, and someone has to tell you," the voice replied. "He's gone."

Bright lights up ahead illuminated the car's cabin. An alarm sounded. "Divert! Divert!"

Kay looked up to see a car coming right at her. It dodged her, but there was another one behind it. She had meandered into an oncoming lane. She made a hard right with the wheel. The tires screamed. A second later and she would've been her own headline.

Back in a safe lane, her well-styled hair frayed across her face, Kay composed herself and was just about to respond to the mystery caller. But the informant was gone. The call had been disconnected. Kay slammed the console with her hand in frustration.

{ }

Quinn and Jasper surreptitiously followed the action behind the window of their editor's office as they worked. Eddington had frequented the newsroom more in recent days, and Quinn was increasingly uneasy with the publisher's presence.

The view in that window became a silent television screen broadcasting a semi-daily drama. In the latest episode, Eddington shook a copy of *The Observator* in the editor's face, then threw it on the desk as the editor nodded repeatedly.

Behind the glass and the closed door carrying the

nameplate of editor Joe Cano, Eddington circled closer to a suspect. He looked out the window, observing the newsroom, and sighed.

"Haskell's being a rabid pit bull over this," Eddington told Cano. "He insists the story came from someone on our staff."

"Does he have proof?" Cano asked.

Eddington looked back to him. "I don't know. I need to make a move. Now." He returned to observing the newsroom.

"Who's the reporter this falls under?" Eddington queried. "Wasserman, is it?"

This was an Eddington trademark—an honest mispronunciation of a name or a purposeful mangling to underscore the person's insignificance.

"Kellerman," Cano replied. "Quinn Kellerman."

"Kellerman, yes," Eddington acknowledged. "Talk to him ... No, *don't* talk to him."

Eddington briefly contemplated that choice, then nodded to himself, affirming his decision. He had a better person to keep an eye on Quinn.

{ }

Kay had an internal switch that was helpful at times. Depending on the situation, she could talk to you, appear to be so engaged, yet inside she could care less about the chat. Your yammering would continue, but in her mind she would hear every word, recall them, carry the conversation seamlessly, while fixating on more important matters—the spot on your collar, the top news picks for her next show, what hidden truth she had to cull from her father.

Then, flip the switch. Kay could still care less, and now you would know it—the look on her face, the slight wandering of her eyes, or her outright expression of impatience.

Not even the temptation of cupcakes satisfied Kay right now as she and her team were live on *Super Morning with Kay, Nicky & Gonzago*. It was the program she disliked the most. Shallow small talk. Zoo animals. Cooking classes.

The problem for Kay was that she looked the part so well for such a show, yet her deepest desire was to be a serious journalist. And she was. But she had "the look" for lighter fare, and that's where the best money was. The morning romp was her penance for doing the work she preferred.

Today's chef du jour shoved a cupcake at her, nudging Kay out of her veiled disinterest.

"There's nothing to fear, Kay," the hearty woman said with glowing confidence. "These are a bitingly sweet twist on my vanilla cinnamon recipe."

Kay took the treat.

"Yeah, but it's cayenne," Kay's bumbling wire frame of a cohost, Gonzago, said with some worry.

Kay took a bite. She closed her eyes.

The chef beamed. "See? What did I tell you?"

"She's right. Incredible," Kay approved with a light laugh as she tried to speak with her mouth partly full. "You'll want to make these, and you'll learn how after this break. Come back for our Cafe Spotlight."

Delicious food and bottomless cocktails were a perk of this assignment. As soon as the *On Air* sign went dark and the commercial countdown started, the drinks came out from behind the desk, or fresh ones were made off-set by visiting mixologists from local establishments. Lemon drops were Kay's favorite.

"Hey boss!" yelled Nicky, a jovial chunk of a guy with an attitude who was the other member of Kay's morning team.

Eddington emerged from the shadows of the studio, looking on the scene and his employees with the air of a proud overlord.

"Good show so far," Eddington said, hands in pockets, relaxed and affable.

Kay spotted him, but she was not keen on talking to him. It had been three days since Owen's removal from the bistro and subsequent disappearance. She grew concerned every hour that her brother didn't call or text to say hello. There were no visits with Dad in the office. Nothing.

Given the mystery call she received after Owen's departure on her birthday—and not a word from Dad about his whereabouts since—she knew her father had to know something he was unwilling to share.

Eddington approached her with a smile, arms outstretched.

"Hello sweetheart," he said. His left hand gently touched her right shoulder.

"Can we talk in my office when you're done?" he asked quietly. The question caught her interest. Was he finally ready to share something about Owen?

"Sure," Kay replied.

Eddington nodded, patted her shoulder, and headed back into the shadows.

"We got what, fifteen seconds?!" Nicky blurted practically in Kay's ear out of nowhere. "Where's Gonzago? Hey! Gonzago!"

Kay wanted to slap the guy for being so damned loud. But then again, that was his role. It annoyed her to no end, especially the more he had to drink.

"Clear the desk!" the floor director yelled. Back under the table went the cocktails. It was time to bake some cupcakes.

{ }

Eddington wasn't one to show nerves. An astute person could pinpoint a small sign of them, depending on the circumstance. The tapping of an index finger, for one. He stood at his office desk, facing away from the closed doors, his right hand tightly holding a small cell phone, pressing it against his ear. And the sign of nerves percolating to the surface—his index finger tapping slightly against the back of the phone. He appeared to be chewing gum, though he really wasn't. Again, nerves.

"You push things too far. It adds up, you know," Eddington said.

"You'd certainly know," he heard Haskell remind him through the line. "There's time to sort this out."

"Time. Yes."

Eddington heard one of the doors open behind him. It was Kay. He immediately ended the call and tossed the phone on the desk, which landed next to a mug. The patriarch grabbed the cup, looked at the view outside the windows, and took a sip of coffee.

"I'm beginning to question the wisdom of having alcohol on the set," he quipped.

Kay found it unusual to see her father appear startled, vulnerable.

"It helps pass the time, especially now," she replied, glaring at him from behind. "It's not like we're doing serious news on that show anyway."

Eddington turned to face her. It was obvious the show wasn't really the thing on her mind. She stood there expecting an answer about Owen. She expected this meeting was about her brother.

Eddington, however, was fixated on the idea that someone within his own news group was responsible for leaks to the black market press. His son was in serious trouble, yet he behaved as if his own newsroom's problem was more important.

It wasn't that Eddington didn't care. At least he knew where Owen was. He was alive. Stable. There just wasn't anything he could do for him at the moment. That knowledge alone allowed Eddington to compartmentalize that piece and set it aside for the time being.

"eState's pressuring me again," Eddington told Kay.

Her shoulders sloped. "Now what?"

"They seem to think we have employees ... well at least one who works on the black market."

"What's that have to do with you?" she said impatiently. "Do you think I know something about it?"

Eddington approached her.

"No. But I want you to get to know someone who might. In our newsroom."

Kay tilted her head, unimpressed. "So I'll be spying on

one of my colleagues now. That's pretty ironic, Dad."

"I just need to know whether anyone is causing trouble," Eddington said, raising his hands in deference. "That's all."

Kay thought about it. Then she realized this was her shot to find out if her father was hiding anything about her brother's whereabouts.

"One condition," Kay said.

"Name it," he replied without hesitation.

Eddington knew what was on his daughter's mind. There was no need for him to wait for her demand. Still, he was reticent, but it was clear she was hungry for an answer.

"He's in prison, Kay."

She was infuriated. The confirmation didn't satisfy her, not because of where Owen was, but because Eddington took so long to say anything, and under the guise of seeking her assistance with something that had nothing to do with him.

"I got a call on my way home that night," Kay said, simmering. "Probably one of his colleagues; I couldn't really tell because the voice was distorted. They said I'd never see him again. And you said nothing. For days."

"I had to find out what his status was before I could tell you ..."

"I want to see him," Kay interrupted. "You said name it. Now that I know, I want to see him."

Eddington's mood grew darker. He absolutely did not want Kay seeing Owen in the condition she would find him.

"It's eState prison."

Kay shrugged, clueless of her father's concerns.

"Prison's prison. They allow visitors and you have influence. I have a right to see my brother!"

Eddington took her by the shoulders.

"You are not prepared for what you'll find."

His genuine worry startled her, but she was unfazed and adamant.

"If I'm spying for you, you'll do this for me."

{ }

Despite the daily mediocrity Quinn endured working for Eddington's Citizen Group, he still got opportunities to report some significant news, or at least try to.

At the moment, he was attempting to sift through the new layers of eState bureaucracy as it enveloped San Diego's City Hall. If the City Council had been disbanded, who were the elected officials making decisions? How would they be elected? Was there to be a reorganization of departments and leadership? And forget the city. What about the entire county?

Quinn had been on the phone for about two hours trying to get such questions answered. He massaged his forehead, growing tired of the non-answer answers thrown his way.

"Well, how's this supposed to work?" he asked some low-level public information officer. "If you don't have a city council, who meets when and where?"

As the PIO spouted more empty information into his ear, Quinn thought about how much easier it would be to just do the real digging on the black market and run it in *The Observator*.

Jasper was sympathetic. He looked over at Quinn, raised his eyebrows. Quinn glared back, shaking his head as he started typing some notes.

"What about public participation?" Quinn continued. He closed his eyes at the rambling on the other end. "Can the public still attend meetings! That's what I'm asking!"

Kay approached Quinn from behind. She gave Jasper a modest wave.

Quinn began typing again, repeating the source's information as he went. "The public are shareholders. As shareholders, they can attend meetings. Got it."

By this point, Kay was leaning on the table, right next to Quinn, observing him.

Jasper flagged his attention.

"Boss's daughter. Behind you," he whispered.

Quinn looked up at Kay and melted slightly. With a hasty goodbye and "thank you" to the woman on the call, he hung up and leaned back in his chair.

"Katherine Eddington. Nice to see you out of the cave," Quinn teased.

"What's new, Kay?" Jasper said, trying to divert some of her attention his way. Jasper knew that was a lost cause, seeing how Kay and Quinn often loosened up around each other. He still found it amusing to try, especially since he wondered whether the two understood their affinity.

Kay was not amused by Quinn's comment. It was common slang from the writers to the broadcasters.

"The cave people need enlightenment," she replied. "I want to get more serious content on the morning show."

Quinn didn't know what to say. She actually appeared sincere about it. In fact, her enthusiasm for the idea grew the more she talked. And her eyes never left him.

"We have enough kids, puppies, and food. We need

stronger, civic-minded stuff. Simple on-air discussion about what's going on, twice a week, especially about home base. We're eState's front line right now."

Quinn pondered the idea, but he was unsure.

"I don't think I'm good for TV," he said.

She leaned into him, bracing her arms on the desk.

"Of course you are. You guys are boots-on-the-ground reporters," she pitched. "Viewers will take you seriously. My job is to push their buttons and give them cotton candy. That only goes so far."

Quinn's reluctance mystified Jasper. "Take the offer, Quinn. The boss's daughter's asking you. I wouldn't say no."

Jasper looked at Kay with a glint in his eye, snapped his finger and pointed. "Remember that."

Kay smiled, keeping her focus on Quinn. It was that on-the-air, welcoming, friendly presence that Quinn first noticed about her on TV when he was in college.

"I'm serious," she said with incisive confidence. "You're perfect. You're a gritty bit of reality the audience will devour. And don't worry. You'll have a pro keeping an eye on you."

08: A DISEMBODIED PLEA

The reels of a cassette tape slowly turned in a 1980s-era player. There was no sound other than the slight whine of the tape moving across the playback head. This was a cassette that contained information, not music, and it was being downloaded onto a computer as archaic as the player.

Lines of code appeared, row after row, on the black-and-white tube monitor of a first-generation personal computer, circa 1979 or '80. As the code appeared, it would take a couple of seconds before it changed into lines of text. The computer interpreted the code into various items—large sums of money associated with names, bank account numbers, addresses, other items of business.

The computer emitted an occasional *beep* or series of sounds—much like that of an old dial-up modem—as tasks were completed along the way.

Quinn jotted notes as he sat at the computer and watched the screen. His eyes were bloodshot, a mix of pain, screen fatigue, and the late hour. He was back in *The Observator*'s newsroom. Work was underway on the next edition following the report on eState's buy-off of the San Diego City Council.

The tape was the one Mayor Day handed Quinn at

Lake Miramar. Quinn studied every line of information for something explosive, as Day had promised. Maybe it wasn't one singular thing, Quinn thought. Maybe it was cumulative. Either way, the research was going to take a long time at the current pace of download.

Behind Quinn, the newsroom was the usual busy, living time capsule he and his underground colleagues had grown to embrace. It was a necessary way of doing business if you were to stay off the grid. Analog methods. Outdated digital technology with no possible connection to the wireless world of data clouds under which every person was now a subject.

"Stone knives and bear skins," Quinn often called it, in reference to a classic episode of a now-obscure science fiction TV show from the 1960s.

Jasper walked up from behind Quinn and leaned in to look at the elder-machine marvel. He also noticed Quinn's fatigued, almost sickly look. It worried him.

"You okay?" Jasper asked.

Quinn rubbed his eyes. "Staring at this machine too long."

That answer didn't square with Jasper. "You're hurting."

Quinn closed his eyes and nodded.

"Sorry," Jasper said. He looked at the screen. "You getting anything?"

Quinn pointed to certain pieces of code that were not being translated.

"There was a lot of money shifting around," Quinn observed. "But look here. See these lines? The app's not decoding this for some reason."

Jasper thought about it for a moment but couldn't

come up with a theory. The pained look in Quinn's eyes was bothering him more than anything. He patted Quinn on the shoulder.

"Go home, buddy," Jasper told him. "Rest up. I'll see you later."

Quinn wasn't going anywhere. It was just past 9:30 in the evening, and the night was early as far as he was concerned.

Jasper went to his desk, grabbed his coat and cap, gave Olivia a quick goodbye, and headed for the hallway. His mood turned melancholic once he was out of their sight. As he walked down the narrow hall, which was just as well-worn as the rest of the building, he thought about Quinn's pain. He dwelled on its source.

He was sometimes jealous of Quinn's strength of character to endure being torn apart by a bomb, reconstructed, and continue living. Whether that required an occasional narcotic in the form of drops or the support of technology to keep his body together and functioning didn't matter. It was an inner strength Jasper thought he had until that day, that moment, when he abandoned his best friend. It was a strength Quinn discovered *because* of that day.

Jasper also felt guilt as much as jealousy. Perhaps more so. The volatile mix of such emotions could lead normally ethical, moral people to do detestable things.

Hidden emotions. Conflicted intentions. They were in keeping with the climate. On the exterior wall next to the door Jasper exited was a small office sign, barely noticeable from the sidewalk unless a passerby knew to look for it—*Western Earnings Group*. Certainly not the name for a newspaper. When you're underground, the last thing you would do is post a sign screaming your existence to the powers that be. It's the kind of tactic a man like Jasper would use to mask behavior he wouldn't dare reveal.

{ }

Jasper had been on the train for about fifteen minutes. He was alone. Without any distraction, except for the occasional lurch to the side as the train made its way along the rails, he thought about the person he was about to see, the information he would share, and what he hoped to get in return.

A few minutes more, and Jasper arrived at his destination. He was downtown, looking up at a towering skyscraper, eState's regional headquarters. The highest floors were barely visible given the height and light evening fog. Red, white, and blue strips of neon, blade-like in appearance, cast a glow into the misty air.

Jasper headed for an out-of-the-way, unmarked side entrance with a small scanner next to the doorknob. He placed his right thumb on the gadget. A small red light turned green, a *beep* sounded, and the door unlocked.

Jasper walked down an austere, nearly all-white hallway that seemed to have no end as it faded into darkness. It was deserted. Fluorescent ceiling lights engaged ahead of him with a metallic *tink*, then shut off behind him, as he walked. This late in the evening, with daily business finished, even an economic colossus like eState cut corners where it could, right down to basic lighting.

At an intersection with another passage, Jasper came across a corner security station walled off by floor-to-ceiling windows. The light through the glass in the dark gave the corner a crystalline look. Jasper took out an eState identification card and flashed it to the officer manning the station, who acknowledged it with a brief glance.

Jasper eyed a row of elevators. He entered one, pushing the button for the eighty-seventh floor. The elevator shot up, ticking off nearly two floors per second. Jasper saw endless layers of himself in the elevator's mirrored walls. He massaged behind his ears as pressure built floor by floor. Finally, he arrived. The doors opened into the executive foyer of Bruce Haskell's office.

Jasper walked to the closed office doors. He paused for a couple of moments, shut his eyes, and collected his thoughts. Then he knocked. The doors opened automatically, revealing Haskell, who appeared as a flat shadow against the glow of the fog-infused skyline seen through the windows.

"Come in, Mister Craig," Haskell said. He turned and walked toward Jasper.

Haskell lightly pinched Jasper's jawline, patted him on the face, and smiled.

"So. What's new?"

"Nothing," Jasper said nervously.

"Nothing?" Haskell chided with minacious disappointment. "You work with these people. I know there's a lot of information about me traded on the black market."

Haskell dug his finger into Jasper's chest.

"I'm paying you, quietly, to figure out what they know about me so I don't appear in print so often. So, do you have a better answer than 'nothing?'"

Jasper gave in. "One of the reporters at The Observator

is trying to decode some information ..."

"Which reporter?" Haskell cut in.

"I can't tell you that right now," Jasper replied.

"I want the reporter just as much as I want the information," Haskell insisted.

"I can tell you that the information is about you but I don't know the nature of it," Jasper clarified, a slight quiver in his voice. "So when I say it's nothing, I mean I don't have anything of substance yet."

Haskell's mood lightened. He was mildly impressed with Jasper's explanation.

"You're very good with your phrasing," Haskell said.

He returned to the window and took in the view.

"What do you need the money for?" Haskell asked.

Jasper didn't answer. He feared giving any hint would reveal too much about the person behind the need. Haskell continued to prod.

"What do you need the money for? For this job? Your hesitance tells me you wouldn't be a spy unless you absolutely felt you had to do it."

Jasper's eyes welled with tears.

"I owe a big debt to my best friend," Jasper revealed.

"He's like family to you," Haskell replied in a deceptively sympathetic tone. "That's what I thought."

{ }

Kay was back on the morning set with her sidekicks, Nicky and Gonzago. She sipped a lemon drop alone at the table of a sponsoring pub and kept her eye on the news desk at the other end of the studio. She wasn't entirely impressed with this particular version of the cocktail. How good it was never really mattered, though, as long as she could enjoy something other than that dreadful Chillax at the end of each show.

A few members of the studio crew walked by her as they went about their duties in the last couple of minutes before the break was over.

Kay paid little attention to them. She was distracted. Concerned, actually. Quinn's first appearance on one of her shows was this morning, and he wasn't in the studio yet. *There's no way he'd blow off a chance like this*, she thought. His job would be in jeopardy if he was that sloppy. More importantly, the stunt she had planned for live television depended on him.

Just as she looked at the clock—one minute to go—Quinn entered the studio. She smiled in relief and downed the rest of the cocktail.

Quinn hadn't noticed her yet. But she noticed him—something about him. It was a nuance she missed in the times they passed each other in the building. Perhaps it was something new she was seeing, about the way he walked. The regulated, nearly perfect movement as he stepped up onto the set, to the way he sat down. Maybe he hurt his back or pulled a muscle, which forced him to be more careful. She noticed such things.

Kay and her sidekick entourage arrived on set with just a few seconds to go. She and Quinn gave each other a quick nod. The clock hit zero, and they were back on the air.

The snake-like movements of the cameras caught Quinn off guard. He knew to ignore them, but being in front of them was a different thing. The more they moved, the more nervous he grew. His heart began to race. Not because he was nervous being on TV, but because there was something about the cameras themselves. Their behavior elicited a tremor akin to panic.

The intro music played. The announcer's voice boomed. Still, Quinn was stuck on the motion of the cameras. One of them set up in front of him. At that point, Quinn could swear he heard the drones of three years ago. He stayed still, shifting his eyes to search for the sound's source. There were, of course, no drones in the room. He fought to keep the unease at bay as Kay began her next segment.

"If you follow this network, you know News United has its national headquarters in San Diego. And you know the region was the last official holdout against corporate governance in California. Affiliate reporter Quinn Kellerman is here to get us caught up on the region's historic transition to eState leadership. Will a corporate government model work here amid vocal resistance?"

"Bow down to the corporate master!" Gonzago barged in with cheesy menace, ruining Kay's serious lead-in to the segment.

In her classic style, Kay ignored Gonzago completely and turned to Quinn, whose nerves eased thanks to her presence.

But Kay's sidekicks weren't finished.

"You know, here's something," Nicky added. "Maybe they'll finally get something done about the sewage in the surf. When I go out for a few sets in the morning, it'd be nice if I didn't have to swallow people's crap, you know?"

"Tell us what happened this week," Kay said with unwavering attention to Quinn.

"The City Council made the transfer official," Quinn told her. "In the next month, eState shareholders ..."

"The shareholders being San Diego residents," Kay clarified.

"Right. They'll vote on a slate of executives who will make up a new board of directors."

Quinn observed a mischievous look in her eye. It was as if Kay had set a trap. He couldn't pin what the vibration was.

"So here's a question," she said.

Kay pulled a copy of *The Observator* from under the desk.

"What do you make of this?" she asked. "This black market paper says the council was paid off."

"I never trust anything I see in print," Gonzago interrupted.

The *On Air* sign began to flash, usually indicating a wrap-up to the segment. Quinn said nothing, unsure what to do. Kay's eyes didn't stray from him. She was probing, maybe even toying with him.

"You think there's some truth to it?" she persisted.

"Something for everyone to ponder," Nicky broke in. "We'll be back after this."

The *On Air* sign went dark and a new countdown began. There was stunned silence on the set. Nicky glared at Kay. His lighthearted goofiness disappeared.

"Enjoy your vacation, Kay," Nicky mocked.

Kay turned to her coworker, ready to launch a nuclear comment in return.

"You know, Nicky, the only sewage you should be worried about is what comes out of your mouth."

She stormed off the set.

{ }

Kay stood alone in a hallway just off *The Citizen* newsroom. She had been there for some time, contemplating her next move after pulling the stunt with Quinn. She dabbed tears, a mix of self-pity and performance, waiting for who would walk by to react.

Quinn entered the hallway on his way back to the newsroom. He spotted Kay and walked over to her.

"Did they suspend you?" he asked.

She nodded. "A week."

Quinn genuinely felt sympathy for her. But he also knew that she couldn't have pulled that off—talking about the black market press on nationwide mainstream television—without knowing there would be consequences.

Kay looked at him sadly.

"I don't know you, really," she said. "We're all part of the same product but no one works *together* here. I thought I'd get in some real news, or just talk about it at least."

She dabbed more tears, then smiled a bit through the sadness. "They shouldn't let us drink on the job."

Quinn was increasingly, perhaps surprisingly, unmoved by her.

"The daughter of a media magnate doesn't push buttons live on the air without a reason," Quinn said.

Kay shook off the tears in a nanosecond. There was that narrow-eyed stare of hers, now directed at him.

"We didn't get to hear your answer," she said piercingly. "Is it true about the payoff?"

Quinn thought carefully. He now realized there was

something more going on, and he had to choose his words wisely.

"Hard to say," he answered.

Kay raised her eyebrows and left. He watched her as she walked away. The tears weren't entirely an act. He could sense that. It was as if she was using real pain, which she could turn on and off at will, for any number of motives.

"You *are* upset," he said. "But it's not about being suspended."

She stopped and faced him again. Her wistful aura returned.

"No."

{ }

Kay's ability to use her emotions, wit, and knowledge to shape situations and outcomes was a solid asset, but it also clouded her ability to truly get close to someone. Unless such a person was familiar enough with her to understand this complex recipe, it was easy to misunderstand her on a personal level.

Her interest in Quinn grew after their interaction in the hallway. He demonstrated an instinct that forced her into an uncomfortable corner, to defend her professional game against someone who could see past it. She found it refreshing, but it saddened her that she couldn't tell Quinn the real reason behind the tears, for the task she now faced.

Kicked off her newscast, Kay had the afternoon free, a perfect time to get to the bottom of what happened to her brother.

Against her father's wishes, she was at eState's county prison. Kay had covered stories at prisons before, early in her career, but this institution looked like nothing she had seen.

The facility was void of outward security. No checkpoints. No officers anywhere. It comprised several connected blocks, four stories tall, pure unpainted concrete, no windows except at the entrance.

Kay walked in, trekking through a maze-like series of corridors with concrete walls two stories tall and an open-air ceiling of cork four stories above. It was dark, intimidating, cold, lit only by a few round, blue-hued industrial lights at the ceiling.

At the end of the maze, Kay found herself at a single desk where an attendant sat, a thin woman in a gray suit, light brown hair pulled back in a bun, and a lit red monocle. Kay wasn't sure what to do at first.

"I have an appointment to see Owen Eddington," Kay said.

Without even acknowledging Kay's existence, the attendant entered some information on a tablet at the desk. The attendant's eyes darted back and forth as information appeared on her monocle.

"Eddington, Owen," the woman confirmed. "Index two zero, four one, zero five. Entrant one nine one, two eight."

She looked at Kay. "He's being uploaded now. Come with me."

The woman headed toward a beige metal door a few steps to her right.

Kay hesitated. She was confused. *Uploaded?*

The door, which had no lock or handle, opened

automatically. The attendant escorted Kay through. Kay observed several open doors along the right side of a windowless hallway and expected Owen would be in one of them, waiting for her.

The attendant motioned for Kay to enter through one of the doors. Kay obliged, but she didn't see what she expected. Like the hallway, there were no windows, only one ceiling light and a small security camera barely visible in the right-facing corner. The walls were rust red. The carpet was charcoal-colored and worn, nearly threadbare in some spots. In the middle was a single wooden chair, positioned at a well-used metal table, battleship gray. On the table sat a narrow, vertical, black computer console and thin monitor. Blue light radiated from a small lens at the center top of the screen. There were no wires, no obvious power sources.

The room's dilapidated simplicity and stale plastic odor struck an uneasy chord in Kay. Nonetheless, she sat at the table. A few moments passed. Then, small white text appeared on the monitor's black screen.

2041-05: 19128: HELLO SIS.

Kay's disorientation turned to something gut-wrenching. She wasn't sure what she saw in front of her, and she couldn't identify what she felt at this point. She turned to the attendant, who remained at the door.

"Do I need a keyboard?" Kay asked, mystified.

The message repeated on a second line.

2041-05: 19128: HELLO SIS.

Kay's confusion grew. "Visits aren't in person?"

"This *is* in person," the attendant answered. The woman left, closing the door behind her.

Now, Kay identified what she was feeling. Horror.

"Hello sis" repeated three more times as Kay tried to sort out what to do, how to respond. Finally, another line.

2041-05: 19128: ARE YOU THERE?

"Yes," Kay said, trying to figure out whether she had to look at the screen itself or the lens at the top. "Where are you?"

2041-05: 19128: HERE.

"Can you see me?" she asked.

2041-05: 19128: YES.

Kay felt ill the more she began to comprehend—however slightly—who or what she was interacting with. She needed proof it was Owen.

"Before we had dinner for my birthday, what did Dad give me in his office? What was the gift? You were there."

She counted the seconds, waiting for an answer. Her suspicion grew the longer she sat there without a reply.

2041-05: 19128: SILVER. NECKLACE.

Kay let out a sob—an amalgam of relief and revulsion at

what her brother had apparently been reduced to. Whatever that was. The mystery behind the interaction deepened her terror.

2041-05: 19128: TOUGH ONE. A GOOD ONE TO TEST ME WITH.

She laughed through her despair. No doubt, *that* was Owen.

"What's going on? What's happened?" she asked.

A message filled out haltingly, a word or two at a time.

2041-05: 19128: I CANNOT EXPRESS EVERYTHING HERE. I KNOW WHAT HAS HAPPENED. I CANNOT SAY MORE.

Then Owen's communication ceased. Kay's pupils dilated. She prayed for another word, some short phrase.

2041-05: 19128: HELP ME.

A shiver moved through her. There was no way to answer such a disembodied plea.

HELP ME.
HELP ME.
HELP ME.
HELP ME.

{ }

Eddington decided to spend a late night at the office, mainly because he knew who would storm in demanding answers. Sure enough, just after 10 p.m., Kay practically ripped the doors off the hinges when she entered.

"What did they do to him?!" she shouted.

He stood at his desk. Shadows cast by a nearby lamp gave him a sinister, authoritarian presence.

"I warned you not to go," her father said, balancing rebuke and solace. "You weren't prepared."

The wrath behind Kay's entrance quickly evaporated. Her voice weakened.

"Would I ever be?" she replied with a hopeless shrug. "Where is he?"

Eddington paused for a moment and relaxed, glancing between Kay and the walls as he cautiously formed his words.

"eState's prisons are indexing inmates now," he explained.

"eState" was the only word with any ring of normalcy to it. Everything else Kay's father said was foreign to her.

"What does that mean?" she asked, bewildered.

The problem for Eddington was that his words were just as foreign to him. How could he possibly explain where Owen really was? Owen's incarceration was an abomination, a cross-section of mad science and technology gone bad.

"He's asleep, Kay," Eddington said, almost impotently, as a bit of his untouchable facade crumbled. "Inmates are put in hibernation, fed intravenously, connected through a network of some kind. That's the best I can describe."

Kay was practically shocked by her father's change of

demeanor. She approached him but hid any sign of sympathy. She was daughter, sister—and reporter.

"What's he in prison for?" she fired off. "His own people arrested him on my birthday. What are you doing to get him out?"

Eddington had no answer. In yet another unusual turn of personality, he looked at his daughter blankly. She nodded in disappointment. She knew that when it came to Dad, it wasn't so much an inability to act as it was an unwillingness, usually for his own power position, however mysterious.

"Well," she said scoldingly. "Let me know what I can do."

As Kay turned to leave, part of her wondered if maybe her father really was at a loss this time, that this new situation was so overwhelming it was unraveling even him.

"Kay!" he called out. "Have you broken the ice with that reporter?"

Her hopes for a moderately changed man were wrong. He was still his old self. She stopped and faced him, her own fierce disposition returning to match.

"Yeah, my suspension did the trick." She walked back to him. "There's something you're not telling me about Owen. And if you're not going to tell me, then I'll start digging."

Eddington raised his hands, as if to plead a case.

"Kay, please. Let me handle this."

She was unmoved.

"Like you handled things with Mom? How's that working out?" she replied.

Kay yanked the left door open and slammed it behind her, leaving a thunderous rumble as the double doors pulsated in wake.

{ }

Quinn had been suffering more lately than he was letting on. He was good at hiding pain or discomfort—emotional or physical. But Jasper knew. So did Kay, even though she really hadn't gotten to know him yet.

Often, Quinn would dismiss anything he felt, believing he could solve the problem before anyone he cared about or respected would get too close to offer help. Almost equally as often, Quinn would simply be in denial.

That might have been Quinn's problem this particular morning. He was out for a run along the lake, his favorite spot. He needed the diversion from Kay's stunt and the return of late nights at *The Observator*, going over reams of data on the tape provided by San Diego's former mayor.

His running was effortless, as usual. But he had developed a tick that required attention. He knew what the likely cause was, but he didn't have the means to address it. Health plans covered only the most important basics—anything else could take years to pay off, especially if it was deemed a luxury item.

Searing electric shocks bolted through Quinn's legs, like misfired connections, as he continued down the path. He lost his footing, staggered to the side, and collapsed.

Quinn winced as he grabbed his right thigh and massaged it. Then he tried to extend the leg. It pulsated in occasional fits. He closed his eyes tightly, calming his breath, trying to exert control over his connection with it.

The leg began to calm. Quinn flexed it, mostly back to normal. He stood up carefully, tried a few steps, then slowly limped down the path.

09: ALLIED RIVALS

Quinn kept his eyes closed as the elevator breezed through the floors toward *The Citizen* newsroom. Until he could figure out what to do about his leg, he would have to be more careful with his steps. For the moment, he was focused on keeping himself balanced, standing as still as he could.

In those rare times when he would suffer an outward reminder of his injury in a way he couldn't hide, Quinn would have to endure curious side-glances and the occasional assumptions, always made by observant people who knew from the way he walked that he had more than a sprained ankle.

War injury?

Accident?

The inquiries were well-meaning, and Quinn knew that. He didn't blame them for being curious. If anything, he was more mad at himself for not being able to conceal the truth from even the most schooled observer.

The elevator bell rang, the doors opened, and Quinn exited—limped, though barely detectable. He wasn't in pain. He was just weak.

Quinn got to his desk and sat. Jasper noticed and was concerned.

"When did it start?" he asked.

"This morning. On my run," Quinn told him. "It's okay. I'll deal with it. I've been pushing myself too hard anyway."

Jasper knew this was the start of larger trouble. "Yeah but when the other ..."

"I said it's okay," Quinn interrupted. "Don't worry."

{ }

Quinn sat as much as he could throughout the day, except for an occasional break. At one point, around 1 p.m., he headed to the Commissary for some coffee. He was anxious over what to do about his predicament. At home, drops were a great cure for pain and poor sleep. They provided an emotional escape, too. But Quinn really preferred the energizing comfort of a hot mug of coffee.

Like booze for the broadcasters, Eddington's empire spared no expense when it came to fine coffee. It was probably the best thing about being employed there, as far as Quinn was concerned, alongside working with his best friend and having enough money for food and a roof.

Quinn stared into the Jupiter-like swirls of cream as he prepared his drink at the Commissary coffee station. His back was to the room's entrance, far enough away so that Kay could observe him unnoticed. She began to approach him, but he turned to leave. They met halfway. She noticed his limp.

"Hamstring?"

"Yeah," Quinn replied dismissively. "No martinis on the set today?"

"Hey," Kay bristled.

"I know what you tried to pull the other day." Quinn kept his voice down, taming his resentment. "Having me on the set? Do your own fact-checking."

"Did you write it?" she asked.

Quinn paused. *She had to go there,* he thought. *Does she know or is she acting on a theory?*

He played ignorant. "What?"

"That story, in The Observator. Do you work on the black market?"

Facing the daughter of one of the most powerful men in the country—asking him if he was a journalistic double agent—Quinn knew it was better simply not to answer. He wouldn't win with a denial any more than he would with a confirmation, so he went for the exit. Kay followed.

"Because if you do, I need your help."

Quinn didn't expect that turn.

Unlike his last encounter with her, Quinn saw no change in disposition, no narrowing of the eyes, no inkling of an ulterior motive. Kay stood there, pleading.

"We ..." she started, halting as someone passed by. "We can't talk here, though."

Quinn's eyes darted about her face, continuing to search for a hint that this was some kind of ruse. But the look wasn't there, and neither was the vibe.

"Okay," he granted. "Coffee after your last show. Downtown."

{ }

Jasper stood in stock-still silence the second he walked in on the sordid scene. He had gone to Bruce Haskell's office with a potential problem that could strain his work for the corporate despot. Jasper's guilt for willingly going under Haskell's thumb was bad enough, but the depths of that guilt reached new levels.

He knew something was up when he passed an eState executive in his forties, gray tweed suit, flaxen pompadour and beard, sitting on the foyer couch. The man was despondent, leaning on his thighs, eyes directed toward the brown carpet. The receptionist's desk was unoccupied. Jasper knew better than to ask the man what was wrong, so he continued through Haskell's office doors. He knew he was expected. What he saw, however, was not.

"I didn't mean to interrupt," Jasper said uncomfortably upon witnessing the late-afternoon rendezvous.

Haskell was standing behind his desk with a young man, around eighteen years old, straight brown hair, light brown eyes, thin, wearing a blue cardigan over a white T-shirt, mustard pants, and white sneakers. He massaged the kid's neck, nudged his cheek near the right ear as he pointed to some documents. Haskell looked at Jasper and smiled. He mussed the kid's hair.

"Go see your dad. We'll catch up later," he told the youth.

The teen quickly left, avoiding eye contact with Jasper as he passed.

"It's no bother," Haskell said with a light laugh.

There was a precarious lull between the two for a couple of moments.

"The batteries I need cost more than I expected," Jasper said.

Haskell didn't seem surprised. "Oh?"

"Fifty thousand."

Haskell pursed his lips at the price. "Fifty thousand dollars for two batteries. You're a loyal friend to help him like this. And I'm delighted to help you."

Jasper's stomach sank at what he knew was coming next—the "however" attached to Haskell's help.

"This actually works out perfectly," Haskell said brightly. "Because this friend of yours has information that's sensitive."

Jasper had enough interactions with Haskell to know that the more earnest he got, the more dangerous he could be.

"You can't hurt him; that's not what we agreed to," Jasper said.

"No, no, of course not," Haskell assured him. "He's been harmed badly enough as it is. I know that just as much as you do. That's not what this is about. Knowledge is power, Jasper. I want to keep that knowledge quiet. That's all I seek."

{ }

At the Red Mug coffee shop, not far from eState's sword in the sky, Quinn and Kay were about to have an after-work chat as well. Kay reached for her cash card to cover the drinks—basic decaf for her, triple-shot espresso for him—but Quinn beat her to it, flashing his own.

"On me," he said.

"Thanks."

Even Kay's modest gratitude seemed uncharacteristically

sincere for someone he considered disappointingly shifty. Perhaps Kay was honest in opening up to him. He would have to test that notion to be sure.

The barista scanned his card—eState titanium resembling currency, with a set maximum of ten thousand dollars and the face of President Ronald Reagan on it. Kay, with Quinn's apparent injury in mind, carried their beverages as they looked for a place to sit.

The Red Mug was an unexpected respite from the sham world of eState and overall modern living. In the heart of a new downtown core with freshly built skyscrapers of progressive design and breathtaking height, many of San Diego's remaining small historic structures somehow managed to survive. One remnant, a two-story red brick building about a hundred twenty-five years old, housed this quaint outpost of tag-sale couches, tables, chairs, and bookcases. It was the kind of place where people could talk business and not feel they were being overheard while still at the center of it all.

The cafe was also a return trip to the days of Quinn's recovery, when he discovered the tranquilizing brume released from the drops he would come to know so well. The chemist next door was Quinn's supplier. He could smell the anodyne now, mixed with the toasty coffee beans freshly roasted at the back of the shop.

He never forgot the first time he caught a whiff of the concoction when he passed the small white warehouse on his way to meet Olivia and Jasper at the Red Mug. He was fresh out of rehab, filled with pain and uncertainty. The incense created by the fusion of narcotic and coffee was a welcoming, calming salve.

Today's outing with Kay reminded him that he was due for a refill. No prescription was needed. The mix of organic and synthetic compounds was as freely available, and lawful, as liquor.

Quinn spotted an out-of-the-way table for two. The chairs would normally be comfortable, but Quinn struggled to find a preferable position at first.

"You really hurt yourself," Kay said as they sat.

"It's okay," Quinn assured.

The pair sat quietly at first, sipping their coffees. The lull wasn't awkward. It was more of a break to collect their thoughts, even to ponder if there might be some level of attraction at work.

Quinn had a professional crush on Kay back in grad school, when her national spotlight was starting to shine. He never expected to see her in person, let alone work with her, or have coffee with her. Kay had no idea Quinn existed until he joined *The Citizen*, and only then she would see him passing in the halls. The writers and the broadcasters didn't mingle much. But there was always something about him that struck her. A quiet intensity. Kindness tinged with pain. The glasses. The dark hair that fell across his forehead.

All that aside, they still had interests to tend to, and a host of reasons for mistrust.

Quinn took another sip of coffee. His eyes never strayed from her, scrutinizing with skeptical penetration.

"Before I tell you anything, what does your dad want with me?" Quinn asked.

Kay took a deep breath.

"He suspects you're working on the black market," she

volunteered. "I know it has something to do with that eState exec. And it has to do with the buyout of the City Council."

Over the past several days, Quinn had started to suspect that Eddington was on to him and Jasper, or maybe just one of them. But he didn't expect this. The actual *truth*, a confirmation coming from Eddington's daughter.

Kay looked away briefly.

"It's become more than that now," she continued. "My brother's life is in danger."

The conversation went from there. Kay offered details about her brother's work with eState as its chief of internal security, a convoluted position that was part attorney general, part secret service, part police commissioner, with a web of people serving under him. It was a mishmash of duties that kept the concept of law enforcement jumbled enough to deflect criticism and obscure malfeasance.

Eddington and Kay both thought that with Owen in charge of eState's security apparatus, they had someone they could trust in Bruce Haskell's corporate inner circle. It was a form of leverage to protect Eddington's interests that backfired horribly.

Kay was convinced Owen had something significant on Haskell.

"Something career-ending, even threatening to eState's credibility. It has to be worse than simply paying off a city council."

Quinn listened to her story, at the same time sifting through his own recent observations to find connections. He said nothing—a common tactic when interviewing a source, a way to get the subject to fill the dead air, keep them talking.

"If you do work on the black market, you've got to be able to find out something," she said.

Without directly confirming he was part of the underground, he let slip one clue.

"The code I can't decipher," he said aloud, thinking to himself. "I might already have something on this."

Kay's face brightened. Her ears perked.

Although Quinn's doubts about her intentions were strong, he sensed a somber honesty in her demeanor, enough to give in a little, if for no other reason than to uncover his unexpected role in the Eddington family's intrigue.

"I might be able to help."

{ }

Eddington hated impropriety, no matter how hypocritical that stance could be.

For all of his strengths as a businessman and (for the most part) father, he had one fault that the family worked diligently to keep quiet. The few times it was discussed, it usually came out in angry bursts from Kay, primarily as verbal knife strikes to remind him that he was not everything he often thought or claimed he was.

Like you handled things with Mom? How's that working out?

I wonder what Mom would say about that?

Which anniversary are you celebrating this time?

Eddington's forty-two-year marriage was the product of friendship more than love, emphasis on product. In recent years, he and his wife had rarely been seen together except for social occasions where the appearance of being a couple was necessary. They were partners in raising two things—businesses and children. But the heart of a deeper relationship eluded them. The blame for that was shared. Still, it was largely Eddington's doing.

His latest diversion was "artist" Junice Fawn. She really couldn't sing. She really couldn't act. Nor could she really draw, paint, write, whatever the pursuit might be. But she was a star. That was also Eddington's doing.

Eddington aptly understood that audiences were built using the basest performers possible—his daughter and select others the exception. Junice caught his eye on one of his network's talent shows, *Star Moves*. She was eliminated early, never got close to winning. But Eddington saw that perfect mix of trashy pop and shallow independence that would please the masses.

When Eddington latched onto such a piece, his family suffered. Kay, Owen, his wife—they all had to endure the onslaught of gushing reviews and scandal-sheet chatter. It left the family questioning, *What could he possibly see in that one?* Worse, *Is that what he sees in me?* The rotation of these starlets had become just as much a family joke as a nuisance.

That nuisance was on vibrant display the day following Kay and Quinn's meeting. There Kay was, sitting on her set, Chillax in front of her—Chillax for all today—observing the living disaster, Junice. Nicky and Gonzago stared at her, captivated, glassy-eyed as she talked about her "philosophy" of life on the morning show.

"No one's who they say they are. Who are we kidding?" Junice said in a nasal, brattish voice, flicking aside strands of cotton-candy-pink hair, flaunting her violet-blue eyes, showing off her busty figure in a tight black dress. "Keeping things real means admitting that, up front. Full frontal honesty about the fact we're all dishonest."

On a superficial level, it all made so much sense to Kay's cohosts. To Kay herself, the irony of hearing it from this one was almost too much to ingest.

This was perfect timing for Eddington to appear in the shadows of the studio, watching, smiling proudly.

"You sure pushed some boundaries in your latest film," Nicky said.

Junice smiled, tilted her head slightly, enticingly. "I'm all about exposure."

Nicky faced the camera. "We'll see if we can get Junice to expose a few more details after this."

Quinn was scheduled to talk city politics shortly. He entered just as the commercial break started. Just in time to see.

Junice left the set and walked over to Eddington, who gave her a light kiss near the lips as he placed his hand at the small of her back.

"Lovely," Eddington said with effervescent approval.

Eddington and Junice exchanged soft innuendo-laced pleasantries, but he drew a bead on Quinn from the corner of his eye the instant he saw his reporter limping into the studio.

Kay was relieved to see Quinn. Within a matter of just a day or two, she now saw him as the sanest person in her life.

Quinn leaned across the desk. "Brutal," he muttered under his breath with a quick glance to the scene behind him.

"You have no idea," Kay replied, rolling her eyes as she scrolled through the next segment's script on her tablet.

Quinn turned to leave. Kay noticed he was still having trouble.

"How's your leg?" she asked.

He shrugged with a half-hearted smile. As Quinn stepped away from the set, Kay observed a change in her father. He was agitated. One of his assistants, a young man in a black suit, was whispering something to him, pointing back toward the door. Eddington gave a resigned nod, kissed Junice on the cheek, and left with the man.

{ }

There was an emergency, apparently. At least that's what Eddington's assistant told him when he said Bruce Haskell was in the building. Anytime Haskell came calling, it was an emergency.

Eddington entered his office to find it had already been invaded by the man. He slammed the door and walked to his desk.

"What do you want?"

"Progress," Haskell ordered. "Anything on that reporter?"

Eddington had concerns about something more odious.

"Water cooler gossip says you're a member of the barely legal club, and you play on both sides."

Haskell laughed the accusation off.

"This coming from the man who's infatuated with his latest starlet. Where did this one emigrate from? Just because you ram her down the public's throat doesn't mean they'll be infatuated with her, too."

"I don't demand that my employees and bureaucrats

lend their children to me for their eighteenth birthdays!" Eddington shot back. "That's a national headline grabber if I ever saw one."

Haskell knew Eddington was right. Which scandal would the public find more abhorrent? He was caught off guard that Eddington knew of his indiscretions, but he hid it well behind his burnished face. The fact that his nemesis knew at all wasn't so surprising. Eddington's business was to know such things. But it was also eState's.

There was a more pressing matter, however. Eddington's son. Owen was an important figure to each of these men on the respective sides of their contest. Neither could afford to admit that Owen's place as a high-profile pawn could turn into a massive mutual miscalculation.

For the moment, at least, Haskell knew he had an upper hand.

"You'll keep quiet as long as your son is in custody," Haskell said. His eyes narrowed as he walked closer to the desk. "You're testing a symbiotic relationship here," he instructed, motioning with his hands in the shape of a globe. "You support eState's efforts and it doesn't go to the mat with you in a hostile takeover. A battle I'd win."

Eddington was infuriated. His core values were being thrown in his face in the name of an oligarchy, and it was dawning on him that in trying to fend off its reach, he was a principal member of it.

"I support free enterprise and efficient government, not a cult!" Eddington declaimed. "I know a lot more than you realize; enough to put an end to you!"

Haskell grew calmer as he watched Eddington ferment.

There was no question Owen's incarceration was the vice he could tighten around the mogul.

"We're in the people industry just as much as you are. More so," Haskell said with patronizing pomposity. "eState has information about every single individual in this country. Every purchase. Every medical condition. Every jog down the street. Every mistress. It's our business not just to know but to control."

Eddington regained his composure. His stare intensified.

"So that's why you need my help?" Eddington noted sarcastically. "Everything's locked in so well for you and eState that you have to hound me about *one* reporter."

Eddington leaned forward on his desk, ready to drop a bomb to send Haskell down a crater of paranoia.

"What would the public think if they knew the truth behind a certain university bombing a few years ago that badly injured a future employee of mine? It's my business to know about *that*."

Haskell's face dropped. He mulled the revelation briefly, then pointed his finger.

"You're not going to say anything," Haskell threatened in breathy panic, now restraining his own agitation. He stormed out of the room.

{ }

Newfound fondness aside, Kay still had a mission. By agreement with her father, she was expected to track Quinn. With the close of the workday, she was ready to step up the game, especially after Eddington told her about Haskell's unexpected visit. He didn't reveal much, but he offered enough for her to know that her brother, perhaps the entire family, was in greater peril than originally thought.

Kay observed Quinn from a safe distance as he hobbled slowly to the newsroom. She actually had a desk on that floor, though she rarely used it for anything more than a place to store stuff. Once she knew that's where he was headed, she took an opposite route to get there. She arrived at her desk just as Quinn entered to gather his belongings for the night.

She feigned work as she carefully watched Quinn put his tablet into a well-worn courier bag and grab his black hoodie. He turned to leave his station but stopped abruptly and winced in pain. Then he spotted her. Kay smiled and gave a slight wave. He acknowledged her and headed for the elevator. That was her cue. She opened a drawer containing a stylish beige coat, also hooded but with a faux fur lining. She put it on and prepared to leave.

Kay surveilled Quinn from a good distance everywhere he went, anticipating his direction in some cases. She didn't need any technical help. There was no tracking device on him. She never once accessed her phone along the way. All she needed were her instincts, a sharp eye, and obscured face, which the hooded coat provided. She appeared remarkably adept at this sport.

From the first floor of the building to the street just outside, from three blocks down to the nearest commuter station, to the rail car itself, Kay managed to go unnoticed.

Quinn took a seat among the eState corporate types leaving work for the day. As usual, they were oblivious to anyone but themselves. Quinn might as well have been invisible. Several rows back, Kay silently, quickly entered just as the doors closed and a soft tone sounded. She kept her head down, hood on, pretending to do some work on her phone. Quinn stayed face-forward, but he was keenly aware of the space around him. He didn't know who was watching him yet, but working on the black market as long as he had, he knew how to divine such things.

Four stops and fifteen minutes later, Quinn exited the train. Kay waited until just before its departure to dash out and follow him. She was familiar with the area. Timeworn, industrial, deceivingly dormant. A blue-gray haze hung over the place, turning the streetlamps into spots casting pools of light on an empty stage surrounded by set pieces. In another era, this could be the kind of zone people would warn others to stay away from. Now, however, there weren't enough people here to justify any crime.

These industrial spaces were perfect for underground operations. They were largely forgotten outposts in a fully digital age where any manufacturing was either outsourced or replicated using vertoprinters.

Kay's familiarity came from her occasional foray into the black market scene herself, seeking information to leverage like she did after the Pacific State bombing.

Quinn struggled for another two blocks. He looked at home here with his hoodie, glasses, and courier bag. He cleared some sweat from his forehead as he went, coughing sporadically thanks to the questionable air. Kay looked entirely out of place, more like a high-end shopper in a bread line. She knew no other way to be, and it was the one giveaway that alerted Quinn to her presence once she was in his domain.

Quinn came upon a row of run-down storefronts. Kay picked up her pace to follow him more closely. Although he still wasn't sure it was her, he knew for certain he was being followed. He stopped abruptly to throw her off. Kay jumped behind the corner of a store entrance. Quinn looked behind him. No one there.

He wasn't satisfied. Kay stood in place as Quinn retraced his steps back toward her position. Kay thought maybe she had dodged him when he passed the corner in which she was hiding. But then he stopped. Turned. Looked straight at her. Still fighting his malfunctioning leg, he approached her haltingly, in shadow, the light from a nearby streetlight combining with the evening's gloom to give him an unnerving aura.

"You're going to turn around, walk back to the rail, and go home," Quinn directed.

"No," Kay replied.

Instead of backing down after being caught, she behaved as if she was entitled to be there, on his turf. Quinn changed his approach. He replaced his order with a query.

"Why are you following me?"

Kay resented being her father's operative. She sought Quinn's help as a way to take control of the situation, to get her own answers. It was time to be up-front.

"Because my dad told me to."

Quinn grabbed Kay's arm and started guiding her back from where they came.

"Then I'm walking home with you," he said.

She yanked her arm away and blocked his path. At an impasse, they paused in the middle of the sidewalk.

"What's in the warehouse?" she asked.

The revelation that Kay even knew the warehouse existed worried Quinn. She had either done prior, deeper homework than he expected or she was asking on a hunch.

"The newspaper," she concluded. "It's The Observator, isn't it."

Kay grabbed him lightly at the shoulders; her eyes widened a bit.

"Quinn, please. Help me. You might have access to answers I can't get."

He took a deep breath. "What's in it for me?"

She stepped back and threw her hands up hopelessly. "Nothing. I don't have anything to offer."

Quinn believed her, but that wasn't enough. "Why should I trust you?"

Kay made her case as best she could.

"You know my dad's tracking you. You know my brother's in prison. And you also know I have nothing to offer you in return."

But was that a case for trust? Quinn still wasn't sure. Her actions were more than just about playing spy for her father. That was clear now. So he decided to take a chance. If nothing else, he could root out what her real motivations were if there was still any doubt.

Without saying another word, he showed her the way to the warehouse. They arrived at a door to the building when Kay had a thought.

"I do have something to offer."

He stopped, waiting for her addendum.

"*My* trust."

Fair enough, Quinn thought. But that didn't encourage him much. Kay could tell.

"I'll admit, I really didn't know what to make of you before," she said. "We'd banter sometimes; people would gossip about how maybe it was more. Maybe it is ..."

"Wait, wait," Quinn broke in. "You're going to play *that*?"

The reaction was automatic given his tendency to doubt so much about the world around him, which applied to people as much as institutions. But he knew his response ran against how he felt. Quinn always liked Kay, even though he was suspicious of her part in the larger machine.

His insinuation stung, but Kay understood that her ability to mold situations for her gain could lead to such dubiety. That's what she now had to overcome. Then a change in his reaction encouraged her.

Quinn dialed back his cynicism.

"Because," he said, pausing. "Maybe it is."

Quinn took out a key and unlocked the door. The *Western Earnings Group* sign elevated Kay's curiosity.

Kay was suddenly, surprisingly, fascinated by the world she entered. The smell of ink and paper. The noise of production echoing through the shabby hallway. It was one thing to go to the occasional underground auction for information, but it was another to witness the inner workings of a black market media squad.

The pair entered the newsroom. Kay's presence rankled Olivia, who bolted from her desk seat. Kay nodded to her politely. Other staff members were just as confounded and rightfully suspicious. Jasper seemed somewhat open to her presence. Kay was amused to see him.

"It's all right," Quinn told them. "She can help us."

"With what?" Olivia protested. "Do you realize what you've done bringing this one here?"

"Please, seriously, give me some space on this," Quinn said. "Give her a chance."

Olivia shifted to Kay. "You can't be here, no more than I can be on your set."

"Maybe it's time to change that," Kay proposed. "It would seem only fair."

Kay's overture dumbfounded Olivia. So did Quinn's insubordinate behavior. But Olivia knew to temper hair-trigger reactions with black-market reality. If a reporter like Quinn, who worked both platforms of the scale, had to bring a mainstreamer like Kay into this domain, there had to be a valid reason. Intuition, tricky as it could be, often worked in Olivia's favor. She decided to let this turn play out.

Quinn guided Kay to the computer terminal, which was still running information from Mayor Day's cassette.

"Let's see what else is on that tape."

{ }

Quinn, Kay, and Jasper huddled around the computer as lines of code continually raced across the screen, still decrypting names, bank account numbers, and financial activities.

Quinn's eyes were glazy. His pain was intensifying. Kay hadn't noticed, however. Her eyes were fixated on the screen. She was fascinated by the old tech's meticulous and transparent translations. The plastic, metallic grind of the tape player moving at slow speed. The sounds of typewriters, wax machines, razor blades against rulers, printers, and conversation behind her.

"So this is the proof; what you published," Kay said. She continued her examination of the material line by line. "So why is my brother in prison? Over this?"

That was news to Jasper. "eState jailed its own security chief? When did this happen?"

"It doesn't matter now," Quinn said, fighting his fatigue. "He knows about something a lot bigger than a political bribe."

Then the screen went blank. A second later, a question appeared.

WHAT IS 56625688?

The trio stared at the prompt.

"What the hell is this?" Quinn asked.

Jasper thought for a moment, then turned to Kay. "Does it look like something your brother could answer?"

Kay looked between the two of them, lost for an answer, recalling the spectacle of her brother reduced to a computer console himself, nothing more than a question in pixels.

"Owen's in a prison like I've never seen," she told them. "Even if he knew, I don't think he'd risk telling me."

Quinn took out a small paper pad and wrote the numbers down. Jasper gave the situation more thought, then turned to Kay again.

"What if I could get you into eState to talk to him directly?" Jasper asked.

The question stunned Quinn. How would Jasper have

that kind of access in the first place? What did he mean by "directly" talking to Owen?

The idea certainly caught Kay's attention. She said nothing specific about Owen's state of being in that place. Jasper's phrasing indicated he knew more.

"How?" she asked.

"I have friends who work there," Jasper divulged. "They're sympathetic to what we do."

It wasn't unusual for Quinn and Jasper, even as best friends, to have unshared sources on deep background. But in eState itself? At the level he was hinting? The journalist in Quinn could resent that kind of scoop, but the notion that his comrade could be involved in such circles disquieted him.

"That's news to me," Quinn said.

Jasper smiled slightly. "I can't work on my own sources?"

{ }

With nothing left to do for the night—the computer frozen on *What is 56625688?*—the trio made their way back to the rail station for home. Quinn was doing worse. His walk was slowing, his gait more unstable. Kay and Jasper were increasingly concerned. Jasper knew the reason, though.

"You pulled more than a hamstring," Kay said. "You should get checked."

Quinn and Jasper exchanged a knowing glance.

"We can walk you home," Jasper offered.

Kay and Jasper supported Quinn at his shoulders so he could avoid full pressure on his right leg. But Quinn knew that wasn't going to work. That wasn't the problem.

Then Quinn's left leg seized, and that was it. He fell to the pavement, powerless. Jasper and Kay tried to break his fall as best they could.

"The other one?" Jasper asked.

Quinn nodded. He broke out in small, brief shivers as a mild current shot through him. His grimaces became more apparent. The pain and shocks got worse each second.

"What's wrong?! Just tell me!" Kay pleaded.

Quinn could no longer answer. He was fading. He grew detached from his sense of place, seeing Kay and Jasper hovering over him.

The evening's haze grew thicker around him. Wisps of white smoke began to mix in with it. The smoke was acrid, almost acidic. Within a few moments, Quinn could no longer see anything.

In the white shroud, Quinn could hear faint cries of agony and terror, growing louder as the seconds went by. Then Quinn was the one in agony. Blood trickled down his face. He felt like a heavy weight pressed into the ground, unable to move. He was back in the moment that shattered him. But something was different this time.

A woman's hand caressed his face. He couldn't see through the veil of smoke, but he knew it was Kay.

10: CHILDREN OF eSTATE

Quinn's vision had gone dark. He felt untethered to space or time. He was floating in a quiet, comforting vacuum of blackness perfumed by that sweet, earthy scent of escape. The screams of his flashback had been replaced by the measured, soothing sizzle of drops evaporating on a heating element. One sensation lingered from the previous terror—the soft caress of a woman's hand on his face. He knew it wasn't part of his memory of the bombing, but it wasn't a terrible thing to add, either.

Kay sat beside Quinn as he slept in his bed. She held her hand to his face, smiled sadly. One small dresser lamp saturated the bedroom in tranquil warmth to help him rest.

With Jasper's help as they carried him home, Kay connected the pins. Who Quinn was. Where he was. What happened to him three years ago. She got more details from Jasper than any victims list could ever reveal. The names she fought to obtain in the early months after the attack were now eclipsed by the story of pain and rebirth behind just one of them.

Jasper told her about the drops and how they helped Quinn through those dark times of flashbacks, pain, or simple exhaustion. Quinn wasn't an addict, but the escape they provided was hard to resist. Jasper didn't know what sanctioned narcotic was in them. If Quinn knew, he never said. The drops were an equal-opportunity relaxant, and Kay didn't trust what she was inhaling no matter the pleasant scent. She occasionally glanced with suspicious annoyance at the machine producing them.

During the time Kay watched over Quinn after his collapse, she meditated on her attraction to him.

Up until recently, as far as Kay perceived, Quinn was a cog of a reporter in Eddington's clockwork. Yet he always seemed out of place in her father's empire. That was the first check mark on her list. Mysteries intrigued her. Quinn was a walking puzzle.

A loose thread of the best fabric. That was one description she coined in the weeks after his first appearance on the job.

Quinn was easy to spot among the mass of her pedestrian coworkers when he joined *The Citizen* about a year after the bombing. Above all, it was his eyes. Whenever Kay saw Quinn at company socials or at the coffee bar, she had the impression that he could see through every person. More than that. Every door and wall, too.

Kay could also tell that he was attracted to her. At a distance, he generally had his guard up. Closer to her, his shield would turn translucent. The most telling clue was the biting, humorous, personal sarcasm they exchanged every so often. It was the kind of talk that revealed genuine affinity masked in daily work banter. He may have called her one of the "cave people from above," but she never really took offense. And she was secretly delighted when he smiled at the throw of one of her comebacks. Check mark number two on her list.

The third check—discovering Quinn's involvement in the black market. She disapproved of its existence earlier in her career, but it lured her own independent streak. Over time, she saw the underground as a tool at her disposal, the auctions most of all. It was also the domain of fringe-fact, an assault on her family's work. It was a challenge to her sphere of influence, and challenge added to mystery was an appealing combination. She now saw Quinn as the embodiment of that.

Quinn took a deep breath, opened his eyes. Kay's presence lifted his spirits.

"How long have I been out?" he asked.

"A couple of hours," she replied.

Quinn tried to sit up at the edge of the bed, but he couldn't. His legs were out of commission. He closed his eyes, shook his head in frustration. Kay studied his reaction.

"You were *there*," she said, pondering his backstory.

Quinn nodded.

"I'd assumed you were involved somehow but I didn't know how deep," she continued. "Jasper filled in some of the blanks."

Quinn craned his neck to see if Jasper was somewhere in the condo.

"He left," she told him.

A bit of disappointment moved through her. The truth should have come from Quinn, not Jasper.

It wasn't a pulled hamstring, as she speculated. Quinn's right leg had been losing power. He didn't collapse on the sidewalk because of a seizure or anything else. Both of his legs finally gave out, sending stray reverberating shocks of electricity through him as they attempted to reboot and reconnect to the rest of his body.

Quinn's prosthetics were extraordinary pieces of technology that, until this point, allowed him to live without constraint. Normally, eState insurance policies wouldn't pay for such premium treatment, but the company made an effort to quietly cover the Pacific State victims. It was good business.

Given the natural motion and integration into the rest of Quinn's body, few people would notice he had them. Quinn never volunteered the fact that his lower body had been shredded in the bombing. *Why should I?* was his philosophy. As a result, the only people who knew were those closest to him and those who were required to know.

"You could've told me," Kay said.

"It's not important."

"It is," she gently insisted.

Kay kissed him on the cheek. She kept her lips there, closed her eyes. Quinn held her gently at the back of her neck, and from there, a deep embrace.

{ }

Jasper knew it would be a particularly cruel fate for Quinn to have legs that were state-of-the-art but unusable. Even though eState pledged to cover bombing victims' medical needs or families' death benefits, the word "initial" was a substantial qualifier in the insurance contracts. Sure, a victim such as Quinn would get recovery, rehabilitation, and other needs covered at the start, but he was on his own after that.

The situation only deepened Jasper's own pain—the shame, the guilt, for cowering as he saw his friend helplessly mutilated on the concrete of the university's quad. He didn't help then, but he was determined to help now. To finally make amends.

Quinn and Jasper both understood that Quinn's new legs were operating on borrowed time. The power would run out. That's where Jasper saw his opportunity to set things right. It's why he made friends in certain eState circles, as a member of the black market press, working his way up, source by source, to the CEO himself.

It seemed an ideal plan. Leak some benign tidbits about black market movements to eState's nucleus. Report whatever he could back to his underground compatriots. Build enough of a rapport to ask a favor.

Jasper had no comprehension of the price. As Bruce Haskell did with most anyone he touched, he found ways to corrupt Jasper's good intentions, to manipulate Jasper's weak spots for his own gain.

"You just earned your friend his batteries," Haskell told Jasper while Kay was back at Quinn's place.

Jasper stood in Haskell's office, petrified as the gravity of his actions began to sink in.

"Don't worry about that studio blonde, either," Haskell assured. "I'll only need to hold her long enough to make a deal with her father."

Even in this moment of awakening, Jasper still couldn't stop himself from blurting out information.

"Quinn's onto the evidence," Jasper said, referring to the information on the cassette.

Haskell was unconcerned. "Human nature tells me he won't say a word if people he cares about are in jeopardy."

{ }

Eddington stood at the elevators on the second floor of his media complex, waiting to be carried to his office. The bell rang, the doors opened, and he was puzzled by what he saw.

Quinn, who had entered at the first floor to start his work day, was now seated in a sports wheelchair, black frame accented with white spokes on the rear wheels. Quinn looked up at him, nodded. Eddington reacted with a slight frown.

"Batteries are dead," Quinn told him.

Eddington thought for a moment, then remembered.

"Oh that's right. I forgot. Prosthetics. Blasted eState plans don't cover much, do they?"

Quinn snickered and raised his eyebrows in agreement.

The elevator arrived at the newsroom floor. The doors opened and Quinn pushed his way out. Eddington's frown returned as the doors closed. He was among the minority who knew what happened to Quinn at Pacific State, a fact he blocked from his daughter.

Jasper was already at work when he spotted Quinn making his way across the newsroom. Once Quinn got settled at his workstation, Jasper smiled to himself. He pulled out a small, brown, unmarked shipping box from an orange backpack and handed it to Quinn.

"Take a look," Jasper said.

Quinn wasn't sure what to make of the unexpected package. He took the box, opened it. Tears came to his eyes when he saw the contents.

The box contained two shiny silver cylinders, each fifteen centimeters long, with small barcodes on them, packed tightly in gray foam. Small print on the labels carried the eState Health brand name and text noting the batteries' twenty-year lifespan. That duration would guarantee consistent power to boost Quinn's legs into his forties.

Quinn noticed Kay sitting at her desk, happily observing the unboxing from afar as she jotted script revisions on a paper-thin digital tablet.

"How did you get these?" Quinn asked.

"I had to sacrifice a lot," Jasper answered. "But it's for you. It's worth it."

Quinn studied the batteries. "Thanks, buddy. Thank you."

{ }

Quinn wasn't ready to install the batteries just yet. There was plenty of work to cover first, especially one item, the riddle presented by the cassette tape back at *The Observator*.

With the workday finished, Quinn and Jasper's jobs continued into the night, now with Kay in tow. Quinn impatiently tapped a pen on the desk of *The Observator*'s computer as the screen's prompt continued to flash, waiting for an answer ...

WHAT IS 56625688?

Jasper and Kay pored over dot-matrix printouts of information already processed from the tape, hoping to find some indication of what all the numbers and names meant.

So far, there was no doubt there were payoffs, graft, and other chicanery of various kinds. It was clear eState built its authority and business model on buying people. But was that enough to begin unravelling its credibility, its very existence, in the eyes of those who mattered most? Would the public really care?

Beyond that, Jasper and Kay had other business to cover. On the rail trip to the warehouse earlier, the two discussed getting full prison access to Owen. Jasper had some news for her on that front. She and Quinn would both be able to see him. Whatever that meant, they were about to find out. Jasper had the inroads to access, even a set date, but he had no idea exactly what was to happen. He was unsure what Kay and Quinn were in for. This uncertainty was not something he volunteered.

Quinn tossed the pen on the desk. He was exhausted and fidgety.

Jasper leaned toward him. "Go home. Rest up."

Then Jasper turned to Kay. "Ready to see your brother tomorrow?"

Kay nodded, but she had misgivings. "I should go home, too."

Jasper gave each of them a sheet of paper explaining the procedures they needed to follow once they arrived at the prison.

"One of my contacts is running the desk for the weekend," Jasper told them. "You're there to visit Owen just like you did before."

With that settled, Quinn and Kay left for the evening. It was just after midnight, Saturday now, as the two of them made their way along the street back to the rail station. The weather had turned cold. The streets were damp. Heat from their breath puffed in vapor.

Kay glanced at the backpack attached to the seat of Quinn's wheelchair. The box containing the batteries was in there, and Kay was curious.

"Are you going to put them in tonight?" she asked.

"Yeah," Quinn said. "I don't know how Jasper afforded them."

"Maybe he can't," Kay speculated. "Maybe he's taken on a lot of debt. Maybe even a debt he can never repay."

Quinn stopped at that suggestion. He turned to her, curious about what she meant. She actually didn't mean anything other than a vague theory.

"That's what friends do," she added.

Quinn didn't reply. *She has a point*, he thought.

"I'd like to see them. Install them at my place."

Curiosity or genuine care, her offer came as a surprise, and it warmed him. Light mist began to fall as Quinn considered the idea.

"Okay."

{ }

Kay lived in a part of downtown populated by new high-end residences, a mix of shorter five- or ten-story buildings and skyscrapers reaching anywhere from fifteen to forty floors, situated in an area known as Bankers Hill. Well-to-do locals and investors flocked to the area for its views of the bay and marshland claimed from San Diego's former airport. The upgraded neighborhood was a major project to replace some of the near-sea-level residential towers that were permanently flooded—and demolished as a result—thanks to environmental changes in recent decades. A few of the old neighborhood's historic homes remained, but necessity required most of Bankers Hill to be mowed down to satisfy the displaced upper class.

Kay's top-floor penthouse was in a building her father owned. A sodden overcast outside clung to the plate-glass windows, cloaking the view in an endless unearthly morass.

Quinn sat on the living room couch, Kay beside him. He took off his sneakers (he didn't need socks). Kay was intrigued by what she saw—feet that were in a natural shape but with no toes, skin of a glossy black material.

As he bridged his legs across to the coffee table and began rolling up his jeans, Kay was able to discern more. The skin wasn't just glossy and black. Hair-thin metallic webbing several layers deep caught the light of the room, giving the limbs an almost semi-translucent appearance. Each of his shins was marked with the outline of a narrow rectangular shape.

"This might gross you out," Quinn lightheartedly warned.

He grabbed his right leg and popped the rectangle open, revealing a shallow battery compartment. Sinewy strands of artificial muscle and real blood pulsed around the now-spent battery. He was surprised to see that Kay wasn't disgusted. She studied the inside of the battery compartment like a science student fascinated by a dissection.

"Can you feel touch? Pain?" she asked while he took one of the fresh batteries from the box.

"It's hard to describe," Quinn said. He worked the old battery out and replaced it. "When I feel pain, it's sharp, almost like a shock."

Quinn grimaced as the new battery sent a jolt through him, returning function to his right leg.

"Touch," he continued. "It's more like the memory of touch. That's the best way I can describe it. It's a dull feeling. Once I got used to it, I could move normally, but getting my bearings took a long time."

He closed the compartment and slowly, carefully tested his range of movement.

"They're built into me. I have full control," he explained, flexing the ankle and foot, extending the knee, then preparing the other battery for his left leg. "They use my blood for circulation and lubrication. They're partly self-powered ..."

He stopped there, reflecting on the one flaw of their design.

"... But they also need batteries."

Kay paused on that thought, too.

"A technological Achilles' heel," she said.

Kay's interest and perception touched a nerve in Quinn. She *understood.* Their eyes locked. They moved closer to each other. The approach turned to an embrace. From there, a deep, passionate kiss. For the duration of the night, the pair would learn much more about each other—and themselves.

The experience was life-affirming. Organic. Synthetic. Electric.

{ }

It was noon Saturday. Rail service was light on the weekends, and Quinn and Kay had the car to themselves. They sat across from each other, the emotional and physical hangover from the night before still wafting through them. There was much to meditate on. Their developing relationship. The visit they were about to make. The layers of corruption they were peeling away.

Their rumination was occasionally interrupted by the jarring screams of wheel against track, the crack of car against car, as the train sped to its destination.

Quinn watched Kay sway with the lurches of the train, her gaze out the window, the random shadow that would wipe across her face from some object outside. He felt a depth to her distant stare that matched what he discovered the previous night—how the professional, proper, even manipulative person he perceived her to be was actually warm, compassionate, truthful. Quinn witnessed Kay's self-importance stripped away, physically as close to perfection as he had ever seen. Aware of, yet undaunted by, his trauma.

Kay might have appeared detached from the moment, but her well-trained anchor's eye monitored Quinn's movements in a way he couldn't detect. When he shifted his look elsewhere, lost in thought as she was, Kay would study him just as closely. She, too, recalled what she saw and experienced the previous night when Quinn showed more of himself to her. The scars where synthetic Quinn and organic Quinn met. High up on his thighs, the O-ring structure of the border where his original body ended and his prosthetics began. And a reaction that surprised her—the instinct to lovingly kiss that line, welcoming his difference as something just as normal as the knife scar on her back, sustained when she fought off a deranged viewer early in her career.

They were vulnerable, together.

After several minutes dodging each other's glances, their eyes met, bringing them back to the present.

"Jasper will be there, too?" Kay asked, breaking a long silence.

"Yeah," Quinn confirmed. He detected a growing level of apprehension in her, however. "Are you sure you want to do this?"

She gave it a brief thought, looking out the window at what ended up a brilliant sunny day. She turned back to him and nodded.

{ }

Kay's nerves were ready to burst by the time they reached the prison. The trauma of witnessing her brother communicate through disembodied lines of text overshadowed her mask of composure. Quinn noticed a quiver to her breath. He placed his hand on her shoulder as they entered.

Kay guided Quinn through the labyrinth of corridors to the attendant's desk. What she saw there was the first red flag.

She whispered her concern to Quinn: "It's the attendant I saw before."

"Go through the same motions," he said. "Don't even think about her."

Once they registered at the desk, the attendant guided them through a dim hallway to a room illuminated by bright pools of light from above, one each at four stations—a terminal including a blue light, camera lens, and monitor resembling what Kay saw before; two empty medical beds;

and a third medical bed holding Kay's brother.

Owen was either asleep or in a coma. His skin was pallid; his hair was gone. A clear bag containing a milky, pinkish substance hung next to him, connected to a tube into his mouth down his throat. Electrodes with flashing wireless receivers were embedded at his temples.

Jasper and two technicians, a young man and woman in turquoise lab coats, stood behind the terminal. The sight of Quinn walking and standing normally brought a short-lived smile to Jasper. The serious business at hand left little room for pleasantries.

"They were able to bring him in from storage," Jasper said as he approached them.

"Storage!" Kay flared at the sickening suggestion.

She went to Owen and studied his condition. A billow of helplessness moved through her.

"So how does this work?" she asked pointedly, turning to Jasper.

"Get on the tables and they'll hook you in directly," Jasper explained.

"What'll that do?" Quinn said.

Jasper's nervousness grew. He kept away from his friend, focusing instead on Kay and Owen.

"I don't know," he admitted. Then he looked back at Quinn and smiled again. "It's good to see you standing."

There had been many times over the years when Quinn was disappointed, amused, frustrated, angered by Jasper's behavior. But now, for the first time, Quinn was suspicious of him.

He first got that sense when Jasper presented him with

the batteries. They cost fifty thousand dollars. How did Jasper secure that kind of money? He knew Jasper's parents could easily have given him that sum, but Jasper was long on the outs with them. Besides, his parents barely knew Quinn. There would be no interest beyond God-fearing charity, and even that was unlikely. So what was going on here?

Jasper's odd involvement in this development was a red flag to Kay as well. It's one thing for a journalist to have contacts within an organization. But a hand behind the scenes?

Jasper convened a quick, hushed meeting with the technicians, who then instructed Kay and Quinn to lie on the tables. Under normal circumstances, the two of them would have headed for the door. But Kay's brother was lying in front of them. There were answers to be found somewhere in this room. They moved forward with the mission despite their doubts.

The spotlights above practically blinded them. The technicians, now silhouettes overhead in the light, placed wireless diodes and visor-like strips across their foreheads.

"A couple of deep breaths," one of the technicians, the young woman, instructed.

A tide of fear began to rise inside Kay. How could she have been so foolish not to consider that she was also about to be put under—imprisoned—just like Owen? Her eyes widened. She broke out in an icy, nauseating sweat.

Then she turned to Quinn.

He looked at her, no trace of fear. Quinn had been through this before. The unknown. Life under threat. He survived that. Not even death itself fazed him. It was a strength that impressed even him at this moment, and it was an affirmation that he was a survivor. Quinn's calmness put Kay at ease. She looked back toward the light, maybe not ready for what was next, but at least knowing she was not alone.

"There will be some pain but you'll fall asleep quickly," the technician informed them as her colleague typed a command.

SEND

There was a shrill alarm. Kay and Quinn cried out in spasm.

{ }

Quinn sensed he was asleep, yet still awake, fully conscious in the transition from where he was to wherever he was going. He saw nothing. Felt nothing. He was floating. Disembodied. In the dark. He had every reason to be fearful, yet he wasn't. He wasn't anything.

Slowly, in whatever brief time had transpired, he began to feel momentum forward and downward. Along with it came an unusual sound, a *rush* somewhere between the snow of a television without a broadcast and a distant waterfall.

The sound faded as Quinn felt his body return to him. He was now standing. His vision was still dark. Then the nebulous shroud began to lift. The first thing to appear—a man dressed in a black suit, his back to Quinn, standing a short distance away.

Quinn's vision expanded, revealing the interior of a long-closed supermarket in disrepair. He couldn't spot any windows. As best he could tell, he was near the back of the store. Spotty light came from a mix of random fluorescent ceiling fixtures and pools of brightness from no identifiable source.

Quinn looked to his left. Kay was standing beside him. Both felt tremendous relief once they realized they made it through together. Kay was still timid, but Quinn found the whole experience fascinating. He smiled as he observed every detail around him.

"It's a lucid dream," Quinn said.

"A what?" Kay asked.

"Being awake in a dream," he explained as his eyes continued to wander. "It's called lucid dreaming."

Quinn came to realize that something felt different—about himself. It was actually an impression of *not* feeling different. It took him a few moments to take in the sensation. He looked down at his legs, knelt, and rolled up the right leg of his pants, revealing natural skin, warm to the touch. Quinn moved his hand across his right calf, the shin, the ankle. He moved his toes.

Caught in the wonder, Quinn disengaged from place and purpose. But he quickly snapped out of it. There was a mission to complete, and however long he preferred to savor the return of his whole body, Quinn wasn't going to sacrifice his real life for some surreal existence in a dark, eternal, creepy grocery store. He was content to carry a fresh memory of his old self from this brief intersection of illusion and reality.

Quinn stood. He noticed that Kay wasn't so fascinated with this false world. She fixated—trancelike—on the male figure before them.

Kay was fairly certain the man in the suit was Owen. But why wouldn't he face her? More concerning to her was the world in which he was thrown. This was a nightmarish existence. The more Kay dwelled on it, the more angry she grew at her father, her work, even herself. What kind of human beings could create and promote a state of such efficiency and "freedom" while being so void of conscience? Unable to fully process this intolerable situation, she entered a kind of stasis, almost like an artificial intelligence going haywire over its own ignorance of the world in which it was created.

Quinn gently took her hand. "Is that him?" he asked softly.

Kay took a breath. "Yeah, I'm pretty sure."

Together, they approached the man in the suit. He slowly turned to face them. It was indeed Owen. Expressionless. Void of emotion or recognition.

"Owen," Kay said, hoping to elicit some feeling of familiarity.

Her brother appeared more like a hologram, perhaps filled with half a soul. That was her initial fear as she observed his inability to focus on her. Owen looked at her fleetingly, as if she were part of the disjointed world around him.

"I used to work here," Owen said distantly. "I was a bagger. It was my first job. Remember?"

Owen focused more on Kay as he appeared to awaken from his daze.

"You're here," he said, puzzled by her presence. He looked at Quinn. "Who is this?"

Quinn held out his hand in greetings. "I'm Quinn."

Owen didn't reciprocate, something out of character for him. It was a product of confusion rather than rudeness. In the days since his imprisonment, he increasingly lost his sense of self as the occupier of a virtual cell. His sister's puncture into this world was slowly bringing him back.

"You're visiting, too," Owen said to Quinn, more as a query than an observation. "The last time she visited, I could only see her there."

Owen pointed to an old-style tube television set, vintage 1960s, to their left. It was freestanding, with a sixty-centimeter screen framed in brushed metal, a V-shaped antenna sticking up from the back of its dark wood cabinet. The screen showed no reception, only static.

Something clicked inside Kay as she examined the mysterious antique.

"The console at my first visit. It had a camera on it," Kay told Quinn. "I wonder if that's how he was able to see me."

"But you couldn't see him," Quinn deduced.

"No, I just got text on a screen," she said. More pieces fell into place for her. "The console in the room we're in now. It has the same setup."

"That means they can probably read what we're saying," Quinn theorized.

The snow on the television screen began to clear as an image scrolled. Once it stabilized, they were able to see a feed of the room they were in. The black-and-white video showed Kay, Quinn, and Owen asleep on the tables. Jasper and the technicians were visible in the background monitoring the room.

Kay turned back to Owen. She opened her mouth to say something, but Owen put his hand up to stop her.

"Don't worry about that," Owen said.

The more he interacted with Kay and Quinn, the more

himself he became. He did have something to share with them, but he had to be careful how. Even in this environment, the technicians could track mostly everything that was going on. *Mostly.*

Exactly how this blend of technology and brain science worked, no one knew. But it had its flaws. Owen, Kay, and Quinn had the visuals. It didn't work the other way around. The technicians could only see in lines of text what was being said aloud. If there was one possible silver lining to the hell of being in this system, it was that the flaw worked in Owen's favor.

"Why were you silenced?" Kay pressed.

Owen put his hand up again, this time more forcefully. It was imperative that no answers be spoken. Four young people, roughly ages seventeen to barely twenty, entered the dilapidated grocery store aisle from behind him. Among them were Alexis Mott and the young man Jasper happened upon in Bruce Haskell's office.

As Kay and Quinn looked at the kids, trying to discern some meaning from their appearance, the scene on the television changed. Jasper was no longer in the picture.

{ }

Unknown to the trio, Jasper had gone into the hallway outside the room where they were being held. Haskell was waiting for an update on the operation.

"They're talking," Jasper told Haskell, who nodded approvingly.

"Good. We can wait a few minutes," Haskell said.

{ }

Continuing their quest in Owen's grocery store dreamworld, Kay and Quinn observed the four young people who appeared before them. The kids stared back with empty eyes. Were they apparitions? Or were they hooked into this virtual prison as well? The potential answers horrified Kay.

Then more young people entered from behind Owen, gathering in a group around him. Four became ten, then twelve, fifteen, and more.

Kay studied her brother's reaction to the visitors. Owen recognized them. Then Owen faced his sister. Kay instantly understood. The young ones were the unspoken message—figments of Owen's will, a visual tip for Kay and Quinn.

Among them, however, another person appeared. A doppelgänger. Quinn's.

The double emerged at the back of the group, bloodied, shivering, drilling through Quinn with an almost accusatory, angry glare. Owen seemed oblivious to the doppelgänger, making it likely that the double was a creation of Quinn's mind.

"Don't say anything," Owen warned. "Just look. Remember."

Quinn was increasingly riveted by his double, contemplating what he could represent. His eyes shifted between the mix of late teens and early twentysomethings and the doppelgänger, trying to sort out the blurring lines of symbolism behind it all, to the point he had practically forgotten about Kay.

"Who ... ?" Quinn asked Owen.

"The children of eState," Owen interrupted.

"Quinn!" Kay screamed in panic. "*Quinn!*"

Quinn turned to her, but she was gone. On the television screen, he could see that Kay was awake, struggling, held down by the attendants as eState security officers rushed into the room. He looked back at Owen.

"The children of eState," Owen calmly emphasized, taking a couple of steps toward Quinn.

{ }

As if being roused from a deep sleep, Quinn jolted awake. The return trip to reality was far quicker and easier than the arrival. There wasn't a second to dwell on the travel's hangover, though.

Kay was dragged out of the room by security.

Two more officers ripped the diodes off Quinn's forehead and yanked him from the table. Quinn looked for Jasper as he was led out of the room, but he wasn't there.

The officers escorted Quinn into the hallway. He saw Kay and the other officers a short distance away.

Then he saw Jasper. With Haskell.

eState's Alpha had his left hand on Jasper's upper arm like a trusted consort. Had Quinn's legs been organic, they might have buckled under him. But they kept him standing strong as he realized that his suspicions—his worries—had been confirmed.

"What did you do?!" Quinn yelled, gritting through his teeth, even spitting a bit in fury, as he struggled to break from the officers.

Quinn jammed his left foot into the foot of one of the officers, who howled and fell back in agony. That gave Quinn the window to break free of the other officer, who he kicked in the midsection with such force that the officer flew back nearly four meters before hitting the floor.

Then Quinn lunged toward Haskell, going past him to Jasper, gripping his best friend hard by the throat and jamming him against a wall.

"Why?!" Quinn cried as he tightened his grip.

The officers charged back at Quinn, wrenching him off Jasper. Quinn struggled so fiercely that one of the officers took out a small weapon—a brown plastic rectangle with metal teeth—and jammed it under Quinn's right jaw line, instantly neutralizing him with a loud electric current.

Jasper's penitence about leaving Quinn to suffer alone after the bombing doubled with the crisis of conscience he now felt. Seeing Quinn immobilized by the officer thrust the point even further into Jasper's soul.

Haskell, satisfied, turned to Jasper nonchalantly on his way out.

"Well. Our business is done."

11: PAWNS AMONG GAMES

Kay paced the length of a rectangular holding cell. Quinn sat on the room's single metal bench. He leaned forward slightly, bracing his chin on his hands, lost in a mix of disbelief, grief, and mystery.

Small ceiling fixtures flooded the room in sterile light, revealing every hairline crack and uneven surface of three concrete walls. The fourth wall—a long portion making up the rectangle—was some other material painted pristine white like the ceiling and floor. There was one white metal door and a large mirrored observation window. As Kay paced, she glanced periodically at that window, seeing her reflection, knowing they were being observed. She estimated they had been locked up for about an hour. That was her best guess without a timepiece.

"Children of eState," Kay thought aloud. "What did he mean?"

She sat next to Quinn, who stared blankly ahead.

"Why was I there?" he said under his breath.

Kay wasn't sure what he meant. She hadn't seen the doppelgänger herself and therefore had no reference for his question.

"Did you suspect anything with Jasper?" she asked.

"We shared pretty much everything," he replied as he wiped his face. "Then I find out he has contacts here? I figured we should be careful but I didn't see this."

It was increasingly evident to Kay that Quinn's issues with Jasper were long-standing, simmering underneath, in danger of erupting with the right pierce through a protective membrane.

"What happened to him in the bombing?" she inquired.

Tears returned to Quinn's eyes.

"I got blown apart, and he cowered under a bench and walked away," he said through a cry. "We were brothers, you know? I thought I let it go. But this ..."

Quinn turned silent again. Kay held his face and kissed him softly on the cheek.

On the other side of the glass, in a dark observation room adjoining the cell, Eddington and Haskell watched and listened.

Eddington was not pleased by what he saw—his daughter's emotional investment in the man she was originally supposed to surveil. Haskell turned to him.

"You didn't know?" Haskell asked. "Your daughter. Your whole family, for that matter. You're the real mess I can't control. Except in one way."

Haskell went to a guard, a hefty man about age sixty, waiting at the door.

"Release Kellerman," Haskell ordered. "The other stays."

Eddington didn't show it, but Haskell's decision worried him deeply. First, Haskell got his son. Now, it was his daughter.

"What are you going to do?" Eddington asked.

"Hold her for now," Haskell replied, waving for Eddington to join him as he and the guard left the room.

Haskell's statement was a somewhat encouraging sign. Eddington had hope that Kay might be spared the kind of incarceration Owen was under.

Kay continued to comfort Quinn when the cell door opened. Haskell and Eddington entered with the guard.

"Quinn Kellerman," the guard called.

Quinn hesitated as he stood, looking back at Kay. He wasn't worried about himself. He was worried about why only he was called, leaving her behind.

Then Kay rose, kissed him once more, and smiled. "It's okay. Go."

Eddington could barely stop himself from rolling his eyes in disappointment over their chemistry.

"I'd like a minute with my daughter," Eddington told Haskell as Quinn left with the guard.

"Of course," Haskell said.

Eddington was about to go to her when he realized Haskell was still standing there.

"I know you'll hear everything anyway but could you at least leave the room?"

Haskell bowed partly, almost mockingly, as he backed out.

"I won't eavesdrop," Haskell promised, closing the door behind him.

Eddington relaxed. He was still displeased by Kay's choice of suitor, though.

"You two?"

She nodded.

"He's a little low in the ranks, isn't he?" Eddington panned.

"Dad."

"Aside from roping you into this, he'll grow on me, I'm sure," he said tersely.

That didn't sit well with Kay. Quinn didn't rope her into anything. Her involvement began with Eddington's desire to keep an eye on him.

"I got involved because I chose to! This all started with you!" she told her father. "You wanted me to spy on him! You wanted me to track down whatever it is about Haskell he supposedly knows!"

Eddington raised his hands, as he often did, to explain the situation like an expert.

"Your brother's the one who knows everything. He's at the core of this! I don't mean to say Quinn's at fault. The way this all fell into place, it's just how it is."

"Then fix it!" Kay demanded. "For all of us!"

{ }

Quinn was now grappling with the idea that he was a pawn in more than one game, none of them his own making, none of which he was the master. Saturday had entered evening, and Quinn was traveling on the rail to confront Jasper at *The Observator*, the most likely place he figured his friend would be.

As his travel continued, despair and rage simmered in him. Quinn was generally good at hiding extreme emotions because he knew they were passing flashes, not how he truly thought or behaved, so he suppressed them. But he faced them more often than anyone realized. Quinn was not a volatile person. He was good-natured. What he couldn't deal with now was the overwhelming sense that he had been used thanks in part to that good nature.

More than any of that, he simply couldn't understand Jasper's role in all this. How could his best friend think that falling under Haskell's influence could be helpful, even for batteries? There had to be something dysfunctional to Jasper's core. He had to be inherently untrustworthy. Weak. Jasper was an enemy.

The rage went from simmer to boil, to the point where Quinn didn't even recall stopping at his destination and getting off the train. Through eyes he could barely see with thanks to an uncontrollable flood of grief, Quinn suddenly realized he was just a block away from *The Observator*'s building. He gathered his composure as best he could.

Quinn entered the building, avoiding eye contact with anyone he passed, staring straight ahead, undiverted. He got to the newsroom and saw Jasper sitting, talking with Olivia at her desk. Jasper had his back to Quinn. He had no idea what was about to be unleashed. Olivia knew, though. She could tell instantly by the look on Quinn's red face, his eyes zeroed in on his target. She stood to intervene.

"Quinn, before you say anything, Jasper has a ..."

Before Olivia could finish, Jasper turned and stood to face Quinn, who promptly, rapidly punched Jasper twice in the face. Each hit landed with a watery crack of flesh and bone. Jasper fell to the floor in a daze. Quinn stood over him.

"I was blown up and you cowered under a bench! And *now* what did you do?!" Quinn spattered.

Quinn turned to leave. Jasper got up to follow him.

"I didn't care about Eddington and Haskell! I cared about you!" Jasper yelled back, almost like a plea, running his excuses aloud in a stream of thought as blood trailed from his nose. "I got the batteries for you! I wanted to help you! I did it for you! I didn't mean for this to happen!"

Quinn turned back and delivered a swift, effortless push-kick with his right leg, full force, to Jasper's stomach, sending Jasper flying to the ground in a heap.

Jasper was immobilized, gasping for air, crumpled like a coat on the floor. Quinn stood there, startled by his own strength. Olivia and two other staff members came to Jasper's aid. Quinn's fury melted.

"Is he okay?" Quinn asked, almost at a whimper.

Olivia ignored him, attending to Jasper.

"He should be checked out," she told the staffers. "Get him to a clinic."

Then she turned her attention to Quinn. "Go home and settle down!"

{ }

Quinn hopped the rail after the blowout, no particular destination in mind. He exited somewhere in downtown San Diego. He didn't pay attention to the stop.

The look on Olivia's face haunted Quinn as he walked the deserted streets, the light of brilliant neon and digital displays dancing in the night haze. Her expression was a disturbing mix of disappointment, anger, fear—and sympathy. That's what Quinn interpreted.

He also dwelled on his reaction to Jasper and the resulting damage he inflicted. From the time he spent on the train to his seemingly never-ending, lonely trek from the whole situation, Quinn gripped his phone tightly in his right hand. He called Jasper repeatedly. No answer. Straight to voicemail.

He texted.

I don't know my own strength anymore, I'm sorry, are you okay? I'm sorry!

No replies.

By the time Quinn arrived at the Red Mug, which was a twenty-four-hour spot, he felt increasingly ill at the thought that he might have actually killed Jasper.

There were no other customers at this late hour. The place was his except a lone employee behind the counter, a young woman with straight purple hair the consistency of straw, wearing a black apron over a weathered white shirt and jeans, and combat boots. Quinn ordered a green buddie—genetically engineered cannabis-infused coffee with a minty zest—only because he loosely understood that such a combination had a way of blurring one's memory. He sat at a corner table, sipping the brew, smacking his lips occasionally at the odd flavor.

About three hours had passed since Quinn left Jasper in a heap on *The Observator* newsroom floor. It was close to midnight, nearly the start of Sunday.

He sent another text to Jasper.

Brother, let's sort this out. Please tell me you're okay.

He prayed for a response.

Then one came.

On the tracks.

Quinn wasn't sure what Jasper meant. If it was code, he didn't know what it could be for. Quinn's concern deepened. He texted for a clarification.

??

I'm on the tracks. Find me.

Jasper followed his reply with coordinates for Quinn to enter into his phone. Quinn obliged, and the phone's map pinned Jasper's location. He wasn't far, just a couple of kilometers northwest. But the confirmation alarmed Quinn. According to the pin, Jasper was indeed on the tracks of a commuter rail.

{ }

Jasper paced between two sets of tracks in a neglected, unoccupied corner of town. It seemed as if he was the only sign of life aside from the trains that would race through the area. None had passed since he arrived, but the heaviest, saddest part of him wished one would.

The tracks emitted a low, subdued hum from the current running through them. While they were safe to walk on, it was not advised. He did so anyway, occasionally wondering what would happen if Quinn were to step on them.

In the half hour he spent walking on the rails, Jasper thought about the alien character who inserted himself into their lives. The man named Bruce Haskell, who sat next to Jasper on a train one inauspicious day not long after the bombing three years ago.

The memory enveloped Jasper. He sat, facing east, on the tracks. The unending hum took him back to that moment when Haskell seemed to appear from nowhere, sitting to his left on a ride home after a visit with Quinn. He pictured Haskell leaning into him with that quiet, predatory stare. There was no need for an introduction. Haskell's face was ubiquitous.

"I know who you are," he recalled Haskell saying. *"Both of you. But it's you I need to see."*

Haskell knew that Jasper and Quinn were aspiring journalists caught up in the attack. He knew they were the kind of living collateral damage that could present problems in the future if the two cared to dig. He was also aware that Jasper and Quinn were ripe for the black market. So Haskell had an offer.

Jasper stopped the recollection there. He couldn't bear its burden. He stood on the tracks again, staggering for a moment thanks to the wounds dispensed by Quinn to his midsection, looking south down the ribbons of rail that faded in the darkness, waiting for the sound of a distant horn, a train approaching.

{ }

Quinn ordered an automated taxi to the spot pinpointed by his phone. He was fidgety the entire ride. With scarce traffic at the late hour, the trip was short. The taxi stopped at a dilapidated sports field beside the tracks. He got out.

Quinn could barely see Jasper, facing away from him, standing on the tracks in the gloomy light of a nearby utility lamp.

"Jasper?!" he called out.

Jasper turned, revealing some of the results of Quinn's pummeling—face severely bruised and swollen. It was difficult to see a lot of detail in the poor light, but Quinn was devastated by what he could make out. Jasper's anguish. That look said everything.

Quinn took cues from Jasper's behavior and choice of location, realizing that caution was needed in the minutes ahead. Still, Quinn had to ask.

"Why Haskell?"

Jasper left the tracks and walked toward him—to Quinn's relief.

"He was just there sitting next to me," Jasper answered, the emotional weight revealing itself in his voice. "I didn't know where he came from. The second time we met Olivia, it was after that. I was on my way home after I left you at rehab. There was a stop and then he was there. He knew who we were."

"What did he want with us?"

"It was me," Jasper revealed, fighting the urge to cry. "He wanted me. He knew how bad you were hurt. He wanted to know, if there was anything in the world I wanted, what it would be. It was to make you whole."

Quinn shook his head and shrugged slightly, unsure where Jasper was taking the story.

"He'd help me if I told him about what we were doing," Jasper explained. "He was obsessed about the bombing and the media."

The worst thing, man. The worst, Quinn thought. He circled a few steps, exasperated.

"It was perfect!" Jasper assured him. "It was *perfect*, Quinn. I gave him little bits, stuff to satisfy him and keep him away. But I got on the *inside*. If he was going to use me, hell yeah, I was going to use him, too."

"But that's not how it worked!" Quinn erupted. "Look at what's happened! How far did you have to go?!"

Jasper walked back onto the tracks. "I just ... stayed."

"Yeah but what reason?!"

"There *is no* reason, Quinn! That's the problem! He guarantees a promise and then he plays with you. He has this force of will about him. You don't realize you're in until after he has you. And then you start thinking about all the ways you can justify being in the circle as he raises the stakes."

The storm between them seemed to die down, but the two kept to themselves in the quiet.

Quinn so often fought the instinct to blame his friend for walking away after the attack that could have ended his life. He speculated whether his outbursts were more damaging to Jasper than the incident itself. He saw Jasper's presence on the tracks as poignant validation.

Reparation absorbed Jasper post-bombing. Quinn didn't wholly fathom it until this moment.

"Could you walk on these?" Jasper asked, glancing at the tracks.

"I wouldn't chance it."

Jasper nodded sorrowfully. "I didn't think so, either. I'm sorry you can't. You should be able to."

Quinn squinted in frustration, briefly breaking eye contact with Jasper.

"I don't know why you think that attack was your fault."

"You hinted enough times," Jasper said. "It didn't matter. It's what I felt anyway, that I hurt you. I abandoned you."

Quinn shook his head, realizing that his own jabs over time were only half of Jasper's affliction.

"You act like you're hurt, when you're not," Quinn told him. "It's not like me, physically, that's not what I mean. You're not ... we're not ... *hurt*. You get what I'm saying?"

Quinn felt a slight vibration in the ground. A distant metallic grind followed, growing louder by the second. From what he could detect, a train was approaching from the south. Then a beam of light appeared in the near distance.

This was the scenario Quinn feared.

Jasper pushed a smile through his tears. He stepped backward onto the tracks nearest them. Quinn glanced to his left, trying to avoid breaking full eye contact with his friend while observing the train. He nervously waved for Jasper to get off the tracks.

"Seriously?" Quinn could barely ask under his breath.

Jasper shrugged. "Maybe."

Quinn tried to mask his terror at what could happen

next, but his shallow breathing was a giveaway.

The train wasn't far now. Its horn blared. The sound carried a deep, thunderous bass that trespassers could feel as much as hear. Within no time, the train seemed just a few meters away.

Jasper's mood lightened. He went to step off the inner rail. Quinn headed for him, left hand outstretched, relieved. But Jasper slipped on the near-polished metal, somehow lodging his left foot behind the outer rail in an effort to catch himself. Jasper cried out as he stumbled. He was barely able to work his foot free.

A surge of air blew through ahead of the train. The vehicle seemed nearly on top of them when Quinn lunged forward and pulled Jasper away, dragging him to safety as he scurried. In a *whoosh* of speed, the train was gone. Quinn offered his hand to help Jasper up.

Jasper backed away once he got his footing. He put his hand up to block Quinn from coming closer. The move wasn't hostile. Quinn could tell.

Stay away. I'm toxic.

That's what Quinn read in Jasper's expression. And he was right. It's exactly what Jasper felt.

Jasper, still wobbly from the close call and Quinn's kick a few hours earlier, turned away and clumsily walked into the darkness. Quinn started to follow, but he stopped. He recalled from his own experience how annoying—intrusive—it was when people didn't heed his own unspoken demands to be left alone.

{ }

A light mist began falling, morphing into a mix of drizzle and heavy fog by the time Quinn made it home. He watched the swirls and sheets of vapor outside as he sat on the couch, looking out the window of his living room, pondering everything that had transpired.

The hangover from his bizarre visit with Kay's brother lifted a while ago, but the image of his own doppelgänger lingered. Quinn wondered if the vision was a messenger of some kind, a warning to acknowledge a seething fury best brought to light and dealt with. He came to realize that what he saw was a reflection of an underlying self—a persona that served to agitate, not heal.

Did he really have so much hate in him that he couldn't forgive Jasper's behavior in those moments after the bombing, as he thought he did? Did he have so much inner rage that he was willing to propel his new legs into his friend, to inflict potentially lethal damage? Or did he just not know the depth of his own strength? Was he the kind, open, mild person he thought he was?

Maybe all the questions were ultimately meaningless, only fueled by the haze and spicy, woodsy scent of drops disappearing with a crackle on the heating element in the kitchen.

Quinn lay on the couch, shifting his gaze between the mist falling outside the window, the dew falling off the leaves of plants and eaves silhouetted by streetlamps, and the drops hissing and evaporating on the counter, giving him comfort in one of his darkest hours in recent memory.

He glanced at a pad of paper on the coffee table, filled with attempts at deciphering the riddle left on the old computer in *The Observator*'s newsroom. He grabbed the pad and a nearby pencil and pondered the question again. Maybe it was an attempt to divert himself from darker thoughts. No matter. The best he could do was add a few doodles on the page.

Quinn checked the time. It was just past 2 in the morning. Perhaps it was best to sleep the whole waking nightmare off. But the doorbell rang. He stayed on the couch, not sure what to do. The bell rang a second time.

Answer it, his inner voice advised.

Quinn got up and walked to the door. He opened it. Jasper stood there, nose and part of his face severely black and blue, his worn gray-green coat damp from the mist, hair a soggy mess. He had the semblance of a car nearly totaled in a wreck. The two stared at each other for a few moments. The damage to Jasper's face was bad enough, but it was that kick to the gut that Quinn felt worst about. They had two things in common right now—relief at seeing the other alive, shame for what they did to one another.

"You okay?" Quinn asked softly.

Jasper nodded, looking down.

"I'm not used to my own strength," Quinn admitted.

"I'm sorry. About everything," Jasper replied. "I had it coming."

"No. No, you didn't. Not like that," Quinn told him. There was another brief pause. Quinn's mood brightened. "Come on, man. Get in here."

Now they could at least work to reassemble their

relationship, to understand each other's place in events beyond their control.

The friends went to the kitchen. Jasper inhaled deeply, raising his eyebrows and smiling at Quinn's choice of drops.

Quinn looked toward a corner cabinet above the counter and remembered a gift from an old mentor. He opened the door and pulled out a bottle of bourbon, the one Noel gave him in rehab. The moment seemed right to share it. He showed the bottle to Jasper.

"You never opened it?" Jasper said.

"It's time."

Quinn grabbed two small glasses from another cabinet, looked fondly at the EAB logo burned into the bottle's black wax seal, then ripped it off, revealing the cork underneath. With the squeaky *pop* of the cork, Quinn poured a small amount for Jasper, then for himself. They sat across from each other, clinked glasses, and began to hash things out.

"You're right about me," Jasper said. "I could've done more. Made better decisions."

Quinn shook his head. "I shouldn't have blamed you. And that day, what could you have done? Think about it."

Jasper couldn't hold the guilt in any longer, unwilling to believe Quinn's interpretation.

"I should've helped you without hesitating. I thought I was that kind of man."

"No. I mean, what could you have *done* ?" Quinn asked again. "I couldn't do anything for myself. If I'd been a few more meters away I could've been stunned under a bench, too. But I got taken care of, and so did you. And we're here. We're survivors."

Jasper angled his glass on the table, rocked it back and forth, staring through it in plaintive contemplation.

"I wanted to make it right somehow," Jasper said distantly. "I don't know what I was thinking. I had no idea what I was getting into."

Quinn's guilt was equally sincere, but it still only went so far.

"It wasn't worth a kick like that," Quinn said. "A punch, though ..."

The recollection drew a jesting smile from Quinn. Jasper couldn't disagree, prompting a brief chuckle between them. They clinked glasses again.

"You never needed to make anything right," Quinn said, recalling the flood Jasper pulled him out of that summer in Arizona. "You already saved me once. It's the other way around. I've owed you for a long time."

"Not anymore," Jasper told him. "You were there for me tonight."

Although it was unspoken, the two felt a return to balance, a purge of the emotional smog between them.

Quinn took a deep breath. "So we move on?"

Jasper nodded.

"When I got to the newsroom," Quinn awkwardly began. "Before I lit into you. Olivia mentioned your name. I never got to what it was about, obviously."

Jasper spotted Quinn's notepad in the living room. He went over and brought it to the kitchen table.

"I thought it was a cipher," Jasper said as he wrote down the mysterious number they came across on *The Observator*'s computer. "Starting with A equals one, B equals two."

Jasper assigned a letter to each number as he continued to write—56625688 translated to EFFBEFHH. Quinn tilted his head in curiosity as he looked at the translation, the remaining strands of conflict between the friends quickly dissolving.

"But the corresponding letters don't make any sense. They don't spell anything," Jasper showed him. "And when I entered this into the prompt, it didn't work. But my instinct tells me it's a cipher of some kind."

Quinn took the pad, studied the numbers and letters. Then something occurred to him.

"On the black market, we use old tech," Quinn mentioned. "Typewriters, paper and wax, handwritten notes, primitive computers. And why. Because it's tough to track. It's off eState's grid. Or anything's, for that matter."

Quinn started writing more numbers down in a brainstorm—numerals 1 through 9, then 0, each with three letters assigned per number.

"And that goes for old-style phones, too," Quinn continued. "The keypads used to have three letters assigned to each number."

He pointed to the number 6 as an example, which was assigned the letters MNO.

"Six can mean three different letters," he said, pointing to the pad.

Together, they started working on combinations. In the process, Jasper came upon one. A word.

KNOCKOUT

"Knockout," Jasper said aloud to himself.

Quinn studied the word. It seemed familiar. Something he recently heard. Then it hit him.

"That's what Mayor Day said when he gave me the cassette," he told Jasper.

Quinn recalled the meeting on the running path along Lake Miramar. He saw Mayor Day's face, observed his demeanor.

"It's all there. Everything you need. With one final knockout blow."

Quinn remained in that moment, reliving it to see if there were any other hints he could pull. He remembered watching the mayor start to leave.

"What do you mean?" he remembered asking Day.

The mayor stopped and smiled.

"You'll see."

{ }

Quinn and Jasper headed back to *The Observator* early Monday morning to test their discovery. They could have waited until after their shifts at Eddington's company, but the potential access to something pivotal was too important to sit on.

They huddled with Olivia around the computer. Before trying the answer, Olivia wanted an update on what information had been gained so far.

The files gleaned from the tape revealed transactions between Bruce Haskell and the San Diego City Council. There was no disputing that.

Olivia reviewed reams of printouts at the computer table.

"What eState fund did these fall under?"

"They didn't," Quinn said, showing her specific portions of the entries. "These are all Haskell's personal accounts. Payoff after payoff. eState itself had nothing to do with them. So I've got the mayor on record, and these transactions back him up."

Olivia mulled the information's potential impact.

"I wonder what eState's executive board would think about this?" she asked, more to herself.

"Haskell can't do any wrong. What would they care?" Jasper said.

"A lot if they have a reputation to keep," Quinn countered. "They might run state and local governments, but they still fall under some federal regulation."

"For how long?" Olivia pointed out.

The three of them looked back at the computer screen, which still showed that odd question begging an answer.

```
WHAT IS 56625688?
```

"All we have to do is get past this prompt to see what else there is," Quinn said.

Quinn entered the answer.

```
KNOCKOUT
```

There was a single *beep*, and the screen began to show a flood of new information, nothing like what came before.

It was Bruce Haskell's personal calendar. It showed names of San Diego regional officials of all levels, and the names of their children, including dates of birth and calendar entries for Haskell to meet them just after their eighteenth birthdays.

Then another file came up. It was titled *Haskell_Reveal* and appeared to be audio. Quinn entered a command to open it. The computer went through several cycles before launching.

"Teenage years *are* adulthood," stated a voice—Bruce Haskell's—apparently caught mid-conversation. Muffled voices in the background indicated an informal setting. The file was significantly compressed so the old computer could handle it. The voice had some distortion as a result. "If I had my way, personally, voting age would be sixteen. Consent should be fifteen."

"Oh. Well, that could be argued, I suppose," an unknown man chimed in on the recording.

"Relationships, consensual, fifteen and up," Haskell emphasized. The file stopped there.

The calendar and audio unsettled Olivia, although she had no clear idea of the context behind the entries. The connection wasn't entirely obvious to Jasper, either.

For Quinn, however, something clicked.

"The children of eState," he thought out loud.

Olivia and Jasper looked at him quizzically.

"That's what Kay's brother said. We saw kids who looked about eighteen, maybe a bit older," Quinn told them.

"This guy's talking about kids younger than eighteen," Olivia said.

Jasper thought back to the scene he happened upon recently—Haskell and a young man, the son of some executive. Given the suggestive nature of the encounter, Jasper had an idea of where this information was going. Still, he had to ask.

"What would Haskell keep a sked like this for?"

"There's one person who can tell me," Quinn told him.

"Who?" Jasper asked.

"Eddington," Quinn replied, patting Jasper on the back as he stood to leave. "Go home, get ready for work. It'll be an interesting day."

As the discovery unfolded, Olivia felt increasingly uneasy. The revelations were painting a picture that could cause serious trouble beyond Quinn and Jasper's knowledge. Olivia's instinct was to tread carefully—more than carefully.

"Quinn," Olivia called, stopping him on his way out. "We can't go to press about anything until I know more. It has to be bedrock."

Olivia's restraint surprised Quinn. She treated the breakthrough like a nuclear football, based on his reading of her expression. He held off asking her why, heeding her appeal for now, and left without another word.

She went back to her desk, observing Jasper as he made his exit.

"Stay tuned," Jasper told her.

Olivia waited a few minutes after they were gone. It was rare for *The Observator* to be busy off-hours after sunrise. She was alone in the newsroom now, an ideal time to sound a warning, or at least get some information of her own.

She opened the top of her typewriter and reached into a corner near the left spool of the ink ribbon. She felt around for something—a key.

Once Olivia retrieved the key from under the spool, she walked to an out-of-the-way closet nearby. She unlocked the narrow door and opened it. Behind the door, an antique wooden stand about waist-high served as a platform for a beautifully maintained 1960s-era rotary dial telephone. The stand's dark walnut finish accented the phone's bright turquoise color.

Olivia picked up the receiver and moved her right index finger to the circle of numbers on the rotor. She hesitated. Then she hung up and closed the closet door. A call would be her last resort.

12: THE STORY OF THE DECADE

Sharp taps—footsteps—perforated the placid morning atmosphere of the sixth-floor corridor near Walter Eddington's office. Desiree Laberteaux Eddington was on a mission to see her husband. The fifty-four-year-old dynamo walked quickly, with authority, in a black business suit and black pumps with spiked heels, gold earrings and necklace, perfect makeup and champagne hair in a short razor cut.

Eddington's longtime secretary, Ann Wen, a short, brown-haired woman of average looks and sweet disposition, stood when she saw Desiree heading her way. Ann's false-diamond American flag broach caught the overhead lights against her navy blue pantsuit.

Desiree made a beeline for Eddington's closed office doors. Ann tried to slow her down (there would be no stopping her).

"Desiree!" Ann said with a warm smile. "He's in a meeting."

"Isn't he always," Desiree replied with a snap of sarcasm as she pulled on the right-hand doorknob.

Desiree walked in and was unfazed by what she saw—Eddington and that talentless "performer" Junice Fawn, seated together at his desk, leaning into each other, smiling, holding hands. He quickly pulled away as his wife approached.

"Junice, right?" Desiree said, deadpan.

Junice nodded.

"At least I know the rumor's true now," Desiree added brusquely.

Eddington rubbed his forehead in equal parts embarrassment and annoyance.

"Desi, I have something called a secretary. She's at that desk for a reason. I don't like seeing her pay go to waste," he complained. Then he turned his attention to Junice. "We'll catch up on the contract later."

Junice got the hint and complied, giving Desiree a clumsy nod and a smile as she left, closing the door behind her.

Desiree was accustomed to her husband's flings. Their marriage of nearly three decades started strong, but the chill settled in thanks to his penchant for eyeing younger women. Still, they were kindred spirits in business and friendship, so the marriage stood as a formality for the sake of their interests, including their children.

With Junice out of the room, Desiree's mood mellowed slightly.

"What are you doing to help the kids?" she asked.

Eddington hesitated. He seemed lost for a reply, which surprised her. That had to mean the trouble was serious.

"I have options," was the best answer Eddington could muster.

"Walter, aside from business, we don't have much left. Except them. If you have options, then use them!" Desiree pushed.

Eddington overcame his momentary lapse of confidence.

He approached her, regaining his facade of control and composure.

"If you expect our business to continue then you'll let me play this as I see fit," he told her. "I will not give up what I've built to Haskell *and* eState."

"*We've* built," Desiree reminded him. "What *we* have built. Media empire, family, all of it. What does Haskell have on you, aside from the occasional actress, singer, whatever, that you can't do anything?"

Eddington didn't like that, especially since he knew that the indiscretions ran both ways.

"I'm sure he's got plenty on you, too," Eddington noted. "Actually, it's what I have on him that's the problem."

Desiree threw her hands up in a fit of frustration at a fruitless conversation.

"Well if you've got something, what does it matter? Wipe him out!" she ordered, turning for the doors. "Do something to save our children, for God's sake. Or I'll find a way."

Even in times of strife such as this, Eddington was reminded of just how much he enjoyed their sparring. It was that spark that attracted them in the first place. He thought perhaps there was a way for them to come together again, to stop the messing around and find value in each other—personally—as they once did. The recent events with their children got him thinking about such a resolution even more.

"Desi," he said gently.

She stopped and looked back at him.

"Is it too late? For us?"

The question had several layers. Too late for the kids. Too late to protect their mutual interests. Too late for a reunion.

Desiree tilted her head slightly, sadly.

"How many times have you asked that?" she said with a touch of regret mixed with pity, then promptly walked out.

{ }

Quinn and Jasper returned to *The Citizen* after their discovery earlier that morning. It was unsettling to be working in a mainstream newsroom knowing they were sitting on a black market bombshell. It was even stranger that no one on the floor seemed to wonder where Kay was. Her on-air seat was filled with an understudy and a simple "In for Kay Eddington ..." announcement at the start of each newscast. That likely meant they were among a privileged few who knew where Kay was and under what circumstances.

All of that hovered in Quinn's mind as he rode the elevator to the sixth floor to share news of their discovery with Eddington in person. Quinn was practically knocked over by a gust of floral perfume when he left the elevator at its destination. He turned to see who it was. To his astonishment, it was Eddington's wife, whom he had seen only in news reports and whom Kay never talked about. She had already rushed into the elevator before he had a chance to say anything.

From there, Quinn approached Ann at Eddington's reception desk. She was pleased to see him, greeting him with a cheerful "Hi, Quinn" as he walked up to her. Quinn called ahead and was cleared to see the boss, but now he was unsure after the storm that must have passed through Eddington's domain (he could still smell Desiree's perfume).

"Hey, Ann. Should I reschedule?" he asked awkwardly.

Ann picked up her desk phone, pressed a single button, and waited a couple of seconds. "Kellerman's here; do you still have time? Okay." She waved Quinn through with a kindly "Go ahead" as she closed the call.

Quinn entered the lair. Eddington, wearing glasses, looked down at a tablet on his desk, furiously writing notes across it. Whatever transpired shortly before, Quinn assumed it wasn't pleasant based on Eddington's brooding demeanor.

"Sir," Quinn said.

Eddington glanced up at him briefly, expressionless.

"You're still on your feet," Eddington observed. "It's good to see."

"Thank you," Quinn replied. "I know that ..."

"You and Kay have thrown me a real curveball," Eddington interrupted, directing his eyes back to the tablet.

Quinn didn't say anything more at first. He wasn't sure how to reply. Eddington stopped writing mid-sentence, sighed, tossed his glasses on the desk, and stared at him.

Quinn broke the silence. "I know you don't approve, but ..."

"Forget about that, forget about that; it's the least of my worries," Eddington interrupted again. "My children are in prison and my wife-in-name-only is being pushy. What do you have to offer me?"

Quinn crimped his lip, knowing he had something tantalizing to share with him.

"A story that I don't think would get past my editor downstairs unless I went to you directly, because it involves you now," Quinn told him. "Why does Haskell keep a datebook of eighteen-year-olds' birthdays? Kids of eState employees? I have audio ..."

Quinn's nerves jumped when he saw Eddington's face. Maybe it was that Quinn broke protocol and hopped over his editor straight to the top. Perhaps the subject hit close to home in a way Quinn hadn't anticipated. Still, he chose to tell Eddington more.

"This could be the story of the decade if it's what I think it is, and it could be leverage to get Kay and Owen released."

Eddington was unmoved. In fact, he grew angry.

"You have no idea what the story of the decade is," Eddington scoffed. "So what do you have? Some salacious bit about him and his fancy for young adults? I'm not interested. It's not the kind of thing we publish, you know better."

Quinn still pushed it.

"Kids offered up on their eighteenth birthdays on his whim! People have a right to know about this! Viewers will flock to your outlets for it ..."

"I said I am not interested!" Eddington yelled. Then he caught himself and calmed down. "Not at the moment, at least."

"It *has* to publish!" Quinn countered.

Eddington's eyes flashed. He was instantly suspicious of Quinn's implication.

"Where else would you run it?" Eddington asked. "Do you have someplace in mind?"

Quinn paused. What did Eddington's interrogation mean? Did he suspect, or actually know, that Quinn worked on the black market? Had Quinn just given himself away without literally telling Eddington the truth?

"I would hope not," Eddington continued. "If you have

anything more, let me know. But for now, this conversation is over."

Quinn was relieved but terrified. He offered a subdued "Yes, sir" as he was about to leave. Then a question came to him.

"If this isn't the story of the decade, then what is?"

Eddington glared at him, but the expression softened as Quinn walked away without an answer. Eddington had such a story, but he couldn't bring himself to reveal it just yet. His hand against Haskell and the eState machine was built upon both stories, and the longer he could keep them quiet, the more powerful they would be when it came time to weaponize them.

Testing the depth of Haskell's depravity was risky, more so for Eddington personally with the family involved. The game had to be played right. Push Haskell too far, too soon, and Kay could be indexed along with her brother. He feared that his nemesis could even have them murdered or rendered "missing."

Eddington stayed at his desk until Quinn was out the door. He walked over to a small hutch—minimalist, light wood, nondescript in design but impeccable workmanship. He opened it, revealing the same model phone that Olivia had hidden in her newsroom closet. He picked up the receiver and dialed 01.

{ }

Olivia hadn't left *The Observator* yet. She often spent late mornings alone in the newsroom between deadlines doing work without diversion—and away from curious eyes—since the bulk of the staff worked late at night. She was editing a small stack of typewritten stories when the closet phone rang.

She looked toward the door, then took the key from inside her typewriter and went to answer the call.

Closet door open, phone ringing, Olivia glanced behind her to make sure there wasn't a stray worker somewhere to catch her. Finally, she picked up the receiver.

"Western Earnings," she answered cautiously.

Eddington, in his office, heard Olivia's voice. He was just as guarded.

"We have a situation to discuss," he replied.

13: FRACTURES IN THE FACADE

If you wanted to witness good old-fashioned American patriotism displayed on the nose, Fourth of July Promenade was the place to go. It was also a perfect venue for stealth meetings since no one ever actually went there.

The grounds were beautiful, formed out of an old community college campus. It was unsettling, though. All of the college's old buildings were still there, mid-century modern architecture circa early 1970s. Large trees dotted the park. Most of the buildings had windowless four-story facades of white concrete in geometric honeycomb patterns. The designs were striking. But the buildings sat unused, maintained to look fresh and occupied but void of any activity, almost like some kind of utopian replica.

When the college fell victim to declining enrollments and budget cuts, the property went to the county, which Walter Eddington then promptly snapped up in an auction. The first thing Eddington did with the place was christen it Fourth of July Promenade, in honor of "the greatest nation on the planet." Brilliant banners of red, white, and blue now adorned many of the facades. The former college's stately entrance, named Avenue of America, was lined with enormous

U.S. flags. And that was pretty much it. The symbolism stopped there.

Eddington wanted to build some kind of new suburban civic center out of it eventually, but population patterns, economic trends, and environmental challenges were against him as people flocked to city centers, leaving the suburbs mostly empty. eState utility systems favored city hubs, especially when it came to distributing tight water supplies, so suburban services were often *de-gridded*—decommissioned. That left Eddington to pay multimillion-dollar assessments just to maintain the park's grounds and keep the power on. He was too proud of the monument to let it go. Besides, the bills were more than nullified by tax write-offs for "gifting" a public space, vacuous as it was.

And so sat Fourth of July Promenade, pristine and useless. Except for this late Monday afternoon. Eddington called a meeting here with Olivia to discuss the "situation."

Eddington paced under the park's handsome clock-tower sculpture of steel and alabaster, shuffling his feet occasionally to kick away a pebble or two. He spotted someone approaching, squinted to get a better look. It was Olivia. Eddington walked to meet her partway.

"Olivia," he said with a fond smile and a handshake. "How are things at Western Earnings?"

"Quiet but productive," she replied coolly.

"As I'm finding out," he said, raising his eyebrows. "Can we expect a thunderous boom anytime soon?"

Olivia relaxed a bit.

"Political bribes are the least of Haskell's worries," she told him. "Arranging sexual encounters with his employees' kids? *That's* explosive."

Eddington nodded. He surveyed the park, bracing for the answer to his next question.

"I do my best to keep my hands out of the operation, you know that. But it's essential I know. Is Quinn Kellerman writing for you?"

"Yes," Olivia informed him. "So is Jasper Craig."

"Has my daughter been on your premises?" he followed.

"Yes."

Eddington sighed deeply, followed by another pause as he contemplated a demand.

"Hold the story," he ordered politely.

"What?"

Even though it was a directive, Eddington underscored it with a touch of remorse.

"This is a personal request, Olivia. It's deeply important."

"It's a case of the public's right to know if I've ever seen one," she contended. "You've never interfered with our product before, what could possibly change that now?"

"Family matters; that's all I can tell you," Eddington said distantly.

Olivia's ingrained suspicion of authority overrode any sympathy for the man's vague dilemma.

"Family matters. So it really is personal," she gibed before tossing an admonition his way. "I have first call on editorial decisions. That's our agreement. I'll take your request under *advisement*."

Eddington realized his approach was hopeless.

"Pleasure as always," he said tersely, walking away.

"What is this really about?" Olivia asked, sensing there

was something running much deeper with him than a normal editorial disagreement.

In his usual fashion, Eddington was unwilling, or unable, to give a simple answer with even a pinch of truth in the recipe. He continued to walk away, then halted, then started again, unsure how much he could afford to hold back. His cryptic tendency still won.

"Olivia," he said as he turned to face her. "The Observator's benefactor is Western Earnings. Remember where the earnings come from."

{ }

Quinn and Jasper were in a good place. After all the recent strife, the misunderstanding, even betrayal, the two were able to put the bombing to rest and see each other as the buddies they had been for years. Yes, the incident was part of their shared history, but its influence over their lives was far less heavy now. Together, they still sought to blow the cover off eState through Bruce Haskell.

It was dawn Wednesday. They rode their bikes together, shielded behind their dark hoodies, tossing copies of the latest *Observator*—sans any provocative developments—on opposite sides of an urban street. The early morning air was brisk. It was the most normal either of them had felt in many months.

After completing their deliveries, Quinn and Jasper rode the commuter rail, sitting next to each other, bikes beside them, bags empty. It was still early. The car was deserted. Quinn extended his right leg, stretched it, rotated the ankle, and smiled to himself. Jasper was pleased.

The car slowed to a stop. The doors opened. And there was a major problem. Quinn was the first to spot it when he turned behind to see who entered.

"What the hell?" he said.

Then Jasper looked. He was just as alarmed.

Bruce Haskell, his charcoal gray suit blanketed with a black cashmere overcoat, stood at the doors as they closed behind him. The one thing missing was his monocle, which meant he was out on personal business. He looked at them, smiled, and headed their way.

"Got any issues? I'd like to see one," Haskell said with snide silkiness as he sat across from them.

Jasper was shaken by the encounter, and with good reason. He and Quinn were getting past a dark chapter in their lives, and the worst reminder of that nasty business just joined them on the train.

"How did you know where to find us?" Jasper asked him.

"I know everything," Haskell arrogantly replied.

"Do you know Kay and Owen's release date?" Quinn taunted, drilling through Haskell with a stare.

"I'm meeting their mother this afternoon and I'd like to give her some good news about that. But I need something," Haskell said. "Helping eState can be very lucrative. You're already enjoying the benefits, Quinn. You can walk thanks to Jasper's work with me."

Jasper collapsed inside. Haskell's presence was tortuous.

"It's okay, buddy," Quinn said. Jasper avoided eye contact.

Quinn turned his focus back to Haskell. "There are cameras all over these trains," Quinn warned.

Haskell shrugged it off.

"I know, and eState runs them, which means I do, so ... Here's the thing. You have information I need kept quiet." Haskell leaned toward them. "Keeping it quiet can help your girlfriend and her brother. You'll never have to work for pittance again. Or work at all. That's how much I'm willing to pay."

The offer was completely logical to Haskell. Normal business. But he failed to consider the rebels before him, and the turf they occupied. Quinn's rejection was evident.

"No good?" Haskell asked, feigning disappointment. "This *is* the black market, isn't it? This *is* how it works."

For all of Haskell's hubris, his ignorance of the black market was beginning to show. Underground media was not simply transactional. There was a moral essence to it, an ethical center. This was something Haskell was incapable of understanding.

"I want to buy that information, plain and simple. Keep it off the books, as they say. Sort of like how you guys use pens and papers and all that archaic nonsense. Then, I can give Desiree Eddington some great news about her children this afternoon."

The train began to slow. Jasper rebounded once he realized just how out of his league Haskell was. The titan's weakness was showing for the first time—Quinn and Jasper knew they had him. They shot each other a brief glance.

"Time to go," Quinn said. Then he jammed his right foot into Haskell's left shin.

Quinn could have split the man's lower leg in two with any more force, but he stopped short of that. Haskell's howl was satisfaction enough.

"No," Quinn replied as he and Jasper grabbed their bikes to leave.

{ }

Haskell's facade could be described as any common cliché—tough as steel, slippery as a nonstick cooking pan, take your pick. The real material that made him so impenetrable in public was beyond anything like that. It was more comparable to a freakish science experiment, a surface made of some unknown substance forged in a secret lab. There was no way to break it down. Until now.

Quinn literally made the first dent. The pain of it was excruciating. Haskell continued to wince and nurse his damaged shin hours after his encounter on the train.

It was late afternoon. Haskell's office had a sickly hue from the orange haze outside the windows. Haskell was fidgety sitting at his desk, monocle engaged, scrolling through reports on a tablet. He pushed his finger against its surface with enough force to create a thud on each hit, loud enough to be heard a few meters away.

The decision to bargain with Quinn and Jasper would be a minor event under normal circumstances. Such dealing was common. But Haskell was worried. This was the first time a quiet little offer of hush money felt like a major blunder. For Haskell, the problem wasn't the act itself, it was the actors he dealt with. These men were savvy. They were risk-takers whose strength was built on tragedy. He may have been successful at manipulating one of them for a time, but even that unraveled.

That had never happened before.

Haskell's kick to the shin was the first real chip in the facade, and for a man who built his power structure through sheer force of will—bullying, deception, manipulation on so many levels—even one chip could lead to a major crack. His ego may have been akin to granite, but it was close to failing.

Haskell's agitated dive into work was interrupted by the sharp whine of an alert. He tapped his monocle. Through the device's internal earpiece, he got word there was a visitor.

"Send her in," Haskell ordered. He disengaged the monocle and tossed it on the desk.

His office doors opened. The visitor was Desiree Eddington, the wife of Haskell's nemesis.

Haskell stood and hobbled over to greet her. He moved in for a kiss, but she dodged it.

"I said we're done," Desiree told him.

Haskell smirked.

"And in the meantime, Walter dates starlets and Russian immigrants," he quipped.

Desiree pulled away.

"He and I should've divorced years ago," she said, shifting her attention to a gold-framed display case on a nearby wall.

Desiree studied photographs of Haskell and dignitaries from around the world. She had seen the case several times before, but now she needed a reminder of what she was fighting for. Her eyes went to particular pictures, those showing Haskell with various children and young adults, posing and smiling in his office as if they were visiting the president of the United States. Desiree gazed at the images in heartache.

"What did I see in you to blind me to this? If I'd known

what was really going on with you and these kids, we would've never happened. And now you have mine."

Haskell limped back to his desk. She turned to observe him.

"What's wrong with you?" Desiree asked out of amusement more than concern.

"Took a spill on the train," he said.

Desiree smiled. She knew his answer was likely a lie, but she found some delight in seeing his fragility.

Haskell wasn't amused. He resented appearing in any position that advertised weakness.

"You know, this whole thing could've been so much less complicated if you hadn't told Owen," Haskell said.

"Of course I was going to tell him!" she fired back. "This ... interest you have ..."

"Yeah, yeah, but did you really think that was going to work?" he interrupted flippantly. "Look who you're dealing with."

For Haskell, loyalty only applied to those things he could master, and it was a commitment he never made in return. A "leaker" like Desiree was perceived as deadly. Desiree understood this psychology, but she should have known better than to mess with such a man, no matter the attraction or motive. It dawned on her that she might be in physical danger because of it.

"Why am I here, Bruce?" she asked impatiently, attempting to mask her underlying fear.

"Walter's incapable of listening to reason," Haskell surmised. "You know he'd sacrifice his children in a heartbeat to keep his interests protected."

"That's not true!" she told him.

"He's never been pushed this hard before," he said.

In Haskell's worldview, anything was on the table for sacrifice in the name of self interest. It was impossible for one to behave otherwise, so he was prepared to force Eddington's hand, knowing his adversary would break. It was an obvious conclusion.

"He's the last annoyance I have in California, and *this* situation blows up, thanks to you in a lot of ways," Haskell continued, shaking his finger at Desiree.

"What do you want?!" she demanded.

He walked back to her, meeting her face to face.

"Silence. And I'll pay for it. Yours, Walter's, your kids', your companies'. It's all worth something, I know it."

He got even closer, wiping out her personal space.

"I'll never mount a takeover of Walter's interests. I'll leave you all in peace to operate within eState's system, as long as you never talk about or report my personal recreation."

Desiree had enough.

"Recreation?!" she said. "No deal! Ever!"

Haskell grabbed her by the throat. Desiree gagged, unable to pry his hand loose.

"Then your lives are finished," he said. "How many little secrets do you people have? Enough to put all of you under for good reason!"

The less Desiree resisted, the more she relaxed in his grasp, the calmer Haskell became. She finally caught a few shallow breaths. As Desiree reclaimed her composure—taking a chance that Haskell actually wouldn't kill her—she matched his predatory stare with an equally resolute glare.

"Let me go," she rasped. "I'll give it some thought."

He let her loose with a shove.

"Don't think too long," he warned.

14: OPERATION STAKEHOLDER

Even in their safe spaces—today, back at The Red Mug—Quinn and Jasper had grown suspicious of generally anyone who gave them as much as a passing glance. That was necessary now given the arsenal of facts they possessed. It also took away some of the pleasure of simply sitting and observing people, cracking the occasional joke or observation about the clientele around them.

The men and women in business suits (seemingly talking to themselves through their glowing monocles) and the bratty pseudo-hipsters in sundresses or plaid shirts and slacks (the "anguished rich," Quinn called them) were spared the usual jabs.

Instead, the duo sat silently across from each other, Quinn on the couch, his left foot resting against the coffee table as he balanced a notepad on his knee, Jasper on a chair with his pad on the table. They were killing time more than anything, a rare break after work at Eddington's outfit on a late Thursday afternoon. As usual, the job was uninspired, watered down. The black market was always where the excitement was, but there had been no movement on publishing the information they discovered. In fact, Olivia kept mum about whether anything would be published at all.

Quinn thought of one reason. *Maybe Haskell got to her.*

"Why do you think she's holding back?" he asked.

"Hm?" Jasper responded as he doodled silly figures on his notepad.

"Olivia," Quinn clarified. "She hasn't asked us to write anything. She hasn't even planned another issue yet."

Jasper reflected on his experience with Haskell and all the damage done in its wake. He looked at Quinn.

"It's easy to be chained by him."

Jasper's answer gave Quinn pause. It was the response of a broken spirit. It reflected a change Quinn saw in Jasper, not just since the bombing but even more from his interactions with Haskell.

"They're not your chains anymore," Quinn told him. "He tried to injure you like he injures everyone. Thing is, he damages people emotionally, psychologically. That's the pain that doesn't go away so easily. I know. You'll do it. I'll help you."

Jasper tossed the pencil on the table, leaned back in the chair, ran his fingers through his hair. He looked up and stared at a slowly turning rust-brown ceiling fan attached to an aged wooden beam.

Quinn observed Jasper carefully. Then someone passing outside caught Quinn's eye. He couldn't see the woman clearly through the large windows covered with stickers, posters, and fliers, but he was certain it was Olivia. As soon as the woman entered the coffee shop, he knew it was her.

Olivia walked in, browsed the customers, then spotted them. She sat in a chair next to Jasper. Based on her earlier reluctance to jump on the Haskell story, Quinn assumed she was about to tell them something they didn't want to hear.

"We have to do the story," Quinn argued. "He uses people, Olivia. He destroys them. He *is* eState, and if that's what runs our lives, it has to be called out."

"I'm an example," Jasper noted. "Look what happened."

"No. *We* are an example," Quinn replied. Then he recalled what Olivia told him about her own experience. "And what about you? How can you hesitate on anything?"

"You don't have to remind me," Olivia said.

Quinn noticed a slight upward turn at the corners of her mouth.

"We're doing the story," Olivia told them. "That's what I came here to tell you."

Quinn and Jasper undoubtedly supported that decision, but their assumption had been the story was a no-go, too inflammatory even for Olivia's battle-worn journalistic street credentials.

"I'm going against explicit demands of our benefactor, so this might be the last thing we do," she cautioned.

That admission opened the door for Quinn to ask something on his mind for a long time.

"Who *is* our benefactor?"

"I can't answer; you know that," Olivia said.

"If The Observator gets shut down over this, what does it matter?" he countered.

"Oh, it matters. To you more than me," she replied. "Just know that we're moving forward. Let's get to work, all right?"

With that settled, Olivia left without saying anything

else. Quinn and Jasper looked at each other, unsure whether to be excited or terrified.

{ }

Quinn had a visit to make before he launched into a fresh series of late nights and early morning distribution runs.

He sat across from Kay, who was separated from him by glass in a prison visitors room not much larger than a cubicle. She looked well, but stylish attire and perfect hair were replaced by a new fashion—fluorescent blue jumpsuit, hair tied back. Even then, she looked beautiful. Certainly to Quinn. And for the first time in her adult life, Kay found she didn't care so much about appearances. It was actually a relief.

Most of the visit went by with few words. They needed each other's company more than anything.

"Olivia's running the story. Special edition," he told her.

"That's good," Kay said with muted enthusiasm.

"It might not be for you," he warned.

"Don't worry about that," Kay said. She put her left hand on the glass. Quinn met hers against the panel with his right. "When Haskell goes down, there's no way eState will keep Owen and me in here. They'll have to save face."

Quinn's earlier meeting with Olivia left him wondering about who the paper's benefactor was. Perhaps Kay would have insight.

"Olivia said something odd," he mentioned. "I've never seen her hesitate to run something concrete, then go forward full-blown. She said The Observator's benefactor put her on notice. They're watching this one."

"Who is it?" Kay asked.

That was not the response Quinn wanted. Was she withholding information or was she honestly in the dark? He hoped it was the latter.

"We've never known," he said.

{ }

The assault Desiree Eddington suffered at Haskell's hand solidified her conviction that the man was an outright danger, not simply eccentric or perverse. If he was willing to threaten her life, imprison her children, then Haskell had to be exposed for what he was. It further strengthened her resolve to see the story published.

"Walter, this is it now!" she urged her husband during an evening visit to his office. "He choked me when I defied him!"

"I won't tolerate it making news on the black market!" Eddington maintained.

Desiree wouldn't accept his ruling. "It has to run somewhere! Now!"

Eddington actually had a plan to kill Haskell's career, to get him thrown out and shoved into obscurity, but his own tendency toward secrecy and mega-control was close to jeopardizing it. He was beginning to realize that as he witnessed Desiree's torment.

"It will. Just not there," Eddington said. "Including every bit of dirt about us."

Desiree wasn't sure what to make of her husband's insinuation. What exactly was he referring to? Would it be so surprising that he would know of her affair with Haskell? Should she admit it? For the moment, she feigned surprise.

"What dirt about us?"

Eddington wasn't buying her reaction.

"eState tracks everything anyway," he told her. "On top of it, Haskell knows our secrets because he's one of them."

Again, Desiree put up a front, this time a poor approximation of disgust. Her husband still wasn't buying it.

"Oh, please! Let's not compete for scandal of the year!" Eddington scoffed. "I've slept with wannabe stars and you've slept with a man one step above pedophile!"

Desiree was close to breaking down. Eddington closed his eyes, took a deep breath, calmed a bit.

"My point is, Haskell will throw all of that into the open and take us down with him. So we beat him to it," he explained. "We plaster him across the headlines, and we're the tabloid sideshow."

Desiree fought back tears. Eddington approached his wife from behind the desk and held her softly by the shoulders.

"We're our own best story," he continued, sad at the prospect himself. "I meant what I asked earlier, about a new start for us. The taste of this medicine's been pretty sour."

"What about Owen and Kay?" she asked him through a slight cry.

"I'm taking a bet that Haskell won't have credibility to hold them anymore. He might not act like it, but he does answer to a board of directors. He's no god."

"You're gambling with the kids," she noted. "You don't see any other way to get them out?"

"I don't own a mercenary squad, Desi. What are you

expecting? Let's say I did. You think the outcome is any less risky?"

She saw his point.

"All right. If the story won't run on the black market, where's it going to go?"

"Across every news site and broadcast outlet I own," he said with a self-congratulatory smile. "The public will see that I publish the truth, even if it involves me. That's credibility."

Desiree pulled away from him, remembering her husband's typical motive for pretty much everything.

"So it's still all about you."

{ }

While the Eddingtons argued about their next steps, Olivia sat at her desk skimming final proofs of *The Observator*'s special edition. She looked at the front page headline carefully. Big bold type ruled the page with a smaller line beneath it.

Probe Stifled?
Haskell Accused of Having Sex With Teens; eState Official in Prison Over Investigation

Quinn and Jasper stood beside her. She took a breath. Then she slapped her hand on the desk.

"Okay," she said, signing her initials with a red marker on the front page's upper-right corner. She handed the stack to them. "Let's go with it."

They trotted out of the room, each carrying portions of the proofs. Olivia kept an eye on them until they were out of sight. Then she looked toward the small closet holding the telephone.

{ }

Back in Eddington's office, Desiree sat on a small couch close to the desk, watching her husband pace. Then the old-style phone in the glass hutch began to ring.

Eddington answered it. "Yes."

"Olivia, I told you!" he shouted. "God damn it! ... Now just a minute! I ..."

Desiree stood. She smiled in amusement. She might not have known what he was upset about, but if the conversation had Olivia's name attached to it, and he was instantly furious, it meant whatever secret scheme he had was just blown out of the water.

"You will stop those presses, do you hear me?!" he yelled. He rolled his eyes, shook his head, as he listened more. "If you weren't so good at what you do, I'd fire you. Don't bark the contract back at me! I know I can't!"

Eddington slammed the receiver down (any harder and the glass would've shattered). He stormed to a small safe embedded in the wall near his desk and entered a code on a keypad next to it.

"They're running it," he told Desiree as he opened the safe and grabbed a red file folder, then headed for a gray overcoat hanging on a rack beside the doors.

"Good! Let them!" Desiree reacted. "Let this run its course! Where are you going?"

"To The Observator to remind them where their money

comes from," he said in a conniption as he put the coat on. "We're doing this my way."

Before he got to the door, Eddington opened the folder and showed a page to Desiree.

"Just so you know that I *know*," he disclosed. "These are from a while back."

Desiree saw two photos. The shots revealed a mansion terrace, Haskell with his arms around her waist, holding her from behind, his chin on her right shoulder. The pictures appeared to have been taken using a long-distance lens.

Eddington mellowed when he saw her reaction.

She wasn't surprised by the photos' existence. She was embarrassed—for the affair itself and for thinking she could somehow keep her husband ignorant of it.

"I didn't snoop very long," he assured. "It seemed hypocritical."

File in hand, Eddington left with a slam of the door.

{ }

Eddington simmered as his car chauffeured him through the city to the off-color environs of old industrial San Diego. It was an area he really had no identity with, yet his interests were inseverably tied there.

Self reflection was not Eddington's strongest attribute. But when time allowed for it—alone in a driverless car, for instance—it was easy for him to dwell on his choices, what was ahead.

Eddington convinced himself that he had an ironclad vision of how to handle Bruce Haskell, eState itself, as the baron encroached on his business interests and the remaining enclaves of a free press. He understood the irony of buying up news outlets across the country as a way to thwart this encroachment, making him virtually the sole gatekeeper of that freedom. Now, Eddington was about to sink one of the last ships of media independence. Haskell would have done so in the long run anyway, but it was a hand Eddington was forced to play instead.

The threats to his family, his business, American values—Eddington was borderline apoplectic.

The car parked outside Western Earnings, the undercover home of *The Observator*. He took the red file folder with him and walked cold-faced down an alley to one of the building's doors. He was entering an analog domain. There were no iris scanners, thumbprint readers, access cards. Instead, he pulled out an old-style key, something that appeared out of another century, and fumbled with it, fought his own nerves, to get the door unlocked and opened.

As Eddington battled with the simple tool, a deep, roaring, thunderous rumble caught his ear. It came from behind the door.

The publisher knew what a printing press was. In his youth, he enjoyed visiting production plants where newsprint zoomed through drums and plates on machines two stories tall. It was a sound he hadn't heard in many years. And then it occurred to him. He always knew where *The Observator*'s living dinosaurs were, but he never bothered to visit, never thought to find that youthful inspiration that propelled him into the business. In that moment, he realized how brainwashed he had become over time.

Eddington shed the reflection. He got the door open and stormed into the plant.

Press operators supervised the behemoths—stationary creatures of interconnected ultramarine metal blocks pulsing with ink, devouring paper.

Several meters away, Quinn and Jasper examined fresh copies of *The Observator*, unaware of their employer's presence.

"Stop the presses!" they heard a gruff voice shout across the plant.

It was Eddington at the other side, making his way toward the plant manager, an ink-stained man in his thirties wearing a dark blue jumpsuit, hair stuffed underneath a black baseball cap. The other operators looked to see who it was, staring in disbelief at the silver-haired bull who crashed the party.

"I said stop the presses!" Eddington yelled again, turning red-faced.

Quinn and Jasper stepped behind a stack of pallets. They tried to make sense of what Eddington was doing in what they thought was foreign territory to him.

"What the hell's he doing here?" Quinn asked as he heard Eddington's raised voice echoing through the plant.

Quinn felt someone touch him from behind at his upper left arm. Olivia moved past him. Jasper took a double look at her.

"Secret's exposed," she said.

They were dumbfounded to see her approach Eddington and engage him in energetic conversation. The loud machinery overran the talk, but Quinn and Jasper could tell that their two bosses knew each other, and not just in passing.

"Shut them down!" Olivia yelled to the plant manager,

loud enough for Quinn and Jasper to hear.

The manager signaled the rest of the crew, an old-fashioned alarm bell rang several times, and the presses started to slow.

"They stopped the job for him," Jasper observed in disbelief.

Eddington grabbed a copy of the paper and read the front, then thumbed through the pages. He threw the copy to the floor.

"Don't start them up again unless you hear from me!" he ordered.

The bosses walked together toward Quinn and Jasper.

"I'm sorry, Olivia, I couldn't allow it. Not in this way," Eddington said, now markedly calm after taming his ire. Then he turned his attention to the reporters. "Eureka, gentlemen."

The four, collectively speechless to be in each other's company in this environment, headed a short distance through a hallway to the newsroom. Quinn and Jasper found themselves caught in a clash between underground and mainstream. Was a stalemate at hand?

"What do you expect us to do?" Olivia asked Eddington upon entering the office.

"Follow my lead. My significant stake in this outfit mandates it," he told her.

And there it was. A confirmation so damning that it really didn't register with Quinn or Jasper at first.

Eddington faced Quinn directly.

"But I need to talk to the reporter who's going to help me—alone—if you please."

Olivia nodded and started to leave. But Jasper didn't budge.

"Let them talk," Olivia said.

Jasper was reluctant, but a confident glance from Quinn reassured him. Once he left with Olivia, Quinn and Eddington stood face to face.

"Who are you to tell us what to do here?" Quinn asked.

"Who do you think owns this operation?" Eddington implied.

Now the truth settled in. "You?"

"Of course it's me," Eddington confirmed. "How do you think I keep eState in line and my interests protected?"

Quinn recalled the sign outside the building.

"W.E. ... Western Earnings ... Walter Eddington," Quinn thought aloud, to Eddington's satisfaction.

First the bombing. Then Jasper's unintended betrayal. Now this. A third, perhaps final, blow. What was there to hang onto if the very thing that gave Quinn purpose was as corrupt as anything else?

"What good is all this if it's controlled by you?" Quinn asked hopelessly.

"Would you rather have nothing?" Eddington argued.

"If it has to involve you."

"Mind who you're talking to," Eddington warned. "Believe me, you'd rather have me on your side."

"So you're stopping us from running the story. What happens now? How does this help Kay?"

Eddington rolled his eyes at the annoying reminder that his daughter was involved with the guy standing in front of him.

"You and my daughter," Eddington said with a sigh. "Not ideal in my book, but you're growing on me."

Eddington saw something attractive in Quinn, a force of spirit that even he had to acknowledge. There was no doubt the man had qualities Eddington admired.

"You're a survivor," Eddington told him. "You tend to hide that fact. You shouldn't."

Quinn looked away, not in shame but humility. He had no idea that Eddington held him in any level of regard.

Eddington smiled briefly, almost with fatherly pride, at Quinn's reaction.

"You follow through on what's right. It's time I did the same thing. I need to own up to my role in this whole mess we're in."

"By censoring us?" Quinn asked, still suspicious of Eddington's motive.

"By giving you a story that's just as titillating as Haskell and his teens," Eddington said, waving the red file folder. "And one that's just as evil, if not more so."

Eddington tossed the folder on Olivia's desk.

"Read it," Eddington ordered.

Quinn picked up the folder. He leafed through the file. It was a printout of the information Quinn got from grieving mother Theresa Bell, the woman he handed to eState authorities to make a few bucks when he was in college. Proof that eState was manipulating the protest movement against it, to the point of planning "terrorist" hits against organizers and participants.

"Operation Stakeholder," Eddington said. "That's what nearly killed you."

The revelation and depth of Quinn's own betrayal of a despondent woman sliced through him so deeply that he began to tremble. But there was much more. Eddington stood patiently as he watched Quinn absorb the truth.

Quinn continued going through the pages and came across the most devastating facts of all. Pain, rage, regret. All of that filled Quinn like a flash flood inundating a gully. The whites of his eyes turned red.

"Haskell ordered the hit that killed those students and injured you," Eddington confirmed. "It's one of several, as you'll recall. His application of reverse psychology. Those anti-eState 'terrorist attacks' were designed to rally public support for its takeover. Haskell doesn't know I have that file."

"You never reported it," Quinn said, his voice cracking.

"It wasn't in my interest at the time."

Eddington continued to observe Quinn's emotional state as the two faced each other.

"Your reaction's a good one. Quiet rage. That's what you need," Eddington said in a tone half parent, half strategist. "Turn these people's actions against them. They'll destroy themselves."

Eddington calmly—with a shifting demeanor suggesting contrition—sat at Olivia's desk. He motioned for Quinn to sit with him.

"Grab a pad. You're going to interview me," Eddington said. "You'll also want to talk to my wife."

15: THE SURVIVORS

Nowhere. Absolutely ... going ... nowhere.

Quinn scribbled his disappointment in the margins of his notepad. Beyond the revelation of Operation Stakeholder, the interview wasn't panning out. For nearly two hours, past midnight, Eddington shared a trove of information, but the top-heavy load of his grandiose "early years" anecdotes, including his first battles with Bruce Haskell, were drowning the crux of what Quinn thought he needed to know.

Background, he jotted impatiently as Eddington went on.

"I was quite a prankster when I was a kid," Eddington recalled with childlike pride, relaxed, leaning back in Olivia's desk chair, bracing the back of his head with his hands. "I ran early morning paper routes before school, tossing them in driveways, yards, stuff like that."

"But," Eddington said, sitting forward. "Sometimes I'd toss papers thrown by other kids on the roofs of the houses. It was just a prank; I didn't mean anything by it. But I found out those kids lost their jobs over it. I felt really bad; really guilty."

Quinn noticed a change in Eddington's demeanor. The fond memory morphed into serious self reflection.

"That didn't last long," Eddington continued. "Once

I realized I could pick up their routes for myself. Then it became a strategy. It seems everything about me fell into place after that."

Formative, Quinn wrote in a side note as his interest in the man rekindled. His impatience remained, however.

"Sir, with respect, what's the tie-in here? What do you want me to know? We've got Haskell. We've got you. The family. You, in this room with me, where you don't belong. What am I writing about?"

"I don't think I'm much different than Haskell," Eddington went on.

"You're nothing like him," Quinn responded, surprised by Eddington's critique.

"No?" Eddington said quietly, staring at Quinn. "No?"

"My moral shortcomings might not be to his level. But they *are* shortcomings," Eddington conceded. "When it comes to battle, as competitors, we're made for each other."

The conflict was personal and always had been.

Quinn's interview covered Eddington's contentious relationship with Haskell, starting with Haskell's early steps taking over a worldwide brand of discount department stores, then grabbing the globe's leading online retailer, all U.S.-based, all blended to build a corporate juggernaut rivaling the federal government. Entertainment, social media, news outlets, health care, delivery systems—control over the managers and messengers of power—were a natural part of developing eState's empire.

Over time, Eddington's national and global media brand stood as the last mainstream check on Haskell's authoritarian ambition. So did a growing swell of underground resistance, of which black market news was a part. Eddington knew he had to support—own—a portion of that underground to help secure his interests.

That's when Haskell built a network of fake terrorist cells to destroy grassroots opposition. The goal was to call such movements into question as they fed on themselves, accusing each other of the deadly attacks that followed, sowing confusion, sidelining them as fringe-fact conspiracies. Quinn was an unwitting victim of that carnage.

Throwing in the Eddington family's personal entanglements with Haskell and the eState machine, Eddington concluded that he had to force his hand with the black market press.

Quinn's disillusionment and feelings of betrayal returned. He thought he was masking them, but Eddington could tell. Quinn grew increasingly restless. The pen started to quiver in his hand. He stopped writing but kept his eyes focused on the pad. He felt himself sink into the psychological pit he inhabited early in his recovery after the bombing.

"It's all right to feel betrayed," Eddington told him. "I'd feel the same way. You'll get over it."

Quinn looked at him, shaking his head slowly. *You've got no idea*, he thought.

"Stop talking," Eddington ordered, to Quinn's shock. It turned out Quinn said what he thought aloud. "You're a living testament that Haskell and eState actually *won't* be the death of us all. So listen to what I have to say, put the pieces in place, then get it out there."

Eddington wanted the cover blown on three things. First, Haskell's personal proclivity toward twisted "friendships" with the children of his underlings. Second, Haskell's direct hand in the building of a pseudo-terrorist network and its activities. Third, his wife's affair with Haskell, a way to prove to the public that a family even as popular as theirs couldn't escape Haskell's manipulative grip. A fourth piece, eState's payoff of the San Diego City Council to collectively resign and hand over power, was already public knowledge thanks to Quinn and his clandestine colleagues.

Ultimately, Eddington was most worried about timing. As it turned out, circumstances and his own imperiousness left him with less control than he thought.

What was happening now would have been unthinkable just a day before. With Eddington's stop order on *The Observator's* presses, his mainstream and underground resources were now working together to collectively release this torrent of information. Eddington was convinced Haskell wouldn't survive it, nor would eState as a result.

"Now," Eddington said as he took a small phone from his coat pocket and entered a number. He put the phone to his ear, nodded, then handed it to Quinn. "Interview my wife."

{ }

Quinn arrived home that night in such a leaden frame of mind that he scarcely remembered getting there. He ignored calls from Jasper. He just needed to be alone for the night, to imagine being in a cabin in a forest somewhere, a place the ataractic scent of narcotic mist would take him. For the few hours of sleep Quinn got, he was in that forest, away from absolutely everything. He sat in a wooden deck chair, looking up at the sunlight piercing through dense, tall pine trees.

It was a destination that stuck with him the following day, Friday, even after the trip itself wore off.

Kay, again behind glass in a prison visitation cell, wondered where Quinn was as he stared through her into who-knows-where. His drop-induced escape didn't allay his devastation. Kay tapped on the glass to snap him back to her.

"Your dad owns it," Quinn said in a Cimmerian tone that concerned her. "He's the biggest player on the black market. Did you know?"

She shook her head. Kay was just as stunned as Quinn to learn this. Not surprised, though, knowing her father. But now she understood why Quinn could barely get the words out. For him, this was the demolition of a foundation he built for himself after the bombing, and for a moment, Kay pondered whether it was worse to be torn apart physically or emotionally.

"He stopped the story," Quinn told her.

"Permanently?" she asked.

Quinn chuckled lightly in a mix of disbelief and amusement.

"No. For a day," he said. "The Citizen and The Observator are working together."

Kay was too troubled by Quinn's disposition to dwell on the inconceivable partnership. She could tell he had something else on his mind. The reticence was evident.

"Did you know your mom was having an affair with Haskell?" he asked.

Kay closed her eyes, irked but not surprised—again. Her reaction was all the acknowledgment Quinn needed.

"She told me," he said. "Your dad ..."

"Why?" Kay interrupted through a miffed sigh. "Why would she tell you? How do you even know her?"

"Your dad said I should interview her," Quinn continued. "I did. And she told me all about it. I'm sorry; it's something I should've left alone."

"No," Kay said with a pensive shake of her head. "They had their reasons to tell you. When Mom and Dad are at war, they use bedrooms for bombs."

{ }

The Citizen's newsroom had a fresh vibrancy with members of *The Observator* on hand. Its wall-sized monitors now ran line after line of information culled from Quinn's sources. There were collegial arguments between editors and staffers about how to break the information into a series of stories, there was so much material. The newsroom that was gray, metallic, often spiritless, was now awash with unique personalities and opinions.

Walter Eddington marveled at the sight as he peered into the space from around a nearby corner. He recalled his own early days when he and his business were this alive. Eddington headed for the elevators, satisfied he had done the right thing.

It was also a refreshing sight for Quinn and Jasper, who openly worked on stories they would have been shunned for just a few days ago. Quinn smirked as he watched Olivia school her *Citizen* counterpart, the thirty-two-year-old hotshot Joe Cano, about news judgment.

Over the weekend, *The Observator*'s presses roared with a new edition showcasing everything Quinn, Jasper, Olivia, and their colleagues put together. The paper would find its way to sidewalks, trains, and coffee shops by sunrise Monday morning just as *The Citizen* news site would break its own versions of the stories alongside its TV counterpart. The news would spread nationally at light speed.

{ }

It was now 7 a.m. Monday. Bruce Haskell stood at the windows of his office, taking in the bright orange sunlight of a normally gauzy morning. Glare off the nearby skyscrapers gave the cityscape a blazing brilliance through the murk.

He went through his usual ritual. He sipped tea from a fine china cup. He read morning eState division reports through the information stream in his monocle.

Then he turned his attention to the latest copy of *The Observator* on his desk. He smiled with delight when he saw the giant top headline across its front page.

News Mogul Mired in Sex Scandal

The Observator's lead story was exactly what Eddington wanted it to be—his own misdeeds with a half-baked talent named Junice Fawn, the starlet of Eddington's buzzworthy TV show.

Haskell put the tea down and picked up the paper, whipping the creases out of it. He went to his office doors, opening one part-way, peeking out.

"Connie, I love you!" he cheerfully told his secretary, who was sitting at her station near the door. "Thanks for snagging me a copy. This'll keep Eddington busy for a while."

Connie Stimson, a sixty-two-year-old woman in a pressed purple pantsuit, wavy white hair, nodded to her boss dutifully but coldly. Her demeanor puzzled Haskell. She was certainly always professional, and loyal, but never so reserved.

Haskell closed the door and returned to his desk.

"Eddington acknowledged the affair with the actress but also said that he and his wife have been separated for several years," he read aloud. "Desiree Eddington confirmed the couple's long-rumored distance, also admitting an affair with eState's CEO ..."

Haskell's smile vanished. Panic hit. He turned the page, where the story continued beside one of the photos of him and Desiree in an embrace. He dropped the paper on the desk and looked out the windows, broadsided by the story's deeper coverage of his fling with Eddington's wife. An affair would normally not be a big deal. It was the parties involved and his broken demand of silence that gnawed at him.

But that was just the first strike.

Haskell started running through scenarios on how he would handle any backlash from the public and, more importantly, fellow eState power brokers. He thought about what to do with the Eddingtons' children. Maybe it was time to index Kay as he did her brother, put them both to sleep as he negotiated some kind of truce with their parents.

Then the second volley came. The final knockout blow, as San Diego's former mayor called it.

The news ticker running through Haskell's monocle—displaying updates from Eddington's Citizen Group—had more than the black market's *Observator*.

BREAKING NEWS ...

EVIDENCE POINTS TO E-STATE IN TERRORIST BOMBINGS ...

E-STATE EXEC ACCUSED OF HAVING SEX WITH TEENS ...

HASKELL AUDIO: 'RELATIONSHIPS, CONSENSUAL, 15 AND UP' ...

E-STATE SECURITY OFFICIAL IN PRISON OVER OPENING INVESTIGATION ...

NEWS LEADER KAY EDDINGTON ALSO HELD WITHOUT CHARGES ...

The mainstream outlets' coverage, again, was exactly what Eddington wanted it to be. The biggest stories of all weren't relegated to the black market this time, where they could be more easily dismissed as fringe-fact on a rail car floor. These stories, with all the information to back them up, were streaming across every monitor, monocle, phone, tablet, and television in the state and most of the country.

Haskell gritted his teeth. He ran his pasty hands through his oil-black hair. The layers of legal, political, professional, economic, ethical, and moral ramifications would be never-ending, neutralizing his base of support.

The Haskell era was over.

{ }

Warehouse or crypt? It was open to interpretation. Any such debate was nonexistent, at least publicly, given the secrecy surrounding eState's prison index centers.

To the rare outsider receiving a tour, such facilities might appear deceptively clinical given their ghoulish purpose. The warehouse-style buildings were three stories high. Mausoleum slots were stacked in rows, ten per story, with white rectangular metal caps, each engraved with individual bar codes. The lighting was harshly bright, emanating from small circular fixtures in the ceilings. Add several aisles of these rows per building, depending on a site's footprint, and there could be storage for hundreds—thousands—of inmates.

Walter and Desiree Eddington stood on the ground floor, looking upward at an automated lift. The single-armed machine, navy blue, extended from a track embedded in the floor. There were two such devices assigned to every row.

They watched, mournfully, angrily, as the lift slowly moved to the top row, pinpointed a unit, and scanned its barcode. It then attached itself to the unit and pulled it out, lowering it to the floor.

The Eddingtons knew of eState's indexing project, but there was no possible preparation for witnessing such a process. Were it not for Bruce Haskell's act of imprisoning their son for spurious reasons, the visit would not have been allowed.

"Some on the board want this discontinued," a woman standing next to them said. It was Amelia Blasco, an eState vice president who was part of a management team running the company in Haskell's place.

Blasco wore a maroon suit, her graying brown hair wrapped in a bun. The characteristic eState monocle was missing. There seemed nothing artificial about her, from what the Eddingtons could tell, and that put the couple somewhat at ease.

"We'll have him prepped for you," Blasco told them. "You can get your daughter in the meantime."

{ }

Kay had few interactions with the outside world in her days of incarceration. The guards were poor company. Her cell had no television, computer, phone, books, or tablet. No window, either. Not even a small portal. Quinn was the only link she had, thanks to his visits.

The only visible technology were six small, black globes placed evenly around the ceiling—cameras—covering the main space and the bathroom area, which was separated by an aluminum divider.

Like the temporary holding rooms she and Quinn had been in before, the cell was antiseptically clean, with white walls, white ceiling, polished concrete floor, and overly bright illumination from above. The bed was small but comfortable, made of light-colored wood, with army green linens.

Thinking was Kay's only recreation. She wondered how the cells could be so sharp when the rooms where she visited her brother were oppositely ratty. That was empty pondering to pass the time. Then there was the fear that she, too, could be indexed without notice. Would her parents do anything? Could they? Was indexing reversible? She considered that if the cell was her permanent home instead, perhaps indexing was the better option. Which of Quinn's visits would be his last? That was the dark stuff.

She was sitting on the bed, back against the wall, when she heard the brief *ping* of the cell door's alarm. Her parents entered with a guard, a portly woman with short, frizzy hair who stood aside to give the family room.

It was radical for the prison to allow visitors direct access to the cells, so Kay knew there must be a serious development.

"You're out," her father said. "eState's board suspended Haskell."

Kay hugged her parents. Yet even in their moment of relief and reunion, she had to call Dad out on something Quinn shared with her.

"Patron of the black market, huh?" she whispered in his ear.

Bemused, Eddington avoided the subject. "Let's get your brother."

{ }

Owen appeared to be in suspended animation, looking generally the same as the last time Kay saw him in the holding room where she and Quinn undertook their journey to contact him. The only thing different about him was his skin, which was more gaunt and gray than Kay recalled. Her brother was on a gurney in a room similar to the ones Kay had visited before. All tubes and devices had been removed from him except the flashing electrodes at his temples. His breaths were shallow, less than faint.

Kay and her parents stood beside Owen in the darkened room, awaiting some signal to indicate his resuscitation. Desiree swept away tears. Eddington tightened his jaw. Kay held Owen's left hand.

The siblings wore the same style prison clothes, color being the only difference—Kay in blue, Owen in red. Eddington had his white shirtsleeves rolled up, something he often did in a crisis. Desiree could have been mistaken for a mourner in her black blouse and slacks.

Owen's breathing strengthened. Then, with a rapid *beep-beep-beep*, the electrodes went dark. Owen took in a long, deep breath. His eyes opened slowly. He squinted at first, struggling to figure out where he was.

"Hello, son," Eddington said.

Kay was overjoyed to see her brother. But that emotion quickly transformed.

Watching Owen return from suspended animation—knowing the half-world in which he had been trapped and the circumstances of his imprisonment—Kay realized the extent of her disenchantment. She questioned more than her father's attitude. She doubted his world view, hearing his *man to man, welcome home soldier* tone upon greeting his son. As if Owen's journey was a trial to be proud of.

Hypocrisy. Layer upon layer of ulterior motive. Action followed by indecision, and vice versa. The self-interested kowtows to a corporate tyrant. *Isn't my family better than this?* Kay asked herself.

{ × }

Walter Eddington embarked on a victory tour following his brilliant turning of the tables against his eState rival. He enjoyed playing the lead of his own news cycle, supplanting eState's would-be dictator, no longer bound by Bruce Haskell's whims and cult of personality. His daughter and son had been released from prison—but they were noticeably absent.

Quinn was left wondering where Kay had gone. Calls to her home, text messages, even knocks at the door, all went unanswered. He wasn't worried or offended, however. Just as he had to put his life back together a few years ago, he understood that she and her brother were likely doing the same.

About a week had gone by since Eddington's media bombardment. He was now sitting on the set of his daughter's flagship news show. The cans of Chillax Cola were there as expected, but Kay remained on leave, recovering from her ordeal. A look-alike anchor was in Kay's seat. Eddington was contrite.

"It's been no secret, ever, that my wife and I have been separated for a long time, and the fact our secrets were laid bare along with Bruce Haskell's is unfortunate. But, it's given use pause," Eddington said as one of the cameras pushed in for a slowly moving close-up. "His behavior put our children's futures in jeopardy. It's made us rethink a lot of things."

"How are your children?" the anchorwoman asked like a sympathetic counselor.

"They're fine. You know Kay. Rebounds from anything. And she'll be back on the set soon," Eddington said confidently.

"Owen has been vindicated and he's just as resilient. I can't speak to his role in any investigations going forward, but he knows a lot. I'm very proud of them."

For all of Eddington's faults, his plays for power and influence, there was no doubting the admiration he had for his children. The whole ordeal, even through his current victory lap, had indeed placed his life and family in a new perspective. That didn't mean he would change his ways, necessarily.

{ }

Quinn was proud of the work he and his colleagues produced on both sides of the journalistic divide, and he was right to be. But he resented the black market's place as a pawn in a grander scheme, his own relegation to game piece.

He was trapped in a miasma of depression, trying to clear it as he sat on his living room couch, drops sizzling away on the kitchen counter to help lift his spirits.

Quinn held a copy of *The Observator* in his hand. A small, white glass bowl sat on the coffee table next to a box of matches.

On the television across the room, a live broadcast showed a defiant Bruce Haskell sitting before the nine-person eState Board of Directors in a congressional-style inquiry. There was no public gallery. No one sat behind him. It was just the nine and their compromised leader. Three members of the panel scowled at their subject. The text running at the bottom of the screen referred to it as a *Transparency Hearing.*

Looking at the picture, Quinn noticed how diminished Haskell appeared. Even with his bullish bearing, complete with the usual black suit and slick hair, the eState patriarch seemed powerless.

"You sit up there on that board because of me!" Haskell testified. "I made eState what it is! You're falling for the greatest hoax the world has ever seen! And for you to side with the terrorists, the protesters, the underground; you're as disgusting as they are!"

"It's odd you would say that, Bruce, given what the record shows you've done," a woman on the panel, wearing a solid periwinkle blazer, auburn hair teased with highlights, said with the civility of a skeptical prosecutor. A nameplate in front of the board member's microphone identified her as Rhea Nazari.

"I have done *nothing*," Haskell retorted. "Nothing but push the interests of our great country."

She ignored the patriotic line. "When we see the files behind this Operation Stakeholder, the deaths, your deals under the table, demands for sexual favors, pushing the boundary of pedophilia ..."

"You are buying into fringe-fact!" Haskell interrupted, targeting her with his gemstone-green eyes. "It's actually worse than that! It's fake-fact! It's a sham perpetrated by the losers of this society who are out of place and out of time! You believe in fake-fact?"

Nazari dismissed his tirade with a shrug. "I believe in facts established by evidence. It's not just the media reports, Bruce. It's the paper trail, the money, the bodies, the kids of our employees."

Quinn turned off the TV and returned his attention to the newspaper. He began ripping the front page into long strips, placing them in the bowl. His disillusionment grew with each tear.

The drops didn't seem to help, either. That's how deep his depression was. All the pain and success may have been for nothing, as far as he was concerned.

Quinn took the box of matches lying next to the bowl, pulled one out, and struck it against the box. The match sparked and sizzled aflame. He watched it glow, taken in by the burst of vibrant orange and yellow with a bit of violet. He took one of the strips and lit it, then dropped it into the bowl, followed by more. Within a few seconds, a small fire established itself, slowly consuming the cluster of strips. Quinn took another page of the paper, tore more strips, and fed them to the fire.

The doorbell rang. Quinn put the paper down and got up to answer it. He looked through the eyehole and saw Kay standing there, fresh from her own ordeal. Kay put her eye to the glass, then stepped backward and waved. She rang the bell again.

Quinn opened the door. Kay had a lightness about her that surprised him given his disheartened state. It was the first time he saw her in clothes that weren't crisp and perfect in some way (not counting the prison garb she wore the last time he saw her). They were still top-of-the-line labels, but the coat was an everyday style, off-white, nice enough. Her hair was down, presentable but not particularly styled, wisps of it fluttering across her face in the afternoon breeze. Even in as dark a place as he was, Quinn was delighted, relieved, to see her.

Quinn's condition worried Kay, though. She gave him a head-to-toe review the instant he opened the door. His hair was a spiky mess. His eyes were sad, almost half-closed. He wore a gray henley, the top two buttons undone. No shoes or socks. Quinn knew he looked barely fit to see anyone.

"Hey," Kay said softly.

"How are you?" he replied, close to a mumble.

In the time she had come to know him—standing tall, limping, or otherwise—Kay never saw him look or appear to feel awkward. Until now.

"I'm fine," she said. "I'm not sure about you."

Kay gently put her right hand behind Quinn's neck and smiled. Quinn blinked, and a few tears rolled down his face. They embraced and shared a brief, pensive kiss. Kay felt reassured.

"You're high, but you're all right," she said confidently.

"No, I'm not," Quinn insisted.

"Which part of my verdict are you disputing?" she quipped, brushing by into his condo. "Whoa ..."

Kay smelled the caustic mix of drops and smoldering paper, then spotted the smoke rising from the bowl. She ran over to it.

"What are you doing?" she scolded.

Kay took the bowl to the kitchen sink and doused it with water from the faucet.

"Everything I've believed in is a lie," Quinn said, standing at the door as he closed it. "I'm their product. They tore me apart and rebuilt me."

Kay washed her hands and darted to the drop-maker, still sizzling away.

"You don't need this."

She turned the machine off and dumped the vial of

remaining fluid in the trash under the sink.

Then they stared at each other.

"So what do we do now?" Quinn asked.

Kay shook her head. Tears welled in her eyes. She walked up to him, and they held each other tightly.

"We work things out together. And we stay together," she told him. "The rest of the world can go to hell."

{ }

There was a lot more to Kay's answer. As far as she was concerned, the world really could go to hell at this point, especially after what she had witnessed in the past few weeks.

Kay faced just as much of an existential crisis as Quinn. Where Quinn grappled with the sense that parts of his life after the bombing were a lie, Kay arrived at the conclusion that her life was a fabrication—words that essentially meant the same thing but with drastically different contexts and consequences.

Quinn nearly lost his life on a lie, built a new life and career partly on a lie, none of which he had knowledge of or control over. Kay, on the other hand, had a world view and career path manufactured for her in many respects, guided by her father's expectations, interests, and outlooks. For the first time, she was beginning to wonder how much of her life had actually been hers, right down to her core beliefs.

All of this weighed on Kay as she closed her final *News America* broadcast. She wrapped up the headlines, looked seriously, solemnly, at the cameras, ignored the can of that gut-twisting Chillax on the desk. The teleprompter stood ready with her regularly scheduled commentary highlighting more virtues of corporate government, especially its ability to clean house after eState cut Bruce Haskell loose.

But then she tossed the script.

"There's no such thing as 'business as usual' right now. We're lying to ourselves if we think otherwise," she began.

The unexpected opening caught the attention of everyone near a monitor or speaker in Walter Eddington's domain. In *The Citizen*'s newsroom, Quinn and Jasper watched silently with the rest of the staff as Kay's image dominated the walls.

"The days I spent in jail were worrying at best, terrifying at worst," she continued. "Would I be indexed into eState's prison system like my brother? Would my pursuit of the truth end with me? None of that came to be true, thanks to my colleagues, now my friends, who worked collectively in the mainstream and on the black market to make sure the story got out. All of it. My family included."

Eddington was in his office when Kay went on the air. He sat at his desk, glaring at the large monitor on the wall. He furrowed his brow as he parsed his daughter's words.

"So it's with all of this in mind that I make a difficult decision, at least in the short term. I've decided to step out of the spotlight and leave broadcasting for now," Kay announced. "I won't be gone from behind the scenes, but it's time to live without the camera for a while, and the long shadow that too often goes with it."

With that, Kay looked deeply into the camera centered on her across the desk.

"This is Kay Eddington saying goodbye for now, and best wishes to all of you."

The music swelled. The announcer made his usually bold

outro, sounding foolish this time given it was recorded. Kay skipped the Chillax.

After the broadcast, Eddington scoured the halls in a huff, searching for his daughter. He was furious. He tried calling Kay at her desk. No answer. His secretary called her over the building's public-address system. No answer.

Finally, after about twenty minutes, Eddington spotted her a short distance away in a hallway. Even from the back, she was unmistakable in her fire-engine red business dress, cut just above the knee, black high heels, hair in a smart-looking updo. Eddington tried to catch up with her.

"You should have told me!" Eddington shouted.

Kay ignored him, continuing on her way, speeding her pace a little.

"Kay! ... *Katherine!*" he yelled.

When he called her Katherine, she knew a major earthquake was about to break. She stopped and turned to face him.

"You are the face of this organization!" he reminded her. "You're the public face of this family!"

Kay would have none of it.

"No, *you're* the public face of this family!" she countered. "And I'm a journalist! Not your PR agent!"

She stormed away.

"Katherine!" he shouted again. "I have an announcement of my own!"

That sounded ominous. She was too curious to ignore him, so she stopped.

"You will follow me to the conference room," he ordered, somewhat calmer now but still as furious.

Eddington loved conference rooms. There were at least three on every floor of the main building. He would have to be more specific for Kay to budge.

"Which one?" she asked semi-sarcastically.

"Newsroom. Please," he said, motioning her to join him.

{ }

Quinn was looking through some notes on a tablet at his station when Jasper caught Olivia entering the newsroom.

"Look who just walked in," Jasper said.

Olivia walked over to them. While they were happy to see her, it was unusual that she would return above ground again so soon after their forced collaboration with the mainstream.

"Eddington summoned me," she told them, sounding unsure of the reason why.

Then Kay and her father arrived. Eddington pointed to Quinn and Jasper as he approached.

"You and you. In the conference room with us," he demanded.

Quinn and Jasper joined Olivia, following Eddington and Kay into the nearby room. Kay shook her head, just as lost for a reason behind the meeting as Olivia.

Once they were in, Eddington lowered the blinds, an oddly time-consuming process because the room's walls were floor-to-ceiling glass, including the door itself, giving the space a naked feeling. The blinds fell with an ear-piercing crash with each impatient pull of the cords, followed by an equally shattering sound of them being drawn closed so no one outside could see.

Task complete, Eddington turned to face his underlings, who stood around a rectangular walnut table waiting for whatever plot he would lob their way.

"All right. Here we go," he said, clasping his hands. "All of you have done a tremendous service. I mean that. But the black market operation is over. It's time to shut it down."

"And do what?" Olivia challenged.

"Fold what you do into the mainstream," he replied matter-of-factly.

"You own every media outlet in this region, you reach the entire country, and the only advertisers that matter are in your pocket already," Olivia noted, questioning how any alternative media, covert or overt, could possibly threaten him.

"I know that," Eddington acknowledged. "But eState is no longer a threat to me now. Having you here, Olivia, gives me a power team of four. All of you."

Eddington was earnest in his assertion. He really meant it when he told them they were a powerful force united. As far as he could see it, the idea was a win for them all.

Olivia shook her head. She looked fondly at her friends and colleagues. Just as Kay had her intentions already decided before she went on the air, Olivia had a response of her own in case this kind of scenario played out.

"Then I'll move on," she told them. "My work is done."

Olivia headed for the door, but not without one final plea from Eddington.

"I need you to lead, Olivia. I need you here!" he pressed.

She looked back at him just as she opened the door.

"I know."

Olivia's departure unlocked a gate, a challenge to the rest

of them to follow her out.

The crew—especially Kay—understood that defying Walter Eddington could dispatch their careers given the reach of his ownership and influence. Kay also knew that her father's resulting fury would be temporary. The more she weighed the consequences, thanks to her recent experiences, stepping out of her father's shadow was an attractive idea.

For Quinn, threatening to leave Eddington's fold would be an empowering step to the fresh start he needed. While he would never be free of the consequence of eState's actions, he made the life that came afterward truly his own. Eddington and his company might not have been the cause of his injury, but they were complicit just by virtue of their silence. Walking out of Eddington's building would be a symbol of his personal reclamation.

It was the same for Jasper. Leaving Eddington alongside his best friend would confirm his loyalty to a brother, a loyalty he never thought he could redeem after his behavior over the past few years.

The three looked at each other. They knew they all had the same inclination. Almost in unison, Quinn, Jasper, and Kay left the conference room. The mutiny left Eddington thunderstruck. He took a few steps to the door, watching wide-eyed as the trio headed out of the newsroom for the elevators.

Eddington couldn't help but admire his daughter's moxie. Kay banked on it when she chose to walk out with her friends.

It took recent events for Kay to understand just how much of a product she was of her environment. What disquieted her most was the realization that she wouldn't buy that product herself had she seen it on a shelf. That meant she had to change, make herself into her own person beyond the expectations placed on her by family, brand, technology, media, and audience.

While Eddington knew his daughter's mind was settled, he was not going to let Quinn and Jasper go so easily. He charged out of the conference room and followed them.

"Wait!" Eddington called out as the elevator doors opened. He pointed to Quinn and Jasper. "Just you two."

Kay wondered why he didn't summon her as well.

"We'll save family matters for later," he told her.

Kay threw her friends a cautious glance and left.

"I know you don't approve of my methods," Eddington said. "I'm not sure you approve of me at all. I don't care what you think." He looked at Quinn specifically. "Well, in your case, I better care a little since you're dating my daughter."

"I do care about your work," he continued. "If it's sharper stories you want, you'll get them. If it's better pay, you'll get that, too. Bottom line, I—want—you."

"Can you give us a moment?" Quinn asked.

"Of course, but I want an answer now," Eddington insisted.

Quinn and Jasper stepped away and huddled out of earshot.

"What do you think?" Quinn said quietly.

"It could still be to our advantage," Jasper reckoned. "It's not just about being on the inside. Nothing else we do will matter if we're starving."

They turned back to Eddington.

"Agreed," Quinn announced.

"Agreed," Jasper immediately followed.

As long as Eddington wanted them, they would stay. But the friends also renewed a pact with each other.

Once Eddington left them, as they waited for the next elevator, Quinn took a deep breath.

"We keep going," Quinn confirmed.

Jasper nodded.

The underground would remain part of their mission.

"You know, in the chaos of your rebellion a few minutes ago ..." Eddington's voice broke in.

The intrusion startled them. Eddington was standing to their left. Whether he was there the whole time or had just walked up, they weren't aware.

"... I never got a chance to share a tip with you. Word is, Haskell got indexed."

Unlikely, Jasper thought. eState announced it halted the procedure nationwide.

"The company said they were stopping it. A lot of prisoners are getting furloughed."

"You really believe anything eState says?" Eddington replied. "Just passing it along."

Did Eddington know of their intention to stick with the black market? His manner was vague enough to leave the question open. If he did know, he appeared to drop a breadcrumb of acceptance.

{ }

The mood was akin to a pending execution.

Haskell's richly manicured hair was gone. It had been shaved to the scalp. Not even stubble remained. He still looked waxy, although it was not by his own design anymore. The electrodes characteristic of the indexing process had been installed at his temples. He was strapped to a bed—more like a padded shelf—his eyes conveying a rotation of fear and contempt instead of strength.

Unlike the storage houses where indexed prisoners were sent, Haskell was in a space about the size of a storeroom with only fifteen drawers stacked three to a row. Haskell was floor level in the middle row, directed head-first toward his designated unit.

Two technicians leaned over him, making final preparations. In their gray jumpsuits and caps, the men looked more like mechanics without the grime of the work. Haskell mutely scrutinized them as they entered commands on their tablets, checked an intravenous feed of milky pink liquid, and made sure he was connected to a sanitary line.

Haskell never understood the intricacies of the indexing process. He only cared that the technology suited his purposes—and those of eState. His dread deepened the more he realized he was the blemish that needed to be hidden.

The technicians talked to each other as if Haskell wasn't there. Soon, he wouldn't be anyway. Not consciously.

"We set?" asked the man to Haskell's right.

"Yup," the coworker replied.

The men counted in unison. "Three. Two. One."

With the simultaneous press of a red *Engage* button on each of their tablets, the electrodes lit.

Haskell inhaled. He kept his focus on the ceiling.

"I pledge allegiance," Haskell said rapidly. "I pledge allegiance."

He couldn't seem to get more words out.

"I pledge allegiance," he repeated, his voice trembling, dwindling. "Oh no. No, no, no, no, no ..."

The technicians looked at each other, intrigued by Haskell's utterances.

"Wonder where he's headed," said the man to Haskell's left.

Haskell's eyes began to close. He fought to keep them open. Wherever he was going as he faded to unconsciousness, he was terrified.

"The explosions. They're so loud!" he cried out. "They're so loud ..."

Haskell fell asleep.

{ }

eState kept news of Haskell's fate under wraps for weeks. When the time came to publicize it, coverage was subdued. Broadcasts mentioned it only briefly. Online, the stories were two or three paragraphs at most.

"So they stored him away for future use," Olivia said in her singular mix of amusement and cynicism.

Quinn, Kay, and Jasper tried to dig into the details, but contacts were tight-lipped. Even if they had more to report, time and resources were compromised. Collecting news for the underground wouldn't mean much if there was no place to publish it.

The power team's partial defection from Eddington gave them a collective chance to keep *The Observator* alive, to help galvanize the black market and stay true to its purpose as best they could. With the paper's facility shuttered without Eddington's money, work had to be done in much smaller quarters, dispersed among them.

A month had passed since their revolt. It was a Monday night, Quinn's turn to host the newsroom. Olivia and the trio sat around the living room coffee table at typewriters, working on fresh leads and new stories. A steady rain pattered against the windows, the sound merging with that of the strikes against the keys. Quinn wasn't one to flood his condominium with evening light, so they made do with the amber glow of the few lamps he had plus the ceiling light from the kitchen.

Kay struggled with the old technology, pecking slowly, key by key, while the other three typed with expert skill. Quinn smirked, amused by Kay's borderline incompetence. She stopped and flung him a look.

"Any word on how all this gets printed?" Olivia asked, eyes to keyboard, typing furiously.

"I was doing a little research about something called a mimeograph," Jasper said, equally wrapped in his work. "Nowhere near the number of copies, but they don't require power. I might be able to get us one."

"How much room would you need?" Kay inquired.

"It could fit on a small table," Jasper answered, glancing at a nearby stand against a wall that was full of papers.

Quinn saw an opportunity to make an announcement.

"I've got a meeting with an old source tomorrow morning. He could be a new benefactor."

Olivia stopped typing and looked at him, almost suspiciously.

"Who?" she asked.

"Can't say yet," Quinn replied with a cryptic smile. "I'll know more when I see him."

{ }

The overnight rain gave way to one of the finest mornings Quinn could recall in recent memory. With his job at *The Citizen* secure and *The Observator* in a holding pattern—and a bit of personal savings to help keep him afloat for the short term—he had some time to get his life back into a more consistent, healthy pattern.

The weather was perfect for a run along Lake Miramar. He also had an appointment to keep along the way.

Quinn felt more comfortable with himself than he had in a long time, to the point where he wore shorts on his run. The sun reflected in the black semi-translucent skin of his legs, revealing a slight depth reminiscent of the top layers of water on the calm lake alongside the path. The air had a chill, but a long-sleeved shirt under a sweatshirt was all Quinn needed. His legs didn't sense cold or heat unless it was extreme.

About fifteen minutes into the run, Quinn spotted a man in trousers and a fluffy brown coat. It was Elliott Day, San Diego's former mayor. His appointment.

"I thought our business was finished a while ago," Day said as Quinn slowed to greet him.

The two smiled and shook hands.

"Déjà vu," Quinn said.

"I followed up on your message," Day told him. "I inquired about that warehouse you said was for sale. Eddington's curious to know why I'm interested in it."

Quinn's buoyant disposition shifted to worry.

"I told him it's none of his business and to name his price," Day added.

"You think he'll go for it?" Quinn asked.

"Like I said, I told him to name his price. He'll sell it to me," Day assured.

"What about the presses?"

"I'll get them moved to another location if it's necessary. You folks have a new benefactor if you want me. I don't know anything about publishing, though," Day said dryly. "I don't think I knew anything about governing, either. I just want to do something."

Quinn relaxed. "Okay, then. Thank you."

"Not a word to Eddington!" Day lightly warned as he turned to leave.

"Hell no," Quinn replied. "I've got to keep my job there, too."

Quinn heard a jet roaring high above. He looked up to see the plane piercing the clouds. For a moment, he thought about the days not long ago when it could have been eState master Bruce Haskell arriving to false fanfare. It was a time when Quinn knew less about himself and the world around him. That era was mostly over now. Thankfully.

Ready to run, Quinn looked at the path ahead. From this spot, the route east seemed endless, disappearing a distance away around a calm bend into an area of rich greenery.

-30-

CPSIA information can be obtained
at www.ICGtesting.com
Printed in the USA
FSHW020318030220
66744FS